By Kris Tualla:

Loving the Norseman
Loving the Knight
In the Norseman's House

A Nordic Knight in Henry's Court
A Nordic Knight of the Golden Fleece
A Nordic Knight and his Spanish Wife

A Discreet Gentleman of Discovery
A Discreet Gentleman of Matrimony
A Discreet Gentleman of Consequence
A Discreet Gentleman of Intrigue
A Discreet Gentleman of Mystery
A Discreet Gentleman's Legacy (2019)

Leaving Norway
Finding Sovereignty
Kirsten's Journal

A Woman of Choice
A Prince of Norway
A Matter of Principle

The Norsemen's War: Enemies and Traitors
The Norsemen's War: Battles Abroad
The Norsemen's War: Finding Norway

Sempre Avanti: Always Forward (with Thomas Duhs)
Ice and Granite: The Snow Soldiers of Riva Ridge (with TD)
Viking Spy

An Unexpected Viking
A Restored Viking
A Modern Viking

*****

A Primer for Beginning Authors
Becoming an Authorpreneur

Camp Hale Series: Book Three

Viking Spy
The 99th Battalion and the OSS

Kris Tualla

ISBN-13: 9781720914495

*This book is dedicated to Gerd Nyquist,
author of "The 99th Battalion"*

and to

*Roger Hall, author of
"You're Stepping on My Cloak and Dagger"
about his experiences in the OSS.*

*Both books are full of first-person accounts referencing
"maneuvers, challenges, and tests" ~ most of which
leave the specifics of these activities up to
the imagination of the reader.*

*The same holds true when the soldiers were
dropped into Norway in 1945.*

*In this case, the story has been fortified by
the fertile imagination of the author.*

I hope I did them justice.

Chapter One

December 7, 1941
Berlin, Wisconsin

Holten Hansen got the call before the sun came up, which at this time of year meant he was able to sleep past six-thirty. After years of practice he was able to roll out of bed, pull on his cold-weather gear, gulp down a steaming cup of strong black coffee, and be ready to head for the Search and Rescue shed before seven.

"What have we got?" he asked the Search and Rescue team captain.

Jan Ramstad handed him a photo. "Fritz Samelsted, age fifteen, went hunting in the White River Marsh yesterday afternoon. Didn't come home."

Holt frowned and passed the high school photo to the next man. "He went alone?"

"Apparently."

Holt blew an exasperated sigh while he strapped on his cross-country skis. Hunting alone was never a good idea, but it was especially dangerous in the wilds of northern Wisconsin during their brutal winters.

After he got the call this morning, Holt checked the temperature outside. The gauge on his garage read ten degrees below zero.

Without factoring in the wind.

"I'll follow County Road D into the marsh." Holt handed Jan the photo and pulled on his insulated mittens. "Hopefully he didn't stray too far."

Jan nodded. "I'll come with you and bring the toboggan, just in case."

*****

Holt and Jan skied along the single-lane unplowed county road, each one pulling down his scarf and shouting Fritz's name every few minutes. Their breath formed brief icy clouds which the sporadic wind carried away while Holt listened for any response.

The breezy day had dawned quiet, clear, and cold. The slanting morning sun washed the snow-covered landscape in pale pink and all the shadows were blue like the sky. The scene was beautiful and serene.

And deadly.

Holt shaded his eyes against the growing glare reflecting off the snow. He methodically scanned the terrain outside of the road's marked path, looking for snowshoe or ski tracks. Though he knew that their constant wind gusts drifted the snow in open areas and soon blew those signs away, he didn't want them to miss anything. The boy's life depended on it.

The fact that he and the Search and Rescue team even had to go looking for the boy made Holt angry. Fritz should have known better than to go hunting alone. Every young man living in Wisconsin should know better. What was he thinking?

Risks will find you—you don't need to go looking for them.

Holt and Jan stopped to catch their breath and take drinks of icy water from their canteens. Standing still in the frigid cold, Holt felt a deep and familiar ache in his left hip where his pelvis had been shattered in the car accident. Hit broadside by a drunk driver, Holt was lucky to even be alive.

Though the truth be told, he wished he'd been the one who

died and not his wife. He always believed she was the strong one, not him.

Holt capped his canteen and shouted again. "Fritz! Fritz, can you hear me?"

A shot rang out from the woods whose edge was about a hundred yards to Holt's left.

"Thank God," Jan huffed through his scarf

Hoping that actually was Fritz and not another hunter, Holt hollered, "We're coming!"

Holt skied off the road's path with Jan and the toboggan right behind him. They quickly crossed the pristine and snow-covered meadow toward the pine trees. Once they reached the trees Holt scanned the protected ground for tracks.

Nothing.

"Where are you?" he bellowed.

The faint sound of wood-on-wood came from his right now. Holt and Jan turned their skis in that direction.

"Keep hitting the tree, Fritz!"

Skiing over the forest's uneven floor was much harder than in the open meadow so the men's pace slowed. Even though snow-covered obstacles like fallen branches and rocks grabbed at his skis, Holt was able to keep his balance and move steadily toward the rhythmic beat.

When he and Jan reached Fritz, it was obvious that the boy was hurt. The dried blood on his face was gruesome to look at, but the fact that it was dried blood meant his head wound wasn't still bleeding.

Holt took off his skis and knelt beside the teen. "What happened, Fritz?"

Fritz struggled to sit up. "I was charged by a buck. I tripped when I was running and I guess I went headfirst into this tree. That's all I remember."

Holt was glad to see that Fritz was dressed well enough to survive the cold and told him so.

"Otherwise, we'd be hauling out your frozen corpse." He turned to Jan. "Let's get this boy home."

*****

The rescue took nearly three hours in all, with Holt and Jan taking turns hauling out the toboggan onto which Fritz was wrapped for warmth and strapped for safety.

Fritz had suffered a substantial concussion and the two-inch gash extending from his forehead to his hairline needed stitches. He'd also twisted his right ankle pretty severely when he was knocked out.

But, thank God, this one ended well. The boy was alive.

While they'd wrapped and strapped the adolescent, Holt took the time to lecture Fritz on the stupidity of hunting alone.

"You *lectured* him?" Raleigh Burns stared at him, clearly appalled. "Don't you think he'd figured it out on his own at that point?"

Holt considered the woman sitting on the other side of the diner's blue checkered tablecloth. Raleigh's gray eyes narrowed while she waited for him to reply.

He shrugged his concession and signaled to their waitress for more coffee. "Just making sure. You never know what he'll remember after a head injury."

Raleigh loosened the scarf that held back her impossibly red and curly hair and then retied it. Holt recognized that habit as Raleigh taking the time to regroup and not let her temper fly unchecked. That was one of the qualities he appreciated about her.

But the thought that she was a hairdresser by trade, yet always wore her own locks in such a simple manner did pique his curiosity.

"Why do you do that?" he asked.

Raleigh's arms paused mid-tie and she frowned at him. "Do what?"

Holt waved a finger at her hair. "You spend all day fixing up other ladies' hair, but you always just tie yours back."

Raleigh's cheeks pinkened. "Does it look bad?"

"No! It suits you. But..." Holt shrugged.

Raleigh finished tying the scarf. "I just don't want to draw any attention to myself."

Holt thought that was odd. "Why not?"

"My purpose is to make other women beautiful." Raleigh crossed her arms on the checked cloth and her gray eyes darkened. "I want them in the limelight, not me. Never me."

Before Holt could react to that, she changed the subject. "How's your hip?"

Holt hated that subject even more than he hated having her scold him.

"When we got back from the rescue, I took two aspirins and soaked in the tub." Holt winked at her, hoping to deflect further questions. "I'm good as new."

"It's been almost two years," Raleigh ventured. "Is the pain ever going to go away?"

Holt wanted to blurt that the pain of losing Nora was permanent, but held his tongue on that subject. Instead he said, "It's better every day, Ralls. It really is."

"But it's still worse in the cold?" she pressed.

Holt took a drink from his freshly-filled coffee cup to stall his answer. Where exactly *was* the line between honesty and whining? He wished he knew.

"I have three metal plates screwed into my pelvis. That part is never going away." Holt leaned forward and stared into Raleigh's eyes, smiling softly and hoping that would assuage her concern. "But the ache's never so bad that a couple aspirin can't knock it out."

Her auburn eyebrows arched skeptically. "Then why the hot baths?"

Holt chuckled and lied. "I really like bubble baths. Haven't I ever told you that?"

Raleigh threw her napkin at him.

*****

The owner of the diner turned up the volume on the radio. The big band music, which normally filled the backgrounds of Holt and Raleigh's conversations had given way to the deep, urgent voice of a shocked announcer.

Holt stopped talking in mid-sentence and laid his hand over Raleigh's. "Hold on…"

The owner shushed the little Sunday lunch crowd, most of whom looked annoyed at the interruption.

"Something happened in Pearl Harbor," he told them. "I think we'll all want to hear this."

As the broadcaster on the radio recounted a terrible and impossible tale, the visibly stunned customers left their half-eaten meals behind and gathered at the diner's counter so they would not miss a word.

"Japan attacked Pearl Harbor this morning—"

"Where's that?" one woman whispered.

Her husband replied, "Hawaii. Shhh."

"Well that's not even America," she grumbled.

Holt shot her an irritated look. She pursed her lips and turned away.

"The attack was unprovoked and our United States Navy was unprepared to defend itself."

Holt's shoulder slumped.

This is bad.

There wasn't much else that the announcer could say beyond that, except that the attack probably meant that the United States of America was going to war with Japan.

After a quarter hour spent listening to the same repetitious information, which was loaded with wild speculation, the diner's customers wandered back to finish their now-cold meals in near silence.

"What are you thinking, Holt?" Raleigh asked.

"I'm thinking that guy's right about one thing. We are going to war." Holt pulled a deep breath and let it out slowly while he rubbed his eyes. "And at this point I don't think we'll be fighting just Japan…"

December 8, 1941

The next morning, Holt picked up a copy of the *Milwaukee Sentinel* at Berlin's only drugstore. The headline was not a surprise: *JAPS WAR ON U.S., BOMB ISLANDS, SEA BATTLE ON*

The article went on to state that the surprise attack sank four U.S. Navy battleships and damaged four more. The Japanese also sank or damaged three cruisers, three destroyers, and one minelayer. In addition, they annihilated nearly two hundred aircraft.

Twenty-four-hundred American sailors, soldiers and civilians were killed in the attack. Nearly thirteen hundred more were wounded.

Oh my God.

This definitely was an act of war.

Holt took the paper to Raleigh's beauty salon to show it to her. After she read it, she looked up at him with tears running down her cheeks.

"This is terrible, Holt. Really terrible."

He nodded soberly. "I know."

The afternoon edition of the *Sentinel* arrived in Berlin at four o'clock to an anxiously waiting crowd outside the drugstore.

When the truck arrived with the bundled newspapers, Holt grabbed a copy, flipped the guy a quarter, and handed the paper to Raleigh who had closed her beauty shop early to wait with the rest of Berlin's residents for the latest news. The pair retreated to a bench to read the information together.

"It says page two has the main points of President Roosevelt's speech to Congress this morning." Raleigh opened the newspaper and looked over her shoulder at him. "Should I read it out loud?"

Though he was tall enough to easily see the paper for himself, Holt said, "Sure."

Raleigh returned her attention to the newspaper and cleared her throat. "Yesterday is a date which will live in infamy. The

United States of America was suddenly and deliberately attacked by naval and air forces of the Empire of Japan. The United States was at peace with that nation, and was in conversation with its government and emperor to maintain that peace in the Pacific.

"But just one hour after Japanese air squadrons began the attack, the Japanese ambassador to the United States delivered a formal message intended to deceive us with false statements and expressions of hope for continued peace."

Holt's heart beat harder in his chest. "Lying bastards."

Raleigh shot him a concerned glance and then kept reading. "Yesterday the Japanese also launched attacks against Malaya, Hong Kong, Guam, the Philippine Islands, and Wake Island. This morning they attacked Midway Island."

Holt was shocked. "They've been planning this for a while."

Raleigh nodded. "They *must* have been. This is huge."

Holt read the next bit out loud for himself. "The facts of yesterday and today speak for themselves. I ask the Congress to declare that since the unprovoked and dastardly attack by Japan on Sunday, December 7th, 1941, a state of war has existed between the United States and the Japanese Empire."

"It's official," Raleigh whispered. "We're at war."

Holt said nothing. What was there to say?

December 11, 1941

Holt sat on the big comfortable couch in Raleigh's front room and watched her open a cold bottle of beer and pour it expertly into a tall glass. The flames from her fireplace flickered through the amber liquid in a mesmerizing dance.

He accepted the proffered glass. "Thanks."

"You're very welcome." Raleigh opened a second beer for herself.

Their mood was somber tonight. Germany's declaration of war on the United States today wasn't a surprise to either of them. But if Hitler thought that the Americans would be so occupied with Japan that they'd be an easy target, that pompous little ass had another thing coming.

Raleigh sat on the couch next to Holt, kicked off her shoes, and tucked her feet under her so she was facing him. "What are you thinking about?"

Holt flashed a wry smile. "I was only thirteen when the US declared war on Germany in nineteen-seventeen. And now I'm too old to fight them in this one."

Raleigh rolled her eyes. "You're only thirty-seven, Holt."

"Thirty-eight next month, and then I'm out." He took a sip of his beer and tried to tamp down his bitter disappointment.

Raleigh's expression softened. "I don't think of you as old, Holt. Not at all."

Her words stirred something uncomfortable in Holt's chest. Something he couldn't afford to think about. It was time to shift the focus of their conversation.

"Speaking of *old*, my friend…" Holt teased. "You're going to be thirty soon and you're still not married."

Raleigh looked like he'd just slapped her. Her gaze dropped to the tall beer glass which she gripped tightly with both hands.

"I know."

Holt realized he'd taken a bad misstep and scrambled to fix it. "What I mean is, you're *so* smart and beautiful, Ralls. And you own your own salon. When are you going to complete the picture and settle down?"

Raleigh looked at him from under her auburn brows. "Settle down? Or just settle, Holt."

Holt rolled his eyes. "That's not what I meant and you know it."

One brow lifted. "Do I?"

Holt wagged his head, confused by the sudden turn their conversation had taken. "Are we fighting?"

Raleigh's head fell back and she stared at the ceiling. "I do want to get married, Holt. And start a family. You have no idea how much."

Holt snorted into his beer. "Well your future husband's never going to find you if you spend all your free time with an old, broken-down Norwegian like me."

Her head snapped forward and she poked his chest with a stiff finger. Hard.

Hard enough that it hurt.

"You're not old *or* broken down, Holten Hansen!" she growled. "What you are is stubborn. And very, very infuriating."

Holt recoiled. "I just gave you several really nice compliments! How is that infuriating?"

Raleigh slapped her forehead with the same hand she poked him with. "Ugh. I give up."

"Give up what?" Holt pressed, truly puzzled.

"Never mind." Raleigh reached for Holt's half-empty beer glass. "Let me fill that up for you."

He watched Raleigh unfold from the couch and walk toward her spotless kitchen. Her thick woolen socks made no sound on the polished wooden floor in her tidy house.

His relationship with Raleigh started when he got out of the hospital after the accident when she brought him a meal, and their deepening friendship was the only thing that kept Holt sane in the aftermath.

Now the unsettling idea that he risked pushing her out of his life warred with the knowledge that he could never invite her fully in, and that battle made him feel like he was drowning.

Chapter Two

July 1942

The article in the *Milwaukee Sentinel* was so startling that Holt read it twice to discern if it was a prank. Six months after Hitler declared war on the United States, some higher-ups in the military were apparently planning on expanding their European front.

That seemed odd, since America had immediately gone into full-blown production of war equipment with factories running twenty-four hours a day—and they were still trying to catch up with the demand.

Satisfied that he'd read it correctly after his second careful perusal, Holt looked up from the newspaper and met Raleigh's reflection in her salon mirror.

"Hold still!" she yelped. "Unless you don't care what your hair looks like in the back."

Holt grinned at Raleigh via the mirror. "I care enough to come into a ladies' salon once a month and allow myself to be draped in a frilly pink cape just to get my hair cut."

The white-haired woman in the next chair chuckled. "And we are all grateful for the pleasurable view, Holt."

Holt was accustomed to being teased by the women in the salon who were getting their hair cut, colored, or permanently waved. Even so his cheeks warmed at the suggestion that he was a good-looking guy.

He didn't dare turn his head when he replied, "I do what I can for morale, Miss Whitley. We are a country at war, after all."

Raleigh handed Holt a hand mirror, forcing him to put down his paper, and then spun him around. "How's that?"

In truth, Holt really *didn't* care what his hair looked like in the back—he couldn't see it. But he looked into the hand mirror to see his reflection in the big mirror and turned his head side-to-side as if he did.

"Looks good, Ralls. Thanks."

"You're welcome." Raleigh reclaimed the mirror and spun him back around. "I'll clean you up and you'll be done."

Holt wanted to talk to her about the confounding article he just read, so he asked, "Do you have time for lunch?"

*****

Damn it, Holt.

Raleigh hesitated and the hand brushing shorn bits of hair off his neck stilled. "Um…"

"I'll buy this time," he cajoled.

Raleigh glanced at Miss Whitley's neutral expression and wondered what the older woman was thinking.

Raleigh was new to Berlin when Holt's wife was killed, but she still took him a casserole, as all good Midwesterners did. The friendship that blossomed between the widower and the single gal was only acceptable to the grieving townspeople because she and Holt were clearly not *dating*.

Raleigh unfastened the frilly pink cape from Holt's neck and carefully removed it without getting any hair on his clothes. "Let me check the schedule."

Holt stood and followed Raleigh to the counter while he pulled three dollars from his wallet. She checked her appointment book, though she already knew her schedule.

"Looks like I have an hour until my next appointment."

Raleigh accepted the bills and gave Holt his fifty cents' change. "You do know the barber is cheaper, right?"

"Yeah, but he's ugly. The view is better here," Holt quipped and raised his voice. "Right Miss Whitley?"

The long-time Berlin resident smiled at her reflection and waved a thin, blue-veined hand in his direction. "You know it is, son!"

*****

As soon as the pair ordered their food at the diner Holt unfolded his newspaper and jumped right in, eager to share what he discovered with Raleigh.

"You won't believe this," he began. "More than *two years* after Hitler occupied Norway, the United States has apparently decided they need to do something about it."

"What?" Raleigh's brows pulled together. "How?"

"The goal seems to be to form a battalion to liberate Norway, and the Army wants that battalion to be made up of soldiers who speak and read Norwegian." Holt's smile grew slowly. "And the best part is—are you ready?"

Raleigh looked askance at him, still frowning. "I think so…"

Holt tapped the newspaper with his forefinger. "Men who are considered 'too old' to enlist will be accepted anyway if they meet that qualification."

Raleigh's gray eyes blinked. "Wait—do you speak Norwegian?"

Holt recoiled. "Haven't I told you that?"

"No!" Raleigh spread her hands, her expression incredulous. "How do you speak Norwegian?"

Holt ran his palm over his newly shortened hair trying to decide how succinctly he could tell the story.

"When my grandfather, Gustav Hansen, was twenty-one he went to Arendal, Norway with his father Stefan Hansen, and his uncle Leif Hansen, to visit our family's ancestral home, Hansen

Hall."

Raleigh nodded. "Okay…"

"Gustav stayed in Arendal for a year, and while he was there he met and married my grandmother Helga, and then he brought her back to America with him when he returned."

"Of course he did." Raleigh gave him a crooked smile. "I'm with you so far."

Holt moved his hands along the checkered table cloth to indicate the next generation.

"When my father was born, Helga insisted that all of their children learn Norsk. So my father, Lasse Hansen, was raised with Norwegian as his first language."

Raleigh's expression smoothed. "Oh! And then he taught you."

Holt waved a finger at her. "There's more to it than that. My father moved from Cheltenham, Missouri to Oshkosh, Wisconsin to teach at Oshkosh Normal School. And there, he met a beautiful immigrant…"

"Don't tell me!" Raleigh grinned and put up her hands. "She was from Norway, right?"

"Yep." Holt chuckled. "My mother, the beautiful Solli Ellefsen, married my father in the first year of this century, after she finished her teacher training. I was born three years later."

A thought dawned and the question lightened Raleigh's features. "Was Norwegian your first language, too?"

"No, my parents wanted us to know English. The Norsk came mostly from my *Bestemor*—Grandma—Helga."

Holt sighed at the memory of the stern woman with a heart of gold whom he still missed. "We all had to learn to speak it because that was the only language that she would speak to *us*. So if we wanted her sweeties, we had to ask in the right language."

Raleigh leaned back as the waitress set their lunch orders in front of them and gazed pensively at Holt. "Are you fluent?"

Holt salted his fried potatoes. "No, I wouldn't exactly say that. My vocabulary is pretty rusty."

He set down the salt and picked up the pepper. "But my

pronunciation and grammar should still be good."

Raleigh unfolded her napkin and laid it in her lap. "How serious are you about enlisting, Holt?"

Holt took a big bite of meatloaf to avoid answering the same question which he'd been asking himself for the last hour, ever since he read the article. It was easy to be bitter about missing his first chance to fight the Germans—until he was offered the possibility of a second chance. Accepting it meant actually going to war. Death was a real risk.

But have I lived since Nora died?

Holt swallowed the meatloaf and met Raleigh's eyes.

"I don't know," he admitted. "But I'm going to look into it."

*****

According to the newspaper article, when American troops land in any European country, soldiers who speak that country's language are valuable assets.

And because of all her immigrants in the last hundred years, the United States of America currently had the largest bilingual population in the world.

Holt told Jan Ramstad that tidbit while the two men had a beer together that same evening, enjoying the quiet atmosphere of the smaller of the two taverns in Berlin.

"I believe it." The middle-aged captain of the Search and Rescue team shrugged. "So many Americans today were first generation kids who were raised by parents speaking the old language at home."

"Do you speak Norse, Jan?"

He wiggled a flat palm. "I understand way more than I can speak."

Holt drew a steadying breath, and then told Jan about the battalion which was looking for soldiers of any age who were fluent in Norwegian.

"It makes sense, though, if you think about it," Holt opined.

"The soldiers will want to fight for the United States as Americans, sure, but they'll also want to free their homeland. Kick out the damned Germans."

"I can't argue with that." Jan signaled for another beer. "You going to enlist?"

"I don't know," Holt hedged. "I mean, I think I'll drive down and talk to a recruiter in Milwaukee. Just to see what's involved."

"Sounds good." Jan nodded slowly. "So, how's hunting going?"

The change in subject was welcomed. "Good. I have two dozen beaver and bear pelts curing in the barn right now."

Jan peered into Holt's eyes. "You making enough to live on?"

Holt nodded and took the last gulp of his beer. "I still have money from both the life insurance and the lawsuit."

"Okay, then. Just let me know if you ever need work." Jan motioned for the bartender to bring Holt another beer. "His next one's on me."

Holt scowled. "You don't have to do that."

"Call it a thanks for that damned fool you pulled out of the river yesterday. Heaven knows I couldn't have done it."

Holt knew that was true. At six-foot-four he had the corresponding wingspan to be able to reach the guy where Jan literally fell short.

"In that case, I'll take it. Thanks."

Holt handed his empty glass to the bartender and accepted the full one. "But after this one I need to go."

*****

Three days later Holt walked into the Army recruiting station on Wisconsin Avenue in the center of downtown Milwaukee. He couldn't stop arguing with himself about whether or not to enlist and decided that going in and asking questions was the only way for one side to win out.

He hadn't told Raleigh where he was going, and he wondered why he felt like he needed to hide it from her. She was his best friend—if a guy could have a best friend who was a woman. She knew how he felt about missing the first war and then being told he was too old for this one. She'd understand that the opportunity to serve his country, which was now dangling in front of him, was heady stuff.

But she wouldn't want him to go.

Holt wasn't sure how he knew that, but he did. And his friendship with her would be the one thing that could hold him back.

To be honest, their friendship was the only thing that carried him through the last two years. If Raleigh hadn't shown up at his house three days after Nora's funeral, carrying the best dang lasagna casserole he'd ever had, he might never have noticed her.

He smiled at the memory.

That would be a shame.

A corporal sitting at a gray metal desk looked up at him. "Can I help you?"

Holt stepped up to the desk. "I'm here to ask about the Ninety-Ninth Battalion."

"Name?"

"Holten Hansen."

"Hold on a moment." The corporal grinned lopsidedly and picked up the heavy black telephone receiver. He dialed a single number. "Major Eriksen is needed again."

Then he hung up the phone and pointed to a row of metal chairs. "Please have a seat."

Holt joined the dozen or so other men already waiting there. Every single one of them looked half his age. And since seventeen-year-olds could enlist, they probably were. He wondered if any of them were here about the Ninety-Ninth as well.

Holt's knee bounced with nerves. He pulled a deep breath and let it out slowly. He examined his cuticles.

How long would he have to wait?

A thick-set blond man with a major's insignia on his collar walked out of a hallway and stopped at the reception desk. The corporal pointed at Holt.

The major looked his way and met Holt's eyes. "Hansen?"

Holt nodded.

"*Kom med meg, vær så snill.*"

Holt flipped the switch in his head.

Come with me please.

One of the young pups waiting with him grumbled to the guy next to him, "Is he German?"

"Norwegian." Holt stood. "*Jeg kommer.*"

He followed the major into a little office. The officer indicated the chair facing the desk and continued in Norsk, "Please sit down."

Holt knew that all Ninety-Ninth recruits were expected to know Norwegian, but it didn't occur to him that the interview would be conducted in that language. Now that he was here, he wondered how that probability could have escaped him.

"So you want to join the Ninety-Ninth?" The major spoke quickly. Holt listened intently to keep up.

"I am here to ask about it."

"What do you wish to know?"

Good question. "What is the... practice?"

The major's brows pulled together. "Do you mean the training?"

Holt nodded and flashed an apologetic smile. "Yes. I am sorry. I am *out* of practice."

The major steepled his fingers. "How often do you use Norsk?"

"To be honest, not after my grandmother died." Holt did quick math in his head. "That was about nine years ago."

"Were you fluent at that time?"

Holt suddenly realized that he was the one being questioned, not the other way around as he had expected. What if he was refused based on this interview? What if his skills were judged to be insufficient?

What if the major sent him packing?

Holt squared his shoulders and straightened in his seat. There was no choice except to push through at this point and hope for the best.

"I am good with grammar, but my vocabulary is smaller, I think," he said. "But I will improve when I speak with others again."

Major Eriksen nodded. "Your pronunciation is good."

That pleased Holt more than was reasonable. "Thanks."

"Back to your question about training, there will be a focus on Alpine mountain skills and adaptation to extreme cold."

The major watched Holt's reaction as if he expected Holt to be put off by that. When Holt merely nodded, he asked, "Can you ski?"

"Yes." He gestured with his hands. "Both across land and down hills."

"And how do you feel about cold weather?"

Holt smiled. "It is my choice to live in northern Wisconsin."

The major smiled a little as well. "What do you do there?"

"I hunt for fur to sell," Holt replied trying to pull the right words from his fuzzy memory. "And I give time to look for lost people."

"Search and rescue." It wasn't a question.

Holt noted the words and tucked them in his rapidly growing list of renewed terminology. "Yes."

"I assume, then, that you have some climbing skills?"

That stopped Holt. "You mean with ropes?"

"Yes."

How should he answer that?

"I—yes—there are times that ropes are needed. And heights do not scare me," he clarified.

"Good." Eriksen flashed a tight-lipped smile. "How old are you?"

Holt tried to look unconcerned. "Thirty-eight."

The major looked pleased again. That was reassuring. It dawned on Holt at that precise moment that he really did want to do this.

If the Ninety-Ninth would take him, he would enlist today.

A zing of adrenaline shot through his veins.

He looked at Major Eriksen and realized he missed a question. "I am sorry. Please say that again."

The major patiently repeated his query. "Have you been to Norway?"

Holt shook his head, hoping that was not a requirement.

"Do you have relatives in Norway?"

He did—and hopefully that would offset his previous answer.

"Yes. My mother's family is outside Bergen. And my grandmother's family is in Arendal. Which," he decided to add, "is where our Hansen ancestral home is."

"I do hear Bergen in your accent." Major Eriksen's eyes narrowed and his brow furrowed. "Do you know how close Arendal is to Denmark?"

Holt did. "Only ninety miles across the water."

"Are you worried about your family?"

Holt leaned back in his chair and sucked a deep breath. He hadn't ever met his Norwegian relatives, but he knew his mother was worried about her family since Bergen was one of the ports that Hitler initially attacked—and now held on to with an iron fist.

His grandfather and grandmother, both deceased, were his only real connection with Arendal.

"To be honest..." Holt met Eriksen's gaze. "I am worried about the whole country. And America. The only thing to do is to throw all the Germans out."

Apparently, those were the magic words.

"Good." The major leaned forward and clasped his hands on the desktop. "I have one last question. You look like an able-bodied guy, but I am required by the Army to ask if you have any physical defects that would prevent you from successfully completing both the rigorous Alpine training and our anticipated mountain battles?"

There was no way in hell Holt was going to mention the three metal plates in his hip and miss this once-in-a-lifetime opportunity.

He forced what he hoped was a convincing smile. "No, sir."

Eriksen nodded, looking relieved. "Do you have any other questions for me?"

"Only one." Holt steeled himself and dove headlong into his decision. "How soon can I enlist?"

Chapter Three

August 1942

Raleigh volunteered to drive Holt the thirty miles from Berlin to Oshkosh in order for him to catch the Army bus coming up from Milwaukee on its way to Camp Ripley in Minnesota. The four-hundred-mile journey from Oshkosh to the camp would take at least ten hours Holt figured, so he packed plenty of food for the trip.

Raleigh reacted stoically to the news that Holt had enlisted.

"I'm not surprised. And I'm really *not* sad," she insisted while wiping her eyes. "But I am allowed to miss you, and I will. A lot. You have to promise to write back if you get any letters from me."

Holt's eyebrows shot up. "If?"

She punched his arm. "Okay, *when*."

He chuckled and dragged his finger over his chest. "Cross my heart."

After dropping his duffel bag in the back seat of Raleigh's sedan, Holt opened the passenger door and climbed inside. The sun rose over the horizon and shone in Holt's eyes as Raleigh drove straight east on State Route Ninety-One.

"Taking the Ninety-One to the Ninety-Ninth," Holt quipped.

Raleigh groaned. "I will *not* miss your corny sense of humor."

Holt laughed. "Yes, you will."

She glanced sideways at him. "You look really handsome in your uniform."

"Thanks." Holt ran his hands down his thighs, smoothing the olive drab pants. "Bet you say that to all the guys."

"Bet I don't."

Holt looked at Raleigh. Her expression was somber and her eyes were fixed on the nearly empty road ahead. There was very little traffic so early on this summery Sunday morning. A surge of unexpected emotion thickened his throat.

"I'm really going to miss you, Ralls."

She didn't look at him. "I know."

The pair rode in silence for a while. Holt watched the familiar scenery pass by. Cows in the fields were plodding toward their barns to be milked. Green thigh-high cornstalks glowed in the yellow morning's light. Hawks circled above, looking for mice.

"What time are your parents coming to the bus station?"

Holt pulled his attention back inside the car. "Six-thirty."

"I can just drop you and go, then." Raleigh glanced his way. "So you can say goodbye to them in private."

Holt felt a sharp stab of disappointment. "I would really like you to stay. If you aren't in a hurry to get back."

She shrugged like she wasn't concerned either way, but Holt saw her little smile. "No. The shop is closed on Sundays."

Holt knew he should say more to her, but the words were caught in his throat. Feelings for Raleigh, which he had habitually pushed aside, were now demanding to be noticed. Probably because he was leaving and going to war.

When they were just a mile from the bus station however, he forced some of the words out, not caring how polished they were. "I would not have survived these last two years without you, you know."

Raleigh braked at a stoplight and turned to face him. "I know that."

"I really do care for you."

Her lips curled softly. "And I really care for you, Holt."

He heaved a calming sigh. "When I come back, after all this is over, will you still be here?"

Her eyes welled with tears. "If you answer my letters I will be."

Fair enough.

The light changed to green and Raleigh pressed the gas pedal. When she turned into the bus station's parking lot Holt saw his parents standing next to their parked car. She turned off the engine and laid her hand on the door handle.

Holt grabbed her other hand to stop her.

Her wide gray eyes met his. "What?"

"Are you saying that if I write to you, then you'll wait for me?" he asked, his heart pounding.

Raleigh's shoulders slumped and her tone was resigned. "Holt, I've been waiting for two years already. I can risk waiting a couple more."

*****

I should have kissed her.

The Army bus was stopping in Eau Claire, Wisconsin before crossing the Saint Croix River into Minnesota when Holt's regret poked him for the hundredth time.

Why didn't I?

Five hours had passed since leaving Oshkosh, including the half-hour stop in Wausau to pick up a few more guys, but since it was now noon, the stop in Eau Claire would last an hour so the guys could eat lunch.

Holt climbed out of the bus, glad to stretch his legs. He followed a couple guys to a patch of grass and trees across the street.

"*Har du noe imot om jeg sitter?*"

One fellow squinted up at him. "I don't mind if you sit with us as long as you talk English."

Holt chuckled and sat on the bench. "Good. Because my

head's starting to hurt."

He opened his lunch sack and pulled out a roast beef sandwich. His stomach had been rumbling for the last hour but he didn't feel like eating on the bus. After taking a big, satisfying bite, he considered the men he was sitting with.

"This is something, huh?" he said with his mouth full. "A whole battalion of Norwegian-Americans."

"I not American yet."

Holt turned to the man sitting next to him. "When did you come over?"

"We escape when Hitler attacks," he said with conviction. "In fishing boat. We sail two days to Shetland Island."

"Who came with you?" another man asked.

"My brother. But he stays there and is Shetland Bus."

"I've heard of that," Holt said. "It's a fleet of Norse and Scottish fishermen who sail to and from the western coast of Norway."

The guy who asked Holt to speak English looked intrigued. "To smuggle stuff?"

"And people, right?" Holt held out his hand to the young Norseman. "Holt Hansen."

The immigrant shook it. "Roald Rygg. And yes, people."

"My Norsk is rusty. I'd appreciate it if you'd correct me when you hear me make a mistake." Holt took another bite of his sandwich.

Roald lifted his soft drink bottle. "You do same for my English."

"Deal," Holt spoke past the roast beef.

When the hour was up, the men trundled back onto the bus and reclaimed the same seats they had while the guys from Eau Claire had to double up. Revived by the break and the meal, conversation filled the vehicle as the three dozen men on board got to know each other.

"I wonder how many of us will be in the same company," Holt mused. "How many companies are there, anyway?"

"Four, plus HQ and the medics," the Eau Claire man in the seat behind him answered. "And there will be a total of nine-hundred guys, is what I've heard."

The last stop was on the northern edge of Minneapolis.

"Just a hundred miles to your new home, Privates." The sergeant who was riding along and checking in the recruits as they boarded grinned and switched to Norwegian. "Welcome to the Ninety-Ninth Battalion."

*****

It was close to four o'clock in the afternoon when the Army bus rumbled into Camp Ripley.

Camp Ripley was exactly that—a campsite. There were no permanent structures anywhere, only different sizes of tents serving different purposes. As the three-dozen men disembarked from the bus they were sent in one of two directions.

"You are all in Company A," the sergeant explained. "But you are being added to two existing platoons to complete their numbers."

Holt and Roald—who said he was twenty-five—were assigned to the same platoon. Holt evaluated the forty men he was now grouped with and it was clear that the Army was trying to balance the ages in each unit. In spite of the attempt, two thirds of the guys in his platoon were obviously under thirty.

At least I'm not the oldest, he wrote to Raleigh that night. *There are two guys in their forties in my platoon.*

Holt paused, and then he decided to acknowledge what he was feeling at that moment.

> *I know you didn't expect to hear from me so soon, but it's been an interesting day, and I'm so used to being able to talk to you whenever I want.*

> *Anyway, we're being housed in four-man tents and sleep on six-foot cots. Of course, that means nearly all of the Norwegian recruits here are taller than their beds are*

long. We'll see how long we all last before we stretch out on the ground!

Everything here is being done in Norwegian so I expect to improve quickly. And I don't think we'll be here for very long. These tents aren't going to keep out the wind once the weather changes.

Roald popped his head inside their tent. "A bunch of guys are sitting around the fire and one guy brought out a case of beer that he's been ordered to get rid of."

Holt folded his letter to Raleigh and tucked it under his pillow, glad for the interruption. He was in danger of getting maudlin and mentioning the missed kiss.

"I will come."

Roald led the way to the circle of soldiers sitting on logs around a fire pit. The smoke kept most of the mosquitoes away, but not all. Holt was glad for his uniform's long sleeves, and that his trouser hems were required to be tucked into his Army-issued boots—but as he slapped his neck, ending another stinging insect's annoying life, he wished he'd grabbed a bandana.

Of course he knew better. The sun had just set so this was every mosquito's chance to make whining attacks on exposed flesh. But when Roald popped in, Holt was thinking about Raleigh and not the fact he was sitting in the middle of a thick Minnesota forest.

Next time.

Holt followed the conversation, which focused on everyone's skiing experience, and he injected comments here and there when he had something to add.

"I have many experience with, um…" What were the words Major Eriksen used? "Search and rescue," he finished when he remembered. "I go on skis."

"Hey, Gramps."

Holt turned to face Wilhelm Steen and his eyes pinned the young man's. "Are you talking to me?"

"Yeah." He gave Holt a lopsided grin. "Your Norsk is

terrible."

Holt lifted one shoulder in acknowledgement. "I am out of practice."

"Where were you born?" the young soldier sitting next to Wilhelm asked.

"In Oshkosh, Bjorn," Holt practiced his new comrade-in-arms' name. "In Wisconsin."

"And your pappa?" Wilhelm asked.

Holt answered patiently. "Near Saint Louis in Missouri. On the Hansen estate there."

"Huh." Wilhelm lifted one brow. "And his pappa?"

"Same place."

"And *his* pappa?" the kid pressed.

"Missouri."

Wilhelm scoffed. "And his pappa, too, I think?"

"As a matter of fact, yes." Holt smiled at the impertinent youth without mirth. "Four generations of Hansens have been born there. So far."

Wilhelm snickered and shook his head. He looked at Bjorn Lind who had joined up with him, and nudged his buddy for support. "So what gives you the right to call yourself Norwegian, Gramps? You're as American as they come."

Holt leaned back and folded his arms over his chest. "You want to marry some day, Wilhelm?"

That stopped him. "What?"

"What I mean," Holt managed. "Do you have luck with the women?"

"Sure I do!" Wilhelm blurted. "What does that have to do with anything?"

"I guess you never have a steady girl. Or maybe," Holt stroked his chin. "Not for long."

Bjorn laughed and smacked his friend's arm. "He's got you there!"

"Shut up!" Wilhelm growled.

Holt refolded his arms. "The reason I believe this is very simple."

By now he had the attention of every soldier in the circle. No one spoke, and they all stared expectantly at him—especially the younger men.

Holt pointed at Wilhelm. "I believe this because you do not think about the women."

Wilhelm glared at Holt. "What women?"

Holt held up one finger. "We start with my mother, who emigrated from Bergen. That is in Norway, in case you forget."

The kid rolled his eyes.

Holt held up a second finger. "Next is my grandmother who emigrated from Arendal, also in Norway. Hansen Hall is our family's ancestral home since Viking days."

Wilhelm clenched his jaw but didn't otherwise react.

Holt grinned. "And then there is my great-great-grandfather who traveled to Christiania—that is what they called Oslo—"

"I know!" Wilhelm practically shouted.

Holt dipped his chin in polite acknowledgement and continued. "He was asked to be a choice for a reclaimed Norwegian throne in eighteen-twenty."

"He was?" Bjorn yelped. "Why him?"

"Because he was full-blood Norwegian, and his *mother...*" Holt held up a third finger. "...was Norwegian princess. She was the granddaughter of King Christian the Sixth."

No one in the circle spoke.

Holt leaned forward. "So you see, son, you must never forget the women. They bring forth the sons who only *think* they rule the world."

*****

"You shut that kid up good!" Roald laughed as he and Holt walked back to their tent. "And he deserved it."

Holt didn't completely agree. "I made enemy in my platoon, Roald. On my first day. Not a good start."

"If you ask me, you made a very good impression on everyone *else*." Roald pushed open the flap of their tent. "And I think that's going to be a bigger advantage than Steen will ever be a problem."

"I hope you are right." Holt followed him in and let the flap fall behind him. He felt for the pack of wooden matches to re-light their lantern.

Roald waited until Holt lit the lamp then spoke over his shoulder while the flame brightened the tent. "Why have you not married?"

Holt's chest clenched. He knew he'd be asked that personal question at some point. He just didn't think it would be the first day.

Holt pulled his shirt off over his head to hide his expression. "I was married."

Roald waited until Holt looked at him again. "What happened?"

Holt realized that if he answered truthfully every time he was asked this, it would be like constantly poking a bruise. If he was going to lie, here was his chance.

Make it close enough to the truth so it feels real.

"She, uh… left." Holt shrugged. "I did not want her to, but there was nothing I could do about it."

Roald's expression twisted. "I am sorry."

Holt shrugged again and hoped his grimace looked something like a grin. "But now I am in the Ninety-Ninth Battalion. That would not have happened if she was still with me."

"Did you fight in the First World War?" Roald asked. "I am sorry, but I do not know how old you are."

"I am thirty-eight. And no, I was only thirteen at the time."

Roald smiled a little. "So there is something in that, yes? That now you get to fight for both of your countries."

Holt clenched his jaw against a rush of jumbled emotions which he had no time to sort out and slapped his neck. As he stared at the bloody splotch on his finger tips he asked, "You think the medics have something for mosquito bites?"

September, 1942

The headquarters at Camp Ripley started publishing a little newspaper, appropriately called *The Viking*, three weeks after Holt arrived. The first issue listed the classes that the recruits in the boot camp were taking. Aside from physical fitness and basic infantry training, the classes included the life as a soldier, basic first aid when living rough, Army ranks including who to salute and when, and the structure of the Ninety-Ninth Battalion as a whole.

"It also lists Norwegian navigation, identification of enemy planes, and Japanese tactical methods." Holt looked at Roald. "Japanese tactical methods? Are they serious?"

The young Norseman shrugged. "The one thing I understand about the Army is that I do not understand anything about the Army."

Holt wrote to Raleigh again after the second issue, certain she would find the facts interesting.

> *It turns out that out of the two hundred soldiers currently in the camp, the names break down like this: there are 4 Christiansens, 6 Andersens, 11 Hansens, 15 Olsens ~ and one unexplained Italian named Natale DePietropaolo. The sergeant can't pronounce his name, so we all christened him Peder Olsen. So now he answers to Peder Olsen, and all his gear is marked Peder Olsen.*

> *There are also classes in English for the men who spoke Norwegian first or maybe came to America so recently that they haven't learned the language yet. It's an interesting group for certain.*

What he did not write to Raleigh about was the feud that had risen up between himself and Wilhelm Steen. Steen's buddy Bjorn Lind was staunchly neutral, but that could not be said for all of the younger soldiers. The schism was becoming platoon wide and falling along the lines of age.

Something needed to be done, but Holt had no idea what.

On this heavily clouded morning after chow, he stood at attention with the rest of their platoon while their platoon sergeant told them what their day's routine would include.

"We're going on a twenty-mile hike over the river and through the woods, but don't go looking for grandma's house," Sergeant Dagestad quipped.

Holt bit back a smile at the corny joke, and made a mental note to tell Raleigh that he was not the only bad jokester in their platoon.

"We'll be stopping along the way for target practice. Get your field packs and rifles, go to the supply tent for rations and ammo, and then be back here in fifteen minutes."

"Yes, sergeant!" the men chorused.

Dagestad bounced a nod and bellowed, "Dismissed!"

Their field packs now loaded with ammunition and rations—plus camp stoves, sleeping bags, and climbing gear—weighed at least fifty pounds. Holt couldn't say it was an easy load, but he was struggling less than many of his comrades, even though he was nearly two decades older than some of his platoon mates.

Roald hiked beside him in companionable silence. Since they met on the bus journey the young Norseman had attached himself to Holt rather than the guys in his own age group. Holt liked his company. He was a sharp kid. Plus Holt's Norsk was improving practically by the hour whenever they conversed.

The rumble of thunder off to their right wasn't a surprise considering the dark and overcast sky, but the storm was far enough away that there was no discernable lightning yet.

Roald wiped sweat from his brow with his sleeve. "If we get wet, at least we'll cool off."

"And the mosquitoes will be forced to the ground." Holt slapped the back of his hand. That unlucky insect's death was marked by a little smear of blood.

Holt wiped the back of his hand on his trousers. "Some of the guys are saying the mosquito is the Minnesota state bird."

Roald laughed. "Yes. I heard this state is called the land of ten thousand lakes—and ten million mosquitoes!"

The next rumble of thunder was considerably closer and was preceded by a faint flash.

Holt grunted and shot Roald a crooked grin. "Looks like you will get your wish."

Chapter Four

The storm hit within a quarter hour dumping buckets on the forty members of the hiking A Company platoon. Blinding lightning lit up the forest like klieg lights and was accompanied by instantaneous explosions of thunder. Holt figured the violent storm mimicked the chaos of battle and that thought sobered him.

But no one dies in a thunderstorm.

As if to mock his foolish thoughts a tree barely twenty-five yards to his left was struck by lightning. The sound of the hit was deafening and several of his fellow soldiers dove for cover. Every fiber of Holt's body tingled with the electricity zinging through the air. The tree's bark instantly turned black and its trunk was smoldering.

If it wasn't raining so hard it would be on fire.

In spite of the close strike Sergeant Dagestad did not slow his pace, even though the thick layer of pine needles under the soldier's boots was now slippery with rain. When the platoon left the cover of the forest their boots got caked with mud as they hiked through impromptu rivulets flowing down the hills they traversed.

The initial downpour lasted half an hour before calming to a steady rain, but Holt was soaked to the skin within minutes. The air temperature had cooled with the onslaught of cold water from above and Holt was glad to keep moving at a pace which would keep the men from getting chilled.

One extreme to another.

"That must be the river Sarge mentioned." Roald pointed to a small ravine ahead which was flowing with runoff. "Or at least, it is now."

Holt stopped at the upper edge of the small ravine and watched the tumbling and muddy water rushing through it and down the tree-covered hillside.

Their platoon sergeant faced the soldiers. "How are you going to cross this in battle?"

"Run, sergeant," Wilhelm Steen answered. "It's maybe five yards wide and it's not deep."

Dagestad's eyes narrowed. "Who agrees with him?"

Several men raised their hands.

Holt did not.

The sergeant looked straight at him. "You don't agree, Hansen?"

Holt shook his head. "No, sergeant."

"Aw, don't be scared, Gramps," Wilhelm taunted. "It's just water and you're already wet."

Holt ignored the jab and continued. "After a storm like this one there is always the possibility of a flash flood from uphill."

"So what would you do, Hansen?" Dagestad pressed.

"I would use a rope to get across," Holt explained. "And then secure it on the other side for the rest of the men to follow safely."

"Wouldn't that take a long time?" Bjorn asked.

Holt didn't answer, or even look at the young man. In his mind the time was well worth it if his men were safe. He was curious to see how the sergeant would respond.

"Anyone else have a suggestion?" Dagestad asked.

No one did.

Holt was watching the water and the level was rising. The men needed to act fast if they wanted to get to the other side. "I volunteer to cross with a rope."

"Don't bother, Gramps." Wilhelm grabbed Bjorn. "Let's go, men!"

A dozen guys bolted down the side of the ravine and into the water, which was barely thigh high. Seeing that, another bunch of guys followed. Wilhelm stopped in the middle and helped the guys across.

But the water was now up to his hips.

Holt shifted into rescue mode. He shrugged out of his pack and pulled out his rope and leather gloves.

"How can I help?" Roald asked. "What do you need?"

Holt handed him one end of the rope. "Tie this end to a tree above the water's edge."

Holt looped and knotted the other end around his waist. He pulled on the gloves as he side-stepped down the slippery edge of the ravine toward the water, which was now up to Wilhelm's waist. A couple guys stopped and backed up, clearly rethinking their decision to follow the impulsive private.

"Come on!" Wilhelm shouted at them. "Hurry up!"

"He's not going to be able to keep his footing," Holt called up to Roald. "Get that rope secured *now*."

Roald threw his hands in the air. "Go!"

Holt waded into the rushing water downstream from Wilhelm.

"Steen! Get moving!" he bellowed.

Wilhelm turned around to look at Holt. Holt saw the wave just before it hit Wilhelm from behind and knocked him off his feet.

Holt gripped his rope and waded deeper, trying to align himself with Wilhelm's path so he could catch the foolhardy youth.

The wave raised the water level to Holt's chest. Wilhelm crashed into him and would have taken him down if he wasn't well braced for the impact and holding the rope so tightly. Holt grabbed the strap of Wilhelm's pack and held on.

The wave subsided and the water level dropped back to the men's waists—for the moment.

"Get your feet under you!" Holt shouted. "Hurry!"

Wilhelm flailed a bit but did manage to stand.

Still hanging on to Wilhelm's pack, Holt shoved him toward

the opposite side of the now ten-yard wide torrent.

"Go!"

Wilhelm waded through the water which was trying to take both men down. Holt was right behind him. When they reached the other side, Holt let go of Wilhelm's straps and they both scrambled up the edge of the ravine.

A visibly angry Wilhelm whirled to face him. "What were you thinking? Trying to be some kind of hero?"

Holt stared at the kid. "No. Just keeping the platoon safe."

"Safe?" Wilhelm blurted. "You nearly drowned me!"

Holt couldn't believe what he heard. "You went under. I caught you."

"I know how to swim! Next time, just leave me alone!" Wilhelm turned around and stomped away.

The ten guys who made it across the wash exchanged awkward glances. None of them would look at Holt.

"Hansen!"

Holt turned around and looked at Sergeant Dagestad. "Yes, sergeant?"

"Get that rope secured!"

"Yes, sergeant!" Holt untied the rope from his waist and tied it around the nearest tree, using his weight to pull it tight. "All set!"

The remainder of the platoon waded into the wash using the rope to keep their footing in the rushing water. Roald waited until the rest of the platoon was safely on the other side before he untied his end of the rope and secured it around his waist the way Holt had.

Then he grabbed Holt's pack and wore both his and Holt's heavy packs on his back while Holt and another man pulled him through the torrent to rejoin his comrades.

Sergeant Dagestad said nothing about the incident. Apparently he didn't think he needed to. The results shouted which had been the wiser choice for themselves.

Dagestad motioned the troops forward.

"Onward, men."

As the hike resumed, several of the sopping wet soldiers

made point to pat Holt on the back. A couple whispered, "Good job."

Wilhelm marched at the front of the line and never looked back.

*****

Two days later Holt stood in the open flap of Company A's Headquarters' tent and saluted the captain. "You wanted to see me, sir?"

Captain Rolf Berg looked up from his folding desk and waved him forward. "Come in, Hansen."

Holt walked up to the desk as the captain stood and held out a packet. "Congratulations. You've been promoted to Private First Class."

Holt accepted the packet of embroidered stripes, wondering what prompted the promotion. "Thank you, sir."

Berg smiled. "Sergeant Dagestad told me how you kept a cool head and saved the members of your platoon during training."

Oh. That.

"Before I enlisted, I was a volunteer member of my county's search and rescue team, sir," Holt deflected, a little embarrassed by the recognition. "Unlike most of the other guys, that maneuver was not my first experience."

"Where was that?" The captain actually looked interested.

"Wisconsin. West of Oshkosh."

Berg looked at him with narrowed eyes. "That is good to know." Then he sat back down. "Dismissed, Private."

Holt walked back to his tent. On one hand he was pleased that his knowledge had been useful. But on the other, Steen was bound to be furious once he saw the inverted V sewn onto Holt's sleeves.

"Don't worry, Holt," Roald scoffed. "That boy is just a bug

to be swatted."

Holt looked up from his needlework. "You are only four years older than that boy."

Roald chuckled. "But I am a decade more experienced, I think." He pointed at the stripe that Holt was halfway through attaching. "Is that your last one?"

"Yes." Holt stuck the needle through the edge of the stripe. "Why?"

"It is Friday night." Roald grinned. "We should go into Little Falls and celebrate."

Holt hadn't really gone out for a night on the town—even a tiny town—since the accident. Going to the little tavern in Berlin with Jan certainly didn't count. He supposed it was time.

He grinned up at Roald. "I'll be ready in ten."

*****

Wilhelm Steen glared at Holt from across the bar. Holt was wearing his uniform in town—as all Camp Ripley soldiers were required to do—and his brand new Private First Class stripe was displayed on his sleeve as would be expected.

Holt figured Steen could work out exactly why he had been promoted and, in spite of the young man's vitriolic protests to the contrary, Wilhelm had to understand that Holt saved his hide in that ravine.

Roald ordered two beers and paid for both. He handed one to Holt and held the other in the air, beaming broadly. His eyes twinkled mischievously.

"To Private First Class Holten Hansen," he called out. "The first of our A Company platoon to receive a promotion! Skål!"

"Skål!" several men echoed and drank.

"What are you doing?" Holt growled through his grin.

"I think that the expression is something like poking a sleeping bear?" Roald took a long pull of his beer, his smiling eyes watching Holt over the rim of his glass.

"That is the expression," Holt conceded. "But why would you do that?"

Roald lowered his glass and his expression sobered. "I expect that we will be going into battle with these men. Isn't that right?"

Holt glanced at the soldiers filling the tavern and nodded. "Yes. Someone would have to transfer outside of the Ninety-Ninth to fight with a different group."

Holt returned his regard to Roald. "And which of us would do that?"

Roald looked satisfied. "Exactly my point."

Holt frowned his confusion. "What point?"

"You and I will fight alongside Private Wilhelm Steen. So how can I know he can be trusted if I don't put him to the test?"

Now Roald's actions made sense. "Steen needs to show the platoon that his loyalty to the group outweighs his immature attitude towards me?"

"He does."

Holt glanced at the guys standing around Wilhelm. "Did any of those guys drink to your toast?"

Roald's eyes moved to the same spot. "I don't think so."

Bjorn was looking directly at Holt. There was no animosity in his gaze. And when Wilhelm turned around to see who Bjorn was looking at, Bjorn took the moment to raise his glass to his lips, pausing slightly on the way up.

Wilhelm sneered at Holt then turned back around.

When he did, Holt lifted his glass in Bjorn's direction and took a long swallow.

I do trust him.

October 1942

As the approach of winter shifted the weather, the tent-housed Ninety-Ninth Battalion moved to Fort Snelling, one-hundred-and-twenty-miles southeast and just outside of Saint

Paul and Minneapolis on the shore of the Mississippi River.

Here the soldiers were housed in heated brick buildings and ate off ceramic plates in permanent dining halls. The fort's wide paved streets were a welcomed change from the muddy paths of Camp Ripley, making the maintenance of their uniforms and equipment that much easier.

There was even a large gymnasium, a beautiful chapel, and lounges for the privates.

"Don't become complacent," Sergeant Dagestad warned his platoon. "All of our new comforts will be offset by our training."

The sergeant was not joking. Their twenty-mile marches were now thirty-mile marches as the men traversed fields, forests, and country roads. The increased pace was grueling for every single guy in the company, as evidenced by bent-over and panting soldiers at every break.

Though his hip ached from the constant strain and exertion, Holt said nothing to anyone. He slyly took aspirin before bedding down at night and made a habit of sleeping on his right side to relieve the stress on his bolted-together left hip. In spite of the pain, he had never been in such good shape in his entire life.

"That's a good thing," he said to Roald one Sunday afternoon as the men rode a bus into Saint Paul. "Because that means we can eat as much as we want on these invitations to Sunday dinner."

Fully half of the Scandinavians in the United States had settled in Minnesota, and they were eager to entertain the Norwegian soldiers. Invitations to private homes arrived at the fort every day.

"And sometimes I even get to practice my English," the younger man joked.

Holt smiled. "So how is my Norsk?"

Roald gave Holt an approving look. "Good. I think the mandatory classes are helping. Do you feel fluent yet?"

Holt considered the question. "I do find myself thinking in Norsk now. I do not have to translate in my mind."

"Your grammar is better," Roald observed. "Have you

dreamt in Norsk yet?"

Holt shook his head. "I do not think so. Or maybe I am, and I just don't know it."

November 1942

At the end of October, the Ninety-Ninth Battalion stopped accepting new recruits. Just over nine hundred men now filled the four regular companies, plus the medics and headquarters.

Many of the men were from the Norwegian merchant marines, and many of them could not speak English at all. Communication was further complicated by the fact there were so many Norwegian dialects to deal with.

"I hope they learn English quickly," Roald groused. "Because I don't understand half of what they are saying."

Holt thought Raleigh would find that interesting and included it in his next letter, along with other news.

Norway's big military hero, Lieutenant Colonel Arne Dahl, visited Fort Snelling today. He visited us once at Camp Ripley when there were only a couple hundred of us, but now the battalion is at its capacity. Imagine 900 tall, blond, Norwegian-speaking "Vikings" ~ all in uniform, and all as fit as any man could be. It's an impressive sight, that's for sure.

What's more important is that every single man here has chosen to be here. Not one of us has questioned the intensive day-and-night training. We all know that we are preparing to serve both our own country, and our parents' homeland.

Now that we're all here, there is talk that we will be moved to Colorado, to a place called Camp Hale in the Rocky Mountains. We've heard that the Army is building a new camp there because those mountains are like the mountains in Norway, Germany, and Austria. Once we're there our training will focus on skiing and mountain climbing.

It's really hard to put into words, Ralls, but I am very proud to be a part of this battalion.

Holt paused, wondering what else he should say to her. Should he tell her that she was the last thing he thought about every night before he went to sleep? That he missed their conversations over coffee and pie in the diner? That his haircuts here were not the same without that stupid frilly cape?

I want you to know that I actually went out on the town with Roald the day I got the promotion. I use the term "town" loosely, but Little Falls does have three taverns so there is that. The point is, I have not done anything like that since you-know-when.

Please be patient with me, will you? I'm beginning to rejoin the living. And I miss you very much. I want you to know that.

Holt

Chapter Five

November 1942

Before leaving Fort Snelling for Colorado the soldiers were given a week-long leave for Thanksgiving. Holt hopped the train to Milwaukee, and Raleigh drove down to retrieve him.

When he saw her waiting on the cold, windy train platform with her hands stuffed into her coat pockets and her red curls tied back in a scarf, his heart thumped with unrestrained joy.

He strode up to her, grinning like a fool. "It's great to see you, Ralls."

She threw her arms around him and squeezed him hard. "I'm so glad to see you!" Then she let go and stepped back, looking up at him in surprise. "Wow. You've lost weight."

"And put on muscle, I think. They work us hard." He draped one arm over her shoulder as they headed for her car. "So what's new?"

Conversation flowed easily as the pair drove north to Oshkosh, and the surprised look on his parents' faces when he unexpectedly walked through the front door was priceless. Though he went back to his home in Berlin that evening, he and Raleigh returned to his parents' house for Thanksgiving Day.

Sitting at his mother's table, with her grilling him in Norsk, and him answering back while his father translated for Raleigh, had left the quartet in hysterics more than once. The surprising part of the day was how natural it felt for Raleigh to be there with his family.

And when she drove him back to Milwaukee to catch the train to Minneapolis, he did the right thing.

He kissed her.

And then she promptly burst into tears.

Holt was horrified and started to apologize but she stopped him with another kiss.

"I'm just happy," she insisted as she wiped her eyes. "And sad that you have to leave."

If asked, he would have said the same thing. "I'll write."

"You better!"

After one last kiss, Holt boarded the train. He waved through the window until he couldn't see her anymore.

*****

Raleigh stood on the train platform and watched the caboose of the train until it curved out of sight. She wiped her constant tears with her wool mittens until her cheeks were numb.

Holt had finally kissed her.

Not a quick peck of friendship, either. But a warm, deep, tongue-tangling kiss that spoke of feelings far beyond their platonic habits.

He really cares about me.

He couldn't say it with words, yet. And that was fine.

At least now I have hope.

Raleigh turned around and walked back through the station, the sudden heat inside making her cheeks sting. She exited the other side and strode through the parking lot to her car, her emotions in a jumble.

Raleigh signed up at church to take Holt dinner after he got out of the hospital because, even though she was new in town, that's what people did. She heard all about the accident and how his wife, whom everyone in Berlin absolutely adored, was taken 'way too soon' and that poor Holten was devastated.

When she met him, she immediately recognized the pain of

loss, and she decided to come back every week with food. Raleigh hadn't asked his permission to do so, she just made another lasagna or meatloaf or cheese casserole and showed up.

She willingly accepted the risk that he would turn her away, or that her actions might be misconstrued by the people in town, because Holt desperately needed to talk about Nora to someone who didn't know her.

Raleigh was a blank canvas onto which he could paint the portrait of his wife exactly how he wanted to remember her.

When did I fall in love with him?

As she started her car, she tried to pinpoint the day, or the week. Even the month.

Maybe it was the first time he smiled gratefully at her and said, "See you next week."

Maybe it was the first time he laughed—really laughed—at her anecdotes from the salon.

Maybe it was the first time he took hold of her hand across the diner's blue-checkered tablecloth and thanked her for being so nice to him.

Raleigh drove out of the train station parking lot and got onto the highway heading north. Berlin was two hours away so she had plenty of time to ponder the unexpected but very welcomed shift in their relationship. Then a memory appeared, and Raleigh smiled.

It was probably the first time he wore that frilly pink cape and asked me to cut his hair.

December, 1942

As the soldiers of the Ninety-Ninth prepared to board the train to Colorado, their battalion commander Major Harold Hansen sent the Ninety-Ninth soldiers a message which Holt found... odd.

The message began well enough, with the hope that the soldiers would enjoy the trip to Camp Hale. "Colorado will remind you of Norway, and for those of you who have not been to Norway, the landscape will make a vivid impression."

Holt shot Roald an amused look. "Tell me if he is right."

Roald lifted a skeptical eyebrow. "We will see."

The message went on to claim that the men would be participating in 'one of the most interesting and invigorating training programs the Army has to offer' including 'real commando tactics.'

In other words, they plan to work our asses off.

The message ended with a list of instructions that made Holt feel like he was back in grammar school: be considerate, don't throw anything out of the train, don't destroy the railroad's property, don't 'accidentally' borrow another man's property, obey your officers and cooperate.

Holt looked around him at the assembled soldiers and saw the same perplexed looks on their faces as he was sure was displayed on his. Norwegians as a whole were orderly people. Why were they being scolded before their journey had even started?

"I am not so sure about this Major Hansen," Holt said to Roald once the train was well on the way. "I hope he shows more respect for his men once we arrive at Hale."

Roald glanced over his shoulder to see who might be listening, then he faced Holt. "I agree. I felt like I was in the nursery again."

*****

The train carrying the entire Ninety-Ninth Battalion from Fort Snelling, Minnesota to Leadville, Colorado took two full days to arrive. Holt watched the scenery outside the train window change, fascinated by the distant mountains that rose slowly into sight across the flat plains of eastern Colorado.

All the while, he was thinking about how he would describe it to Raleigh.

Now as the Army transport train slowed and curved into little Leadville, Colorado, Holt and the rest of the tired soldiers peered through the windows, examining their new surroundings.

"What a lousy hick town," Wilhelm complained loudly. "Looks like slim pickin's in the female department."

"Aw, don't worry, Steen," one guy at the other end of the train car called back. "I bet that fancy gal on the corner will do you just fine."

"That's one way to spend your pay!" another whooped.

Roald leaned toward Holt and lowered his voice. "That's the only way *he'll* get company."

Holt flashed Roald a knowing smile.

"All right, gentlemen," Sergeant Dagestad barked once the train came to a stop. "Gather your things and assemble on the other side of the station in fifteen minutes. We have a long march to the camp."

The soldiers' cold and windy seventeen-mile four-hour uphill march brought the Ninety-Ninth to Camp Hale's flat snow-covered valley just as the sun disappeared behind the surrounding mountains. Holt was not the only one panting heavily in the increasingly thinning air.

"We are well over nine-thousand feet elevation." Sergeant Dagestad's evaluative gaze moved over the platoon. "Tomorrow we'll talk about altitude sickness. In the meantime, drink lots of water, and let me know if you get a headache or feel sick."

"How you doing?" Roald asked Holt.

"I'm okay so far." Except for his hip, of course, which ached with the cold and the exertion.

"Follow me." Dagestad turned and headed toward one of the completed barracks in the largely still-under-construction Army camp.

The barracks were two-story wooden buildings with space for sixty-three men—an admitted improvement over Fort Snelling, where their mess hall was crowded into their same building and the men slept in bunks stacked three high.

"It's warm inside." Roald sounded relieved. He and Holt claimed spots next to each other before the exhausted platoon trudged through the snow to the big, brand new mess hall.

As they walked across the camp Holt looked up at the moonless sky and the myriad of bright stars, asking God silently to give him the strength to be able to accomplish what was set in front of him.

*****

Training started in earnest the next day. After breakfast, Company A gathered in the gymnasium for a lesson in gear. Spread out on one of the three tables in front of the bleachers were white parkas.

"Snow camouflage," Holt murmured.

Brilliant.

Next to the parkas were colored packets of ski wax, a waterproof box of matches, two pair of white mittens, a scraping knife and pliers, and green sunglasses. Captain Berg named each item as he tucked it into one of the many pockets of the parka.

"This is how you carry all that." He laid the parka down, moved to the next table, and lifted a waterproofed canvas bag. "This is your rucksack."

Again the captain named each item as he put it in the bag: white camouflage pants, underwear, lots of socks, sleeping bag, ground mattress, a green and white reversible mountain tent with poles and pegs, a Coleman gas stove, cooking pots, and rations.

"And on your body…" Berg moved to the third table. "Your rifle, bayonet, entrenching tools, first aid kit, emergency snow shoes—and of course, your skis and poles. Any questions?"

Wilhelm Steen's hand shot up. He looked worried.

"Private?"

"How much does all that weigh?"

"You men will be carrying about seventy pounds of personal gear," Berg stated. "*Plus* ammo."

Holt let out a low whistle. "We're looking at ninety pounds."

Bjorn Lind heard him. He twisted in his seat in the front row and looked up at Holt, his expression incredulous.

Holt softened his expression and gave the young man an encouraging nod.

Bjorn heaved deep breath and turned his attention back to Wilhelm.

*****

Over the next two weeks, Holt wondered if he had completely lost his mind.

What the *hell* had he been thinking?

Next month he would turn thirty-nine years old and he had three metal plates in his hip that seemed to attract the frigid cold of the Rocky Mountains and store it in his core. His sporadic search and rescue missions in the woods of Wisconsin had not prepared him for the rigors of Army war training during freezing blizzards and at high altitudes with limited oxygen.

Company A's last maneuver before Christmas was a two-night campout with a day-long tactical test in between. As had become their habit, Holt and Roald paired up for the challenge. Holt appreciated the younger man's inspiring energy, and Roald said he relied on Holt's previous experience with many of the skills they were learning.

When camping out, two soldiers worked together and packed their equipment accordingly. Besides their personal gear, one man carried the tent and poles, and the other man carried their Coleman stove, extra gas, and a set of aluminum cooking pots.

Hauling over seventy-five pounds each, tomorrow morning the soldiers would ski up into the mountains surrounding Camp Hale and spend two nights in sub-zero weather sleeping on snow.

Holt stood in the shower the night before the maneuvers trying to soak up as much heat as he could. He took three aspirin before he packed the little bottle in his rucksack and hoped for a solid night's sleep.

He heard some of the guys horsing around in the other half of the latrine and he understood why they needed to let off steam. They were nervous about their upcoming test. None of the soldiers in their company had ever experienced the sort of conditions which they were facing tomorrow.

As the raucous play grew louder, Holt turned off the shower and dried off, not wanting to be caught at a disadvantage if the play spilled into the showers. Which it did.

In spades.

"Go long!" Wilhelm ran into the shower area, twisted, and tossed a rolled-up sleeping bag backwards. It flew over the heads of a couple guys straight toward Bjorn.

Bjorn caught the bag and held it like he was going to pass it back to Steen. Three more guys ran into the showers and they all wrestled with Wilhelm to keep him from catching the return pass.

"Over here!" one guy shouted, laughing and waving his arms. "Throw it to me."

Holt stood his ground on the sidelines, holding his towel around his waist and watching the impromptu game. He envied the younger men. It had been nearly two decades since he'd roughhoused with his buddies the same way.

Bjorn's gaze shifted to Holt.

Startled, he put up his free hand. "No—"

But it was too late. The sleeping bag was flying toward him.

Holt reached up with both hands to catch the rolled bag before it dropped into the drain and somebody was stuck with wet equipment. When he did, his towel fell to the floor.

All movement stopped.

Holt's seven platoon mates stared at him, jaws slack.

Holt tossed the bag at the closest guy then bent over to pick up his towel. He rewrapped it around his waist, he praying he would be able to leave the area without being given the third degree.

That prayer was not answered.

"What the hell?" Wilhelm blurted. "I thought you missed the first war."

Holt felt his face flush. "I did."

"Your hip's a mass of scars, man!" Wilhelm stepped closer. "What the hell happened to you?"

There was no way on the face of God's green earth that Holt was going to stand there naked in an Army shower and tell a bunch of guys half his age about his beloved dead wife.

He had to think fast.

What's plausible?

It was safe to say, "I had an accident."

Wilhelm tilted his head. "What kind of accident?"

The only sound in the echoing shower room was the drip of water behind Holt. He bought himself a few seconds by turning around and twisting the handle tighter to stop the flow.

When he turned back, he decided on, "An avalanche."

"Snow?" Bjorn appeared shaken by the possibility.

Holt shook his head. "No. Rocks. A good sized one fell on me."

Several guys winced, including Bjorn.

"What were you doing?" another guy asked.

"Road construction." *This is working.* "Blasting through a granite hill."

"That looks pretty bad, Gramps." Wilhelm's grim expression displayed his skepticism. "I don't think you're up to being part of this battalion."

Holt drew a deep breath, straightened, and glared at the younger man.

"Have I fallen short yet?" he challenged. "Or did I save your hide once already?"

Wilhelm's face mottled. "The *hell* you did!"

Holt grabbed his shaving kit from the hook on the shower stall. Without another word, he pushed his way through the little crowd and left the latrine.

*****

When their Company A platoon reached the designated campsite late the next afternoon, Sergeant Dagestad ordered the men to settle in. Not a moment too soon as far as Holt was concerned.

His legs burned from the uphill ski climb. His lungs burned from panting in the thin, frigid air. His cheeks burned with frost nip and he kept retying his scarf and breathing warmth against his face to keep his skin from freezing.

At least all of that kept his mind off his hip.

"Where should we pitch the tent?" Roald's question was muffled by his scarf.

"Someplace out of the wind," Holt answered as he looked around the area. "In that little ravine."

Roald nodded and the men trudged toward the dip.

Holt dropped his rucksack and pulled out the tent and poles. This was the first time they had set the tent up so it took them a good quarter of an hour before the little shelter was secured.

Holt opened his canteen to take a drink, but the water was frozen. So he sat down in the snow and shoveled a handful into his mouth, letting the icy crystals melt on his tongue.

"Hungry?" Roald asked as he pulled out the little Coleman stove and aluminum pots.

"Starving." Holt fished in his pack for his rations. "Let's give this a try."

The campsite was at twelve thousand feet and the thin air made it hard to light the stove. After striking six or seven wooden matches which quickly died out, the fuel in the stove finally caught fire. Holt and Roald opened their rations and set the tins in the pot above the flame.

A pair of soldiers from a different platoon had pitched their tent next to Holt and Roald, and they finally got their stove lit as well.

"I know the Army wants us to use our equipment," one of them grumbled. "But it is a better plan to make one big fire and share the warmth."

Holt agreed. "That is what we do when we hunt."

"Hunt where?"

"Wisconsin."

"We are in North Dakota. I am Ole Andersen." The man gestured toward his companion. "My brother Ragnar."

Holt shook both men's mittened hands with his own. "Holt Hansen. You speak like a native."

"We came to America four years ago."

Roald shook the brothers' hands as well. "Roald Rygg. I escaped when Hitler attacked."

"We will kill the little bastard, eh?" Ole grinned. "Maybe slowly?"

Holt chuckled. "Hopefully we will get the chance."

The men ate their warmed food in companionable silence, focusing on getting their potted meat from tin to mouth before the air stole what warmth the stove had given it.

When they finished and put the stoves away, Ole offered another piece of advice. "Put your ski boots inside your sleeping bags or they will be frozen stiff in the morning."

*****

After another lukewarm meal for breakfast, Holt and Roald stood in their not-frozen ski boots and waited for their platoon to receive the instructions for the test.

"You will be split up into three squads," Sergeant Dagestad stated. "Each squad must follow a prescribed path to the objective, and arrive within the time limit set. The objective is the same for everyone, but the three paths are different. Private Hansen?"

Holt stepped forward and accepted a packet.

"You are leading the blue squad. Read off the names."

As he did, Holt was immeasurably relieved that Wilhelm Steen and Bjorn Lind were not in his squad. He gathered his twelve men and opened the packet. The instructions were straight forward, though the map was not marked with the route.

He handed the map to Roald. "Will you watch the compass

headings?"

"Sure." Roald pulled off a mitten and reached in his pocket for his compass.

Holt pointed at two other men. "You two also check your compasses and compare with Rygg's. Make sure you keep us on the right path."

They also retrieved their compasses. As the three men huddled over the map, Holt turned to the rest of the men. "We will take turns at lead and change out every thirty minutes. If the terrain is really rough, we will take a ten minute break after each thirty minute hike. Otherwise, just five."

"How much time do we have to reach the objective?" one guy asked.

Holt consulted the instructions. "Six hours."

"How far are we going?"

Holt added up the segments. "Twelve miles."

"Two miles an hour isn't too bad, eh?" he asked hopefully.

Holt huffed. "That depends on the terrain. This is not like marching up the highway from Leadville to Hale."

His gaze swept over his squad. "Let's go, guys."

*****

The first three miles were relatively easy as the squad traversed a high meadow. After that, they descended about a thousand feet and into the tree line where the trees and brush slowed their pace.

"How are we doing?" Holt asked Roald when the squad took their first break. "There should be a creek we need to cross about a hundred yards ahead if we're on the right track."

"I think we are spot on," Roald replied. "Want me to go look?"

Holt considered the squad. No one was struggling after the easy ski across the meadow. "No, I think we are ready to move on."

Sure enough, the forest's snow-covered floor was sliced by a steep ravine with a thick ribbon of ice filling its bottom. Climbing down the sides and up again was going to require the removal of their skis and the stringing of ropes.

Holt gave the orders and the soldiers followed his instructions. It took three-quarters of an hour for the thirteen men to cross the frozen creek. He looked at his watch.

"We have covered four miles in less than two hours, so we are on a good pace." Holt smiled at his squad. "Good job. Let's keep going."

Holt took his turn at the lead. The men were heading back uphill again and, according to the map, would need to follow a ridge to the next mountain. After a break, Roald took the lead and Holt manned the compass. The squad had picked up the pace and he was sure they would reach the objective well under the allotted time.

Roald stopped the line at the crest of a hill. "We have a problem."

Holt skied forward. When he reached Roald's side he looked down at the ridgeline they were supposed to follow. The narrow path was blocked by a massive avalanche. The hill fell off sharply on one side of the path, and inclined at a steep angle on the other.

While the men gathered to consider the scene in front of them, another enormous chunk of snow shivered, shifted, and tumbled down the ridge from higher up before plunging over the edge.

"There is no way we can safely cross that," Holt stated.

Roald shook his head. "No, we cannot. We will need to find another way to get to the end."

"We were told not to deviate from our path," one young soldier pointed out. "Shouldn't we follow orders?"

Holt turned around and addressed the squad as a whole. "I will not allow any of you to risk your lives by trying to follow a path when the snow above it is obviously unstable. If it falls again while you're trying to cross it, it will push you to your death."

"But will we make it back in time if we have to find another route?" the young soldier pushed.

"He's trying to save your life, kid. Let him." The thirty-year-old who spoke up reached for the map. "Let's find another way."

*****

Seven hours after they left the first camp, Holt led his squad into their camp for the night. In order to get there, the men were forced to backtrack to the frozen creek and follow it downstream until they found a road leading up toward the ridge. They followed the road—which was partially blocked by the same avalanche—and rejoined their assigned path on the other side.

"There you are, Hansen. Finally." Sergeant Dagestad looked frustrated. "What took you so long?"

"Our route was blocked by an avalanche, sir, and snow was still falling," Holt explained. "I refused to allow my men to cross at that point and risk their lives."

"So what did you do?"

Holt unfolded the map and traced his squad's path as he recounted where they had been.

Dagestad looked at him from under lowered brows. "You were told not to deviate from your instructions."

Holt was momentarily speechless. "Yes, but—"

"There are no 'buts' Private Hansen. Mission before men. You deviated from your assignment, and you are more than an hour late in reaching the objective."

Holt clenched his jaw and said nothing.

"You failed the test." Dagestad refolded the map. "Your squad will be on kitchen patrol for the next seven days."

Holt's rage fizzed in his veins. His fists clenched. It required every single ounce of his tenuous self control for him to simply grind out the words, "Yes. Sir."

Chapter Six

December 1942

The week on kitchen patrol was a blessing for Holt since his squad was indoors for those hours instead of out in the blizzards, wind, and deepening snow. The men who were being punished with him debated their situation over scraping and rinsing dirty dishes, and between loading and unloading the big steel dishwashers.

"I'd rather be alive and up to my arms in hot dishwater than be dead," Roald stated.

"It's not fair, is all," another grumbled.

Holt agreed, but didn't dare voice that opinion. "Being part of a unit that functions well means everyone is expected to complete their assignment as given. I didn't follow orders."

"But you protected us!" the private yelped.

"This time." Holt shrugged and pulled a heavy rack of clean, steaming dishes from the dishwasher. "Next time it could go the other way."

"Is that why Steen was promoted? Because he was the first one back?" he pressed.

Holt glanced at Roald. Wilhelm's rise to Private First Class rankled, but there was nothing to be gained by letting his squad fellows know that.

Roald flashed him a brief and tight-lipped smile.

"I was promoted because of my actions in the wash," Holt said evenly. He turned his gaze to the irritated private. "Steen was promoted for following directions well and bringing his squad in well under the allotted time. In *that* context, it is fair."

The private grumbled under his breath and shoved another load of dishes into the washer.

*****

Spending Christmas in a military camp was a new experience for the Norwegian recruits. The camp did have a church, and on Christmas Day there was a service in Norwegian just for the Ninety-Ninth.

> *Over three hundred guys attended, Ralls. Hearing that many voices singing Christmas hymns in Norsk was something I never expected to be a part of.*
> *I have to confess to wiping a tear or two.*

Raleigh wrote back before New Year's.

> *I'm so glad you had a good Christmas, Holt. I missed you terribly, but I'm so proud of what you're doing. And you are in my prayers every single night.*

> *Do you remember Walter Schultz? The new barber? He just bought the barber shop now that Heinrich is retiring, and he's been trying to talk me into joining forces with him and opening a bigger shop together. Anyway, he asked me to go to Oshkosh with him to celebrate New Year's Eve...*

Holt stared at the neatly inked words on the paper. Raleigh was going on a date? With a man who wants to go into business with her?

His hand began to tremble and he set the letter down. Holt always felt like Raleigh was his, exclusively his, even though he had never actually said anything to her to that effect. For the past three years he rested in their friendship and the fact that she never spent time with any other men.

But Holt left Berlin five months ago and was not coming back any time soon. And Raleigh would be thirty-one in February.

If he wasn't willing to ask her to be his steady girl—such a stupid way to put it, but what else could he call it?—then he had no reason to object or be upset if she stepped out with another guy.

Holt didn't write his response to her for three days. Instead he wrestled with himself, struggling with what to say. With what to do. And with how he felt.

On New Year's Eve he finally put his thoughts on paper, assuming Raleigh was spending that same evening in Oshkosh in the company of Walter Schultz, barber shop owner.

Happy New Year, Raleigh! We have seen a lot of changes since this time last year, haven't we. America is at war on two fronts, I am in the Army, and training harder than a man of my age (39 in a couple weeks!) ever should be.

Things here at Camp Hale are moving along. The camp is almost filled up now. Nearly twelve thousand American Army guys have arrived since Thanksgiving, and they're calling themselves the Ski Troopers. I know we're headed for Norway, but I don't know where they're going. We don't train together, so we really don't talk to them.

There have been some guys in the Viking Battalion who couldn't cut it, I'm sorry to say, and they are already transferring out. So I guess the Ninety-Ninth will need to start recruiting again.

And you are considering expanding your shop! That was a surprise. I do remember Walter. He's the stocky brunette with the Chicago accent, if I'm recalling correctly. With his big-city background, I'm not surprised he wants to make his shop bigger and better.

But is it a good idea, Ralls? You don't want to risk overextending yourself. And I'm not sure a town the size of Berlin has enough customers, to be honest. Please think carefully before you decide to do it.

Holt paused, his pen hovering over the paper and his heart thudding in his chest. He had to say it now, or be in danger of never having another chance.

And to continue being honest, I confess I was taken back by your New Year's Eve date with Walter. Of course you are free to do as you please, I just never thought about you spending time with another man.

And yes, I ~~was~~ am jealous. You know how much you mean to me. I never want to lose that.

But how can I expect you to wait for me to return? While I certainly have no plans to die, there are no guarantees in war. And as much as I hate the thought with all of my heart, the safe thing for you to do is look for a future with someone other than me.

Holt's pen hesitated again. He drew a deep breath before writing the last sentence.

Please don't misunderstand me, Raleigh. I only want what's best for you because I love you so very much.
Holt

January 1943

Holt forced himself to focus on the marksmanship test, even though the temperature in the camp was thirty degrees below zero with flurries blowing dry snow pellets into his eyes. His platoon was spread in a horizontal line across the white field, advancing from low ridge to low ridge as they moved closer to the targets—first standing to shoot, then kneeling, then lying on their bellies in the crusty snow.

He hadn't heard back from Raleigh for two weeks since he confessed he loved her and was thinking about writing a letter to retract his declaration, afraid he had upset her.

Please God, don't let me have screwed this up.

Stretched out on the frozen ground Holt pressed his rifle to his shoulder and sighted his aim.

Shot after shot, he watched the holes gathering in the center of his target. He made part of his living by hunting bears, after all, and a wounded bear was no joke. Holt had cultivated both a good eye and a steady hand a long time ago.

When he finished his test and went forward to take his turn at manning the targets another soldier from Company A handed Holt his shot-up target.

"Ninety-five percent."

Holt nodded and smiled behind his scarf. "How's everyone else doing?"

"Great. The majority are scoring above average." The private slapped Holt's arm. "Now it's my turn."

Roald fell in step with Holt when they were finished up and were heading back into the camp. "I'm stopping at Company Headquarters to apply for a weekend pass. Want to come with me?"

Holt chuckled. "To Headquarters or on leave?"

"Both!" Above his scarf the corners of Roald's eyes pinched with his smile. "There's a place in Denver I want to visit. The ski troopers were talking about it. It's called the Brown Palace."

"I'll come as far as the office for now," Holt said. "We'll see about Denver."

The pair trudged through Camp Hale in the frigid afternoon as the snow flurries gained momentum. When they reached the Company Command Post Holt pulled the door open and followed Roald in.

"Hansen—you got a phone call this afternoon," the lieutenant on duty said when he saw Holt. "Said she'd call back at seven."

"She? Who?" The thought that something had happened to his father shot through Holt's gut like one of the bullets he spent the afternoon firing off.

"Didn't say."

"Well, what did she sound like?" Holt prodded. "Was she upset?"

The lieutenant shrugged. "Sorry, I didn't take the call. I was at lunch. But come back at seven and find out for yourself."

After Roald asked for two leave request forms he handed one to Holt. "Who do you think called you?"

Holt absent-mindedly accepted the form. "My mother, obviously. I hope my father's okay."

Roald nodded soberly. "I hope so, too."

Holt looked at the form. "I better fill this out just in case I need to go home."

"You'll never make it there and back in forty-eight hours," Roald observed. "Just the round trip on the train takes four days."

Roald was right. Holt handed the form back to the lieutenant.

"I'll wait until I talk to my mom. You go on to Denver without me."

"Are you sure?"

Holt nodded and looked at the clock. It was four-fifteen.

Holt was back in Company A's office by six-forty-five. He sat in a wooden chair, in silence, while the soldier on duty read a book behind the brand new gray metal desk.

At seven-o-five the phone rang.

*****

Raleigh held the heavy black receiver against her ear while the operator connected her call to Camp Hale for the second time that day.

"A Company," the duty soldier answered.

"I'm calling for Private First Class Holten Hansen," Raleigh stated. "He should be expecting this call. Is he there?"

"Yeah. He's here. Hold please."

Raleigh waited on the silent line, heart pounding. After half a minute, the static of the connection resumed.

"Mom? It's Holt."

Raleigh hesitated at Holt's anxious tone, wondering if calling was such a good idea after all.

"It—it's not your mom, Holt," she stammered. "It's me. Raleigh."

"Raleigh!" Holt was clearly surprised. "What's wrong? Are my parents okay?"

Again Raleigh was taken aback. This call was not starting out in any way that she imagined it would.

"I don't know. But I'm sure they are fine."

Holt sounded confused. "Then why are you calling?"

Raleigh scoffed. Why shouldn't she call him? Did he have no concern for her after all?

"Because *I'm* not fine!" she snapped.

"Oh—" Holt sucked a quick breath. "Is that why you haven't written?"

"Yes."

Holt's tone changed. "I'm so sorry, Ralls. What's wrong?"

Raleigh cleared her throat. The conversational ball was back in her court now, and she needed to make sure she communicated clearly.

"I didn't know how to respond to your last letter. Honestly, I was so angry when I read it, I wanted to shoot you."

"Angry?" Holt sounded gob smacked. "Why?"

Raleigh pulled a deep calming breath.

Keep yourself together.

"Ralls, I—"

"Hear me out, Holt!" she interrupted.

"Right. Sorry." Now Holt cleared his throat. "Go on."

Raleigh straightened her shoulders. "After two weeks, I'm still angry. So I figured I should call you instead of trying to explain it in writing."

"I—I don't understand why you're angry, Ralls."

Now Raleigh was surprised. "You really can't figure it out?"

"Are you mad because I said be careful about expanding your store?" he ventured.

"No!" Raleigh huffed. "I'm mad because you said you loved me but I should go find another man!"

Holt was quiet for a moment, and Raleigh could imagine the familiar pull of his brows as he puzzled out his response. "But I was only thinking of you."

"Oh, really?" Her voice dribbled sarcasm through the phone line so heavily that she knew he'd pick it up. "How is that?"

"I want to protect you, Ralls. I don't want you to get hurt. You mean the world to me."

"And *you* mean the world to *me*." Raleigh sniffed and swiped the back of her hand under her nose. "I love you, Holt. I don't want anyone else."

"But..." His frustration was clear in his tone. "It's too risky."

"Why? Because you could go into battle and die?" Her blunt words bludgeoned her own chest. Hard.

"Well... yes."

She shook her head though she knew he couldn't see that. "You have an equal—no a *better* than equal chance of coming home to me when this is all over."

"But next month I turn thirty-nine, and the month after that you'll be thirty-one."

"And?" she challenged, fearing where this turn was going.

"And if these wars last a couple years—which they very well could—I'll be forty-one and coming home to a thirty-three-year-old woman."

Raleigh sniffed again, hoping Holt wouldn't realize she was crying. "Sorry. I have a cold."

Holt ignored that and gently asked, "Don't you want a family, Ralls? To have children someday?"

She sucked a ragged and startled breath. "Are you saying you don't?"

"No, that's not—"

"Women can give birth into their forties," she countered, her tone stern. "And men can become fathers into their seventies."

"True, but—"

"And we're only talking about a couple of years, Holt. It's very possible."

Holt was quiet for a moment. Raleigh knew him well enough to know he was pondering his words carefully.

"What if you wait for me during those years and then I don't make it back?" he prodded. "Then what?"

Raleigh didn't hesitate. "That's a risk I'm willing to take."

"Ralls—"

"Holt, stop. I know you are all about protecting people…" She pulled a raspy breath and laid out the truth. "Because you couldn't protect Nora."

Silence.

Raleigh waited, hoping she had not gone too far.

When Holt didn't speak, she continued, "I'm not afraid to take that risk when the stakes are this high, Holt. You have to believe me. I *am* going to wait for you because, honestly, you're the only man for me."

Holt finally drew a breath so deep Raleigh could almost feel it fill her lungs.

"Do you really love me, Holt?" Raleigh's voice wavered as she pressed him to be truthful. "Or are you arguing with me because you don't?"

"No! Yes!"

"Well which is it?"

Holt heaved a shaky sigh. "I love you, Raleigh Burns. I never thought I would love anyone again, but there it is. You have my whole heart."

"Then when this is all over, come home and marry me."

Holt huffed a chuckle. "Are you proposing?"

"No. I'll let you do that." Raleigh's voice lifted along with her relief at their conversation's new direction. "You'll get down on one knee, with a bouquet of roses, and ask me for my hand."

"And you will say yes." It was not a question.

Raleigh smiled. "I will, soldier. Count on it."

"Then I guess it's settled." Holt paused. "I'm really glad you called, Ralls."

"So am I." Her voice was soft. "And I'm glad we worked this out."

"So am I." Holt cleared his throat. "This call is going to cost you a fortune. We better hang up."

"I suppose so. I love you, Holten Hansen. With all my heart."

"I love you, too. I'll write again soon. Good night, Ralls."

Raleigh hung up the phone before she realized with a start that Holt just agreed to marry her. Holten Hansen would be her husband after all. She never expected that agreement to happen any time soon, let alone tonight.

But she was glad beyond words that it had.

Stay safe, soldier.

Come home to me.

Chapter Seven

February 1943

A full battalion of the ski troopers had been sent on some sort of test on a mountain called Homestake during the first week of February, so the camp was a little less crowded for the week-and-a-half that the soldiers were gone.

But when the soldiers from the Homestake test straggled back into camp it was clear to Holt that they had not been adequately prepared for the extreme winter conditions that they encountered at higher altitudes.

"And that's why we are stepping up our training," Sergeant Dagestad barked. "We're headed up Copper Mountain to twelve thousand feet. The first leg is tomorrow. Have your snow gear packed and ready after breakfast."

Holt and his squad were ready and waiting when Dagestad called roll. There were no trucks in sight, which meant a long march with heavy packs in the freezing wind.

"Our objective over the next couple days is to use our Army equipment as instructed," Dagestad explained. "We're testing it for when we get sent into Norway. We need to know how well it works."

Holt thought that was a reasonable thing to do, considering the frigid Nordic winters. And he figured that the Viking Battalion guys would be dropped in remote areas, out of sight of the Germans.

And probably at night.

"Our first objective is North Sheep Mountain, eight miles north and east. We'll ski march in single file. Let's go."

Holt fell in about half the way back from the front. He didn't want to listen to Wilhelm Steen's annoying chatter all day.

As usual, Roald fell in behind him.

There was no trail to follow so their pace was slow. The soldiers, dressed in their white camouflage suits, herringboned up hills and snowplowed back down though the rough terrain. Holt hated this sort of stop and go. Not only was progress excruciatingly slow, but it put more of a strain on his hip than straight cross-country ski marching did.

As the soldiers continued their march, the weather took a decidedly unfriendly turn. Already windy, heavy clouds were gathering above them as if conferring on how to make the men even more miserable.

Dagestad called a halt. "Ten minute break!"

Holt sat back on his skis, panting, and shrugged off his eighty-pound rucksack.

Roald mimicked his actions. "How far have we gone, do you think?"

"Two miles at least. Maybe two-and-a-half." Holt pulled down his scarf and took a drink of slushy water from his canteen.

Roald did the same and then made a face before pulling his scarf back up. "It's going to be a long day."

*****

It was a long day. The platoon reached North Sheep Mountain after six hours of single-file ski marching over eight miles of rough terrain.

"Set up your tents in rows, get out your stoves, and make your suppers," Dagestad ordered. "We're going to do everything by the book."

Roald and Holt did as ordered, though both men agreed that this was not the best plan.

"I know the Army likes everything neat and orderly, but we should be looking for protected spots out of this wind," Holt grumbled.

"And sharing a fire." Roald struggled to light their camp stove, finally succeeding on the fifth try. He looked up at Holt. "But Dagestad is hell bent on following the rules this time."

Holt considered his young friend. "Maybe there is a point in proving the rules to be wrong."

Roald dug through his rucksack for his rations. "You mean we follow them, but it's a disaster?"

"Something like that. Yes." Holt retrieved his own food. "Hopefully we survive the trial and then we can report back on the problems we encountered."

The men warmed their meal in front of their two-man tent alongside twenty other tents neatly arrayed in two rows across the side of North Sheep Mountain. None of the soldiers looked happy about their conditions, and as soon as they finished eating they retreated into the relative protection of their tents.

The next morning the soldiers heated up their breakfasts, ate, took down their tents, and packed up their equipment before receiving their orders for the day. A low cloud shrouded the platoon in fog, but thankfully the wind had died down.

"Today we are splitting the platoon into two teams," Dagestad began. "Each team will be given a map to Copper Mountain with a different route to follow, but both routes are the same length—fourteen miles. There are flags along the way that you are expected to collect, four each, and their coordinates are marked on the map. You are not expected to reach the objective until tomorrow, but the team which completes the challenge first will be rewarded. Any questions so far?"

When no one spoke up, Dagestad continued, "I have decided to split the platoon by age. Young guys against the older guys. We'll see if experience trumps youthful vigor."

Holt glanced at Roald. The younger man was frowning.

"Everyone from age twenty-nine to forty-five will be in the

older group, the rest of you in the younger group." Dagestad's gaze swept over the assembled soldiers and rested on Holt. "Okay, group up. If you aren't teamed with your tent mate, then figure it out."

Holt looked at Roald and shrugged, sorry to be split from his capable friend but glad not to be teamed up with Wilhelm.

"Good luck with those guys. I'm guessing Dagestad expects your team to kill us."

Roald glanced toward Wilhelm Steen and Bjorn Lind. "We'll see. Good luck to you, too."

The twenty older soldiers huddled around their map.

"Which of us is good at orienteering?" a private first class named Olsen asked. Three hands went up.

Olsen handed the map to one of them. "You start at lead. We'll need your skills in this fog."

"I'll take the end of the line," Holt volunteered. "To make sure no one falls behind."

Olsen nodded. "Let's go."

After a few minutes of getting oriented, the twenty older men skied away from the campsite heading east.

*****

The fog dissipated in the early afternoon as the temperature dropped dramatically and the moisture in the air turned to ice. For four-and-a-half hours the men skied in panting silence, taking a ten-minute break every hour and changing out the leader. The going was just as rough as the day before—if there was a trail nearby their instructions were keeping them away from it.

"When we are dropped into Norway, there won't be trails there either," the oldest member of their team, who was in his early fifties, reminded the group.

One of the three orienteering guys looked up from the map. "At least we have the first flag and, according to the map, the second flag is about half a mile ahead."

Olsen's eyes crinkled above his frosted scarf. "Good. Let's see how far we can get today. I really want to beat those kids."

Holt chuckled. "I really want to beat Steen."

Several of the guys laughed at that. Wilhelm Steen's constant badgering of Holt was obvious to everyone in the platoon, though no one took sides. Better for the group to let it play out by itself.

The soldiers set off again, in the direction of the second flag. A man named Jensen found it tacked to a pine tree about ten feet off the ground. He used his rope and scaled the trunk to reach it, and the group cheered when he held it up triumphantly.

"We've covered six miles so far," Olsen announced and consulted his watch. "There should be three more hours of daylight. Let's see how far we can get."

Holt was panting and sweat was running down his back when it grew too dark to safely continue. An hour ago the icy cloud which surrounded them earlier had let go of its hoard and a heavy snow began to fall on the line of soldiers, slowing their progress.

The line's leader stopped the men at the bottom of a rise. "I can't take us any farther under these conditions. We'll have to make camp here."

Holt looked around the hollow and made a decision. "I suggest that we abandon the Army's plan of tents in a row and look for shelter."

"I agree," Jensen said emphatically. "This blizzard is getting worse."

Holt nodded. "How about if half of us pitch the tents, and the other half gather firewood for a central fire?"

Olsen peered at him over his scarf. "Sounds like you've lived rough before."

"Hunting bear in northern Wisconsin." Holt shrugged. "You learn a thing or two."

The team set to work. Holt partnered with Harald, the twenty-nine-year old who also was split from his regular tent mate. Holt pitched their shared tent in a sheltered spot under a snow drift while the younger man brought wood.

In less than an hour, a shared fire was crackling in the center of the hollow and the twenty soldiers were using it to heat their rations. Heavy snow blew in a crazy wind-choreographed dance all around them.

"This is so much better than last night," one of the men commented with his mouth full of potted beef. "Glad you suggested it, Hansen."

"How far did we get today?" Holt asked.

The man who started the day at lead grinned. "Almost nine miles. Just over five to go."

Jensen whooped. "Let's get an early start tomorrow and be waiting when the young pups get to the checkpoint."

Holt smiled and scooped the last bite of meat from his tin.

I'd like nothing better.

*****

Holt woke in darkness and shined his headlamp on his watch, certain he'd been sleeping long enough.

"What time is it?" Harald asked.

"Almost seven. Time to get up." Holt sat up and pushed against the tent opening. "No wonder we were so snug. We're in a snow cave."

"What?" Harald sat up in his sleeping bag looking concerned. "Are we buried?"

"We're okay."

Holt wrapped his scarf snuggly around his neck to keep snow from falling inside his coat, and then he climbed through their snow covering to get out of the tent.

When he got to his feet he saw big lumps of snow all around the dead fire, each one housing two men in a tent. The clear sky above was lightening from gray to lavender.

Holt put two fingers in his mouth and whistled long and loud.

Looking like gophers emerging from their burrows, the awakened soldiers scrambled from their snow-encased tents.

Holt laughed, his breath clouding in the cold, crisp air. "Time to get a move on, boys, if we want to come in first!"

*****

After a cold breakfast, the twenty soldiers resumed their northeasterly march toward hopeful victory. They found the third flag almost by accident—it was only a hundred yards from where they camped.

Two miles farther along, they reached the edge of a deep but narrow ravine.

"The map says we are supposed to follow the ravine east to its foot, then head back up the other side before turning north." The orienteering soldier looked up from the map. "The fourth flag is on the other side."

Twenty pairs of eyes looked across the ravine.

"I see it," Olsen said. "It's right there."

Holt looked at the trees edging the ravine. "I say we cross here with ropes. What do you guys say?"

Jensen turned to the guy with the map. "How much mileage would we cut if we did?"

The man measured the map. "I'd say a good mile and a half."

"Then we'd only have another mile and a half to the meeting point on Highway Ninety-One." Holt looked at the others for support. "Have any of you done anything like this before?"

Most shook their heads. One guy lifted a tentative hand.

"I can show you if you want," Holt stated. "Or we can ski down, and climb back up."

"Hell, no. Let's do it." Jensen stepped forward. "What do we do?"

Holt grinned.

This was good.

"First, we have to get a rope to the other side and secure it to something." Holt pointed to a broken tree stump. "Like that."

"I can rope that." The guy in his fifties stepped forward and began tying a sliding knot at one end of his rope. "I've roped cattle in South Dakota for years."

The cowboy's first try went off to the left. The second to the right. And the third circled the tall stump.

He grinned and handed the rest of the rope to Holt. "And that's how it's done."

Holt looped the rope around the tree closest to the ravine—twice—then asked Olsen to pull on the loose end while he dug out two carabiners.

He clipped the carabiners to the taut rope. "When the rope is tied on the other side, you'll clip one on each half of the line. Then run your own rope through the clips, like this, to form a loop you can sit in."

Holt ran the loop around his hips.

"Hold onto rope like this so it doesn't loosen." Holt gripped both strands of rope running through one carabiner in each hand.

"Now, if you guys will keep the rope taut, I'll ride it to the other side."

A couple guys stepped up to keep the rope from unwinding around the tree under his weight. Holt stepped backwards as far as he could, then ran the four steps forward and launched himself into the air.

Though the ride was maybe seven seconds long, holding himself up on the single rope made his arms burn. His trajectory was low and without a second stabilizing rope his body turned in the air.

He slammed into the anchoring tree trunk with his left hip.

Searing pain ran down his leg and up his back. He couldn't help but grunt with the impact. For a moment he couldn't breathe.

"You okay, Hansen?"

Holt waved a reassuring hand in the air, unable to speak.

My hip is held together with metal plates.

It can't break again.

Holt forced himself to roll onto his knees. If he could stand, he was still in one piece.

Holt pulled his legs under him and, using the stump for support, regained his feet.

He faced the group on the other side and hoped his grimace passed as a grin.

"Rough landing," he shouted across. "I'll move the rope."

Trying to ignore the excruciating throbbing in his core, Holt bought time by looking around for a tree to tie the rope to higher. Then he lifted the rope from the stump and untied the sliding knot.

With a deep breath, which he held, he took a step toward the nearest tree.

Do not limp.

He could walk. His hip was not re-broken. But he'd bet good money the bone was good and bruised.

And it hurt like hell.

Holt pulled on the shorter end of the rope to even the ends out, then reached up and ran the rope twice around the pine tree and above some branches which would support it. He tied the ends together, using his body weight to tighten the knot.

The rope now stretched from Holt's position, across the ravine, around the first tree twice, and back to Holt.

"Okay!" he shouted. "Come on over."

His twenty-nine-year-old tent mate stepped right up, clipped a carabiner on each length of the rope, and fashioned his loop like Holt had.

"Take a good run at it!" Holt called out. "You need the momentum to make it all the way!"

Harald nodded, backed up, and bolted forward. He let out an excited whoop as he slid across the ravine.

"That was amazing!" he yelped when he stumbled to a stop. He turned around and shouted. "Come on, guys!"

In a quarter hour, all twenty soldiers on the team had ridden the ropes across the ravine. Holt stood by the landing tree the whole time, praying for the pain in his hip to subside.

While Olsen retrieved the flag, Holt remained in place and

untied the rope.

He pulled on one end and coiled the rope around his arm as the loose end dropped into the ravine, the slid up the other side, around the tree trunk, and back in and out of the ravine.

He handed the rope to the Norwegian cowboy from South Dakota. "Thanks. Couldn't have done it without you."

*****

Somehow Holt managed to ski the last mile and a half to the checkpoint at Copper Mountain by keeping most of his weight on his right leg. He knew that leg would be sore tonight, but maybe he could find a way to rest for a day.

I'll pack myself in snow. That will help.

When someone asked him why, he'd just say he was sore from the march. And if he had to claim age, he would.

When the team skied up to the Highway Ninety-One checkpoint, Sergeant Dagestad looked gobsmacked. "How did you get here so soon?"

The soldiers shrugged and exchanged conspiratorial glances.

"We are just good," Olsen offered.

Jensen held out his hand. "Here are the four flags."

Dagestad's eyes narrowed. "Go get in the truck. I'll see you back at camp."

Holt stepped on the bumper of the personnel carrier with his right leg and accepted outstretched hands that lifted him into the vehicle. He sat on the bench in the nearest available spot.

Some of the guys watched him closely.

"You hit that stump pretty hard," one of them said. "Are you sure you're okay?"

Holt flashed a crooked grin. "I'll have one hell of a bruise, that's for certain. But nothing's broken."

"You might want to get checked out at the hospital just to be sure," Olsen suggested.

Holt sighed. "If my hip or leg were broken, I would not be

able to walk, much less ski that last stretch."

Trust me. I know.

When he still faced skeptical looks, Holt offered, "I'll use snow for cold packs to keep it from swelling. I'll take a couple aspirin. I'll be fine."

The men in the truck seemed to believe him and turned back to their own conversations. Except for Harald.

Holt caught Harald's eye and the younger man scowled at him. Holt opened his mouth to say something, and then a shot of realization zinged through his frame.

Harald was in the showers the day Holt dropped his towel.

Harald saw my scars.

Chapter Eight

After dinner Holt undressed behind the shower curtain and examined his hip. The bruise which covered his lower left side was an ominous dark purple rimmed in angry scarlet. While tender to the touch and swollen, the skin had been protected by his winter wear and wasn't split open.

Holt thanked God that the plates successfully held his once shattered hipbone securely in place. Sure, it hurt. Badly. But he was still whole. The pain would eventually subside and he could go on training.

Holt showered quickly, dressed, and went outside. He scooped snow into a towel and rolled it up to make an ice pack. Retreating to his bunk he settled the pack against the bruise, downed four aspirin tablets, and focused his attention on writing Raleigh a letter about how the old guys beat the young ones to the finish line by an hour and a half.

He saw Harald approach out of the corner of his eye and he paused mid-sentence.

"Got a minute?" the young man asked.

"Sure." Holt bent his right leg to make space on his cot for Harald to sit.

Harald glanced around before he spoke. "I, uh. I saw your hip that night in the showers…"

Holt kept his gaze steady. "I remember."

"You hit that tree pretty hard."

Holt huffed a chuckle, deciding to take a lighter path through this conversation. "You're telling me."

Harald's brows drew together. "Are you sure you're okay?"

"To be honest, I've got one hell of a bruise." Holt pulled back his Army issued blanket to expose the soothing ice-packed towel resting against his damage-concealing flannels. "I'm applying ice, which is really all that can be done. I'll be fine."

Harald looked skeptical but conceded the point. "Okay. If you say so."

Holt replaced the blanket. "Thanks for asking, though. I appreciate it."

Harald looked a little embarrassed. "After spending those two days with you, I have to say I might have misjudged you."

That was surprising. "How?"

Harald glanced over his shoulder again before he answered.

"You know Wilhelm. He's always running off at the mouth about how you old guys should be at home in rocking chairs and let the young guys fight this war."

"We old guys missed the last one, you know. We were too young," Holt pointed out. "If the Ninety-Ninth hadn't let us in, we would have missed both."

Harald nodded. "Yeah. I get that now."

"And…" Holt smiled crookedly. He could not resist pointing out the obvious. "We beat the younger team by a significant margin."

Harald chuckled. "Yeah we did." He stood up. "Well, let me know if you need anything."

Holt gave Harald a two fingered salute. "Will do."

He returned to his letter to Raleigh, deciding to add something about the conversation he just had with Harald—just not *why* his platoon mate approached him in the first place. Holt paused and adjusted the ice pack.

Raleigh did *not* need to know anything about him hitting the tree.

*****

Late the next morning, the twenty men on Holt's team were summoned to A Company Headquarters to meet with Sergeant Dagestad and Captain Rolf Berg. The men packed into a small meeting room and perched on folding metal chairs facing a chalkboard, curious to a man about why they were there.

"Men, we need to discuss the two-day training challenge you just completed," Dagestad began. "Do you recall what the goals were of this challenge?"

Olsen raised a hand. "To use our equipment as instructed to see if it works?"

"Yes." Dagestad's stern gaze shifted through the small crowd. "Anything else?"

"Do things by the book?" Jensen offered.

"Exactly." The sergeant clasped his hands behind his back. "And is that what you all did?"

The men glanced at each other, confusion displayed in their expressions, and Holt suddenly realized what this meeting was about.

It was about following rules.

Shit.

Captain Berg stepped forward. "Each team was being followed by a pair of judges. They tracked you and determined if the instructions you were given were being followed."

The twenty men now sat as still as drab-green statues.

"I'm sure you know what they discovered." Berg drew a deep breath. "They discovered the remains of a shared fire used for cooking, and tents placed in a circle around it, not lined up in the required rows."

Holt needed to address that. "Captain, may I speak?"

Berg folded his arms and stared hard at Holt. "Go ahead."

"Sir, we got caught in a wicked blizzard, and our equipment was just not adequate," he said honestly. "The shared fire not only allowed us to all stay warm, but it also heated our rations more effectively than the camp stoves."

Berg tilted his head. "The shared fire would make you targets for the enemy. Was that your plan?"

"With all respect, sir," Jensen ventured. "We were told to

test equipment and collect flags. We were not told to expect enemy engagement."

"That would certainly have changed the objective, sir," Holt conceded.

"In war you *always* expect enemy engagement," Berg sneered. "Now about the route you took."

Shit shit shit.

"Whose idea was it to traverse the ravine to the last flag instead of ski around it as the map showed?"

Holt stood and said softly, "Mine, sir."

Chairs squeaked as the other soldiers turned to look at him.

"And why did you disobey orders, Private?" Captain Berg demanded.

"I didn't consider it disobeying, sir," Holt explained. "We could see the flag, and we were in the right spot. So we used our Army equipment to traverse the ravine and reach the checkpoint more efficiently."

Probably should not have said 'more'…

Berg's face reddened ominously. "Your training in ropes and climbing does not start for two more months. You risked the safety of every man on your team."

"I would never do that!" Holt blurted. "It was a simple process and narrow ravine!"

Olsen stood as well. "We all agreed on it, sir," he offered. "It wasn't Hansen's fault."

"Is that so?" Berg growled. "Who agrees with Private Olsen?"

Jensen and Harald stood.

The other sixteen men remained seated.

"Well then." Captain Berg turned and addressed Dagestad. "Sergeant, these sixteen men who remained seated will have two weeks of extra duty on kitchen patrol for not following the instructions given to them by their commanding officer."

"Yes, sir," Dagestad responded amidst a roomful of eye rolls and grimaces.

"The four men standing will be on latrine duty for the next three weeks," Berg continued. "And Hansen, I'm taking away your Private First Class stripe."

Holt forced himself not to react, but he was seething inside. "Yes, sir. Understood."

"You are all dismissed." Captain Berg spun on a polished heel and strode from the room, followed by Sergeant Dagestad.

*****

Raleigh read Holt's letter about the two-day test, the decisions the group made regarding the tents and fires, and his suggestion that the soldiers cross the ravine by a rope line.

She could feel his anger and frustration in his long rant, and saw it in the dark, angular lines of his writing.

I would never put any man in danger. You <u>know</u> this about me! Just like when I refused to cross the fresh avalanche and risk the lives of my men. I was punished for that, too!

There are times when those men making the rules don't seem to have <u>any</u> idea what it's really like in the field! Otherwise, why would they insist on tents being in a straight line?

What difference would that make in winning the war? Will the Germans see the orderly array of tents and run away in fear? Or even surrender? No!

Raleigh laughed out loud at that. Holt had a very valid point. The problem arose when a lowly soldier brought it to the attention of those men 'making the decisions' that their decisions could actually be detrimental to the soldiers involved.

And as an older man with plenty of outdoor experience, of course Holt felt compelled to bring the errors and corrections to their attention.

I understand exactly how you feel, Holt. And I completely agree with your decisions.

It seems to me that there will be critical instructions which will impact the thing you are meant to accomplish at times. But there are also times when something as arbitrary as how the tents are placed should bow to the soldiers' needs for safety and comfort.

I'm sorry you got demoted back to Private, but be assured that I don't think one whit less of you because of it. In fact, I respect you more for putting the needs of your men ahead of personal gain or loss. Your constant protection of those around you is one of the things I love most about you.

April 1943

Holt survived his demotion with a wounded pride that slowly healed along with his hip. And now that spring had reached the Rockies, the Ninety-Ninth Battalion's training switched from emphasis on snow and skiing to rock and mountain climbing techniques.

A cliff on the edge of the camp was pressed into heavy service for the beginning climbers, and from dawn to dusk everyday it was covered with scrambling soldiers literally learning their ropes, both from the Ninety-Ninth Battalion and the ten-thousand ski troopers at Camp Hale.

The other half of the Viking soldiers' warm-weather training focused on stamina. Long marches with fully loaded packs, taken at double-time in the thin air, pushed Holt to his limit. The only saving graces were first that the men got out from under the soot-filled canopy that fouled the air over Camp Hale, and second that Holt's hip ached less in the warmer weather.

Two things to be grateful for.

Today the Ninety-Ninth was finishing up preparations for a trip south to Camp Carson, Colorado for a personnel review by none other than President Franklin D. Roosevelt himself. And even though it was April, and the Colorado spring was in full force, the official uniform for the Viking Battalion was still ski boots and mountain jackets.

So that was what they cleaned and laundered, and that was what they wore.

Standing at attention in full sun and waiting for the President was uncomfortable at best. Holt could feel sweat rolling down his spine and he resisted the nearly overwhelming urge to wipe his brow rather than allow the sweat to keep stinging his eyes.

After waiting in formation for an hour, President Roosevelt's wheelchair rolled into view and began to make its way down the lines of Army and Air Corps soldiers.

You know I didn't vote for him, Ralls, I voted for Wendell Willkie. But that doesn't matter. Roosevelt is the duly elected President of the United States of America, and for that reason alone he deserves my respect. Lord knows, I'll never be in his position!

It means a lot to all the guys in the Ninety-Ninth that he took time out in the middle of a war to come all the way from Washington D.C. to Colorado just to encourage us and tell us he was proud of us.

I'm proud of us, too.

On a completely different subject, the intelligence officer at battalion headquarters needs maps and pictures of Norway. Could you post notices in the diner, both taverns, your shop, and Walter's barber shop asking if anyone has maps or photos of coastlines and seaside towns? The Army is specifically interested in harbors, airports, factories, and anything else that might be significant to the military.

If they are willing to donate that stuff, or knows anyone who does, please have them mail it to Camp Hale, Attention: Intelligence

And make sure they know that by donating these things that they are helping the Viking Battalion liberate Norway!

Your loving Viking,
Holt

August 1943

Holt stepped out of the train onto the platform in the Milwaukee train station knowing that no one would be there to greet him. He hadn't told Raleigh or his parents that he was coming because it all happened so fast he'd beat the letters home.

And he didn't call because he liked the idea of surprising them all by showing up unannounced.

The Ninety-Ninth had received unspecified travel orders for later in the month, and all the soldiers were told they were being given immediate leave for fourteen days. After they returned to Camp Hale they would be leaving the country.

And because the Army could not legally send any soldiers overseas who were not American citizens, they started checking every one of the nine hundred Viking Battalion guys, and then busing the soldiers who weren't citizens yet into Leadville to swear them in.

There were so many soldiers who needed to be made citizens that it took two full days to make certain every Viking Battalion guy qualified for an American passport.

Holt hefted his duffel bag and flagged a taxi to take him to the bus station. The next bus north through Oshkosh was leaving in just over two hours, so Holt bought his ticket before wandering down the block looking for the closest thing he could find to a home cooked meal.

Four-and-a-half hours later, in the dimming orange light of the summer's balmy evening, Holt stood in front of his parents' front door. He opened it and walked in, grinning like a hyena.

The next morning, he borrowed a car and drove to Berlin.

*****

Raleigh was in the back of her shop mixing hair color for the pastor's wife, who was expected any moment, when she heard the bell on the shop's front door jangle.

"I'll be right out!" she called from the back.

"I just need a trim," a man's voice replied.

Raleigh froze. Was she imagining things?

Could it be?

She pulled back the curtain which separated the front of the shop from the storeroom and peered around it.

A rugged-looking six-foot-four soldier in fatigues stood by the front desk, cap in hand, and grinning so wide that his cheeks nearly obscured his eyes.

"Holt!"

Raleigh dropped her melamine bowl, which clattered noisily on the linoleum floor and spattered the tiles with Brown Number Five. She leapt over the mess and bolted toward Holt at full speed before leaping into his arms.

Holt grabbed her and staggered backward against the front desk, saving both of them from mimicking the bowl's fate.

Raleigh's arms had a locking grip around Holt's neck and sobs of joy stole her voice for a moment. She wiped her cheek with one hand then kissed him, hard and fast, on the mouth.

"Wh—what are you doing here?" she managed.

Holt laughed and kissed her back before she loosened her hold and he set her down on her feet.

"We got our traveling orders five days ago and were given

fourteen days' immediate leave," he explained. "I hopped on the train that same day."

"Why didn't you tell me?" Raleigh asked, still shocked that Holt was standing in front of her.

"I'd beat a letter getting here, and…" He shrugged impishly. "Then I decided not to call and to surprise you."

Raleigh turned her head toward her big wall calendar and made a quick calculation. "Nine days left, minus four days to take the train back, means I have you for five days."

Holt turned her face back toward his. "Let's not waste a minute."

"No," she whispered happily. "Let's not."

His lips met hers and this time he kissed her very, very well.

*****

The five days Holt spent with Raleigh was the first time the couple was together since declaring their love back in January.

While he wondered if Raleigh would want to talk about their sort-of engagement, Holt really hoped she wouldn't. He was never a superstitious man, but he still didn't think it was wise to tempt fate by making plans that might never have the chance to come to fruition.

And with his own experiences with grief, he knew that if he did not return from wherever he was about to be sent, that Raleigh would be better off if everything between them was still in the *someday* stage.

It was clear to Holt that Raleigh felt the same way, because her conversations centered on current events and current gossip. Only her kisses and caresses spoke of her love for him and her hopes for a future together.

Holt made a point of spending time with his parents as well as his sort-of fiancée. He and Raleigh drove to Oshkosh three evenings out of the five to have dinner with them, and on the second night his mother pulled him aside.

"Help me pick tomatoes, Holt?"

"Sure, Mom." Holt followed her out the back door.

"What's going on with you and Raleigh?" she asked him once they were out of earshot. "Something is definitely different between you two."

Holt looked down at his mother, still classically beautiful at sixty-five. "I finally realized that, if I was going to war, I should live again while I still had the chance."

She titled her head and looked up at him. "So you finally noticed what was right under your nose?"

Holt chuckled. "I'd already noticed. I just finally accepted the inevitable."

He bent over and picked a fragrant red tomato and handed it to his mother. "Do you approve?"

"More than." She smiled. "I was hoping you wouldn't mourn forever."

Holt picked two more fruits, deciding what to say next. He settled on, "We'll make it official when the war is over."

"Not before you go?" His mother sounded disappointed.

"No, Mom." Holt picked one last tomato and turned back toward the house. "I want to do it right. For Raleigh's sake."

"*Hvordan er din Norsk?*"

Holt laughed. "*Utmerket. Jeg er helt flytende.*" Excellent. I am completely fluent.

"Well, your pronunciation is a bit accented, but I guess you'll pass." She looped her arm through his as the walked. "I am proud of you, Holt."

He kissed the top of her fading blonde head.

*****

Holt lay on Raleigh's couch and held her close along his body. "I wonder if we should have eloped so we could have a wedding night together before I left."

Raleigh slid her hand into Holt's unbuckled pants and

caressed his very muscular left butt cheek. "This will do for now. You need to have something to come home for."

Holt wiggled a finger into her unbuttoned blouse and traced a delightful path around her bra and down her belly to her panties. "I suppose you're right. But I want all of you."

Raleigh wanted all of him, too. There was no doubt about it. And considering her past history, there was technically no reason not to bed him before the vows were spoken.

Except that this was the man she wanted to spend the rest of her life with, and she did not intend to cheapen their new love by giving in to momentary lust. Especially after everything she had gone through, and the effort required for her to escape and put her past behind her.

She finally had a chance at a normal relationship with a wonderful man, and the possibility of messing that up was one risk she was *not* willing to take.

Holt pulled her into another kiss. She pressed against his wandering hand and moaned a little before reluctantly pulling away.

Raleigh looked into his eyes while tears welled in hers and blurred his face. "Then be sure you come home to me, soldier."

Holt nodded, swallowed visibly, and turned his head toward the living room window.

"The sun is coming up."

Chapter Nine

September 1943

The Viking Battalion's ten-day voyage from New Jersey to Scotland on the six-thousand-ton steamer *SS Mexico* was uncomfortable, to put it mildly. The ship was an old banana boat and every wave between the United States and Scotland seemed to lift her propeller out of the water and then slam the boat back down into the next trough. Seasickness, combined with lousy food, felled more victims than they didn't.

In mid-September the ship mercifully docked in Glasgow, Scotland where the soldiers were met by the Scottish Red Cross. The women served the soldiers coffee and fresh donuts before the men were loaded onto a train heading south into England.

"Best thing I've tasted in over two weeks," Holt told Roald with his mouth still full. "Can I have another, do you think?"

Roald grinned. "Never hurts to ask."

Holt and Roald carried their second donuts and refilled coffees onto the train.

"How far is it to Perham Downs?" Roald asked.

"Sergeant Dagestad said it's eight hours to southern England." Holt claimed a couple of empty seats. "Might as well make ourselves comfortable and enjoy the scenery."

Holt took his own advice and watched the autumn English countryside roll past his window. Green meadows were filled with fluffy flocks of sheep, while multi-hued herds of cows chewed their cud in the pastures. Plastered white houses with grayed thatched roofs stood beside big red barns.

Looking at the countryside, Holt would never guess the country was embroiled in a bitter and violent war—until they passed makeshift airfields with lines of ready-to-go British Spitfires scarring the landscape.

The train carrying the Viking Battalion soldiers reached Andover Station at dusk. A line of British personnel carriers waited to take the nine-hundred American soldiers seven miles to the military camp in stages.

"Probably be faster to walk," Holt grumbled.

"And it would be nice to stretch our legs," Roald agreed.

"If it wasn't getting dark, I'd be tempted to set off." Holt pulled a resolute sigh. "But the country's under blackout orders so it's probably best not to get lost our first night here."

The barracks were cozier than Holt expected—big two-story brick buildings with huge fireplaces on the short walls. Both floors had double bunks, toilets and showers, and even closets.

"Home sweet home—at least for now." Holt claimed a bottom bunk while one was still available.

Roald took the top bunk above him. He climbed up and sprawled on his back. "I thought I'd be happy to have a bed that wasn't moving…"

Holt leaned on Roald's bunk. "Is there a problem?"

Roald groaned and opened his eyes. "It just feels like I still am."

*****

Right at the start of their training in Perham Downs, three hundred of the Viking guys were selected to test new rations, comparing American rations to English ones. The point was to simulate harsh battle conditions and judge the effect of the rations on those lucky soldiers.

Holt apparently drew the short straw and was put on the English rations, while Roald stayed with the American supplies.

"We'll be marching twenty miles a day for the next fifteen days," Sergeant Dagestad warned. "And all we'll have to eat are the rations we have been given."

Holt shrugged. "Maybe I got lucky this time…"

"We'll see." Roald tipped his head toward Dagestad. "Sergeant's on the English rations too, so who knows?"

Darkmore Forest around Perham Downs covered some of the most desolate and impenetrable terrain in all of England. And the majority of the daily twenty mile marches were traversed by the soldiers in typical English weather—cold rain, cloying fog, and more cold rain.

"The only time in my life when I have been more miserable than this was at the top of an ice-covered mountain," Roald grumbled.

"It's a close call," Holt agreed.

He stabbed at his unappetizing English rations—a congealed and unidentifiable canned meat product—while his stomach grumbled in vain. "At least these miserable rations aren't frozen by the weather."

Roald looked askance at him. "From the looks of them, maybe it would be better if they were."

The fifteen days of monotonous marching through Darkmore Forest did eventually come to and end. When it did, the three hundred guinea pigs marched back into camp and headed for the hospital to be weighed in. Roald lost one pound in fifteen days on the American rations.

Holt lost sixteen on the English food. And Sergeant Dagestad lost twenty.

"That settles that," Captain Rolf Berg declared. "I don't know or care what the Brits do, but our guys are going to get American rations and only American rations."

His irritated gaze swept over the bedraggled half of the soldiers who had subsisted on the English tins. "Head over to the mess hall, men. We have our own cooks back and they've prepared a smorgasbord. Lefse and pickled herring for the whole company!"

Holt slapped his hollow belly. "Out of the way guys, it's time to put back some of what we lost."

He grinned at Roald. "You coming? I need you to carry my second plate."

October 1943

The Ninety-Ninth Battalion Commander, Lieutenant Colonel R. G. Turner, assembled the nine hundred Viking guys to make an announcement. As they huddled inside a momentarily empty hangar, Holt wondered if their deployment to Norway was imminent.

"I hope we're getting shipped out soon," Wilhelm Steen unwittingly echoed Holt's thoughts. "We've been training over a year already."

Turner stepped up to a microphone and the battalion guys quieted down. "Good day, men. I have assembled you all here so that General William Donovan from the Office of Strategic Services can address you as a whole."

The OSS?

Holt shot a startled glance at Roald to see if the younger man had any idea what that was about. He didn't seem to.

Lieutenant Colonel Turner turned to face the man standing beside him and saluted the higher ranking officer before he stepped away from the microphone.

General Donovan took his place. For a moment he simply looked out at the crowd of soldiers, his hands clasped behind his back and his expression stern.

"I have come here today with the intention of recruiting one hundred men—eighty enlisted men and twenty officers—from your ranks. These men will receive special OSS training, including parachute jumping, sabotage, and guerilla warfare."

The general paused to let that information sink in.

"That means jumping behind enemy lines," Holt murmured.

Roald stared at him, his expression a mixture of fear and excitement.

"We are looking for officers and enlisted men who want to engage in duty of a secret and highly hazardous nature, and which will involve close combat," the general continued. "Soldiers must be in excellent physical shape and possess a high degree of endurance."

Holt's heart thumped with increasing intensity as he considered the prospect of parachuting into Norway. He was in excellent physical shape—as recently proven by the fifteen days of marching sustained only by starvation-level rations.

And his hip survived the impact with the tree.

I can do this.

"Moving from the Ninety-Ninth Battalion to the Office of Strategic Services—the OSS for simplicity's sake—is completely voluntary, so any soldier who is interested must apply to become a member of the newly forming Norwegian Operational Group."

"Hell, yeah," Wilhelm muttered behind Holt. "This is exactly what I was talking about."

"My assistant and Lieutenant Colonel Turner have applications. Please come get one if you are interested. My office will go through the applications and select those soldiers which we determine are best suited for the tasks that we have planned." General Donovan flashed a tight-lipped smile. "Thank you. You are dismissed."

The murmurs of nine hundred soldiers filled the air as many moved toward the men handing out the applications. Wilhelm was pushing his way toward the front with Bjorn, as usual, trailing along behind him.

"What do you think? "Roald asked. "Are you interested?"

Holt nodded slowly. "I think I am. What about you?"

Roald's expression hardened. "I want nothing more than to jump into Norway and kill as many Germans as I can. Filthy bastards."

Holt clapped Roald on the shoulder. "Then let's go."

As Holt and Roald neared the officers with the applications,

Wilhelm and Bjorn turned around, applications in hand, and faced him. Wilhelm's expression screwed up in disbelief.

"Come on, Gramps. You can't be serious!" Wilhelm smacked Holt's stripeless sleeve. "You've already been demoted for not following orders."

Holt glanced at the two stripes on Private First Class Steen's arm. He narrowed his eyes and stared down the younger man.

"At least I know how to think for myself."

Wilhelm laughed derisively. "We'll see how that turns out for you now, won't we?"

As Wilhelm and Bjorn shoved their way past him, Holt could not help but wonder if Steen's words held any portent.

"Ignore him," Roald growled.

"He might be right," Holt admitted. "My record is definitely not stellar. And if I need Captain Berg's recommendation, I doubt he'd give it."

Roald reached out and asked for two application packets. He pressed one stack of papers into Holt's hand.

"Do it if you want to and don't let anyone else stop you. It's not Steen's decision, is it?"

*****

Holt and Roald headed back to the barracks with the unopened packets in hand. When they sat side-by-side on Holt's bunk the pair discovered that there were at least twenty sheets of paper to be filled out, each one asking for different information than the others.

As Holt skimmed through them, he found one alarming element which was consistent. "Every page asks for the name and address of a person to be notified in case of death."

His arms went slack and the packet dropped into his lap. Holt turned to Roald. "Not serious illness or injury, just *death*."

Roald huffed a laugh as he flipped through the forms. "I guess they're trying to warn us that our obituaries might not contain the words *ripe old age…*"

"I'm not joking, Roald." Holt drew a deep breath. "I'm the only child. I have my parents to think of."

Roald's eyes met his. "And Raleigh. I know."

"What do I do?"

Roald was quiet for a moment.

"All I can say is this…" He paused and his brow twitched a little. "If you are leading my squad, I know we'll be safe."

Those words punched Holt straight in the chest.

"I cannot say the same for Wilhelm," Roald continued. "Soldiers *will* be dropped into Norway. Whether they live and complete their missions, or die because some hot-head leads them into danger, depends on who they are following."

Holt shook his head. "I'm the lowest rank possible. I wouldn't be leading anyone."

"You don't know that." Roald tapped the application packet with a stiff finger. "The OSS is looking for a certain kind of soldier. I believe you are exactly what they are looking for."

A surge of hope released Holt's tightened chest.

Could Roald be right?

"Fill out the damn application and let them decide." Roald handed Holt his pen. "Stop trying to fail before you even begin."

Holt accepted the pen with a sigh if resolution. "You're right. Filling out the application is no guarantee that I'll be chosen."

And no reason to worry Raleigh or his parents until he was.

November 1943

Two and a half weeks passed before Holt was called into the OSS office. In the meantime, at least a dozen guys from A Company had been interviewed and accepted, including Roald Rygg, Wilhelm Steen, and Bjorn Lind.

Now Holt sat in the OSS Office waiting for his turn. Two other guys were called in and fairly quickly dismissed. Neither one looked happy.

"Hansen?"

Holt stood.

"You can go in."

Go in and get out seems to be the pattern.

"Thank you."

Holt walked into the office right behind the reception desk. He closed the door behind himself without waiting to be told to, then faced the major inside and remained standing. Based on those who went right before him, he assumed there was no reason for him to sit.

The major—whose name was Helgesen according to the placard on his desk—looked up at him. "Take a seat."

So this is how we're doing it after all.

Holt stepped forward and lowered himself into the wooden chair facing the desk.

Major Helgesen folded his hands on top of the stack of what Holt assumed were his application forms. "You are an interesting case, Hansen."

How should he respond to *that?*

"Uh… thank you? Sir."

"You are one of our older soldiers. Did you fight in the first World War?"

Holt shook his head. "No, sir. I was too young."

"Is that why you enlisted in the Ninety-Ninth?"

"To be honest, I would have enlisted anywhere after Pearl Harbor," Holt admitted. "But I turned thirty-eight before that was possible."

Helgesen unfolded his hands and rubbed one finger across his upper lip. "Why was enlisting important to you?"

Holt huffed softly. "Because I want to protect my country. Against all enemies foreign and domestic."

"Is that all?"

Holt frowned. "Isn't that enough?"

Helgesen shifted the paper on top of his stack. "And the Norwegian connection?"

Holt pointed at the papers. "You have my family history

there. I may not have been to Norway, but my mother and grandmother are first generation."

The major nodded. "Your Norsk is good."

He smiled and switched languages. "How's your English?"

Holt was so accustomed to speaking Norsk all the time now that the realization he was being interviewed in that language startled him.

Holt switched to English. "English is my *first* language, sir."

"Good." Helgesen nodded and went back to Norsk. "So here you are, on the verge of forty years of age, and while you were initially promoted to Private First Class, you have since been demoted. And you have two disciplinary reports in your file."

"Yes, sir. I understand." Holt stood.

Helgesen looked up at him, bemused. "Where are you going?"

Holt motioned toward the door. "I thought you were dismissing me."

One corner of the major's mouth lifted. "Not yet. Sit down, Private."

Holt reclaimed his seat. His right knee began to bounce.

Major Helgesen lifted a sheet of paper. "You were promoted because you saved your platoon from a flood during a training exercise. Tell me about that."

Holt described the events of the day, the thunderstorm, and the flash flood. "In my civilian life I volunteer with the local search and rescue team. So I've had plenty of experience with that sort of thing."

"Protecting your platoon. Good thinking." The major lifted a second sheet of paper. "In a training exercise at Camp Hale you were given a route to strictly follow, but you deviated from that route which resulted in subsequent disciplinary action."

"Kitchen police. Yes, sir."

"Why did you disobey orders?"

Holt shifted his stance in the chair. "A recent avalanche blocked the path that we were assigned to take across a ridge."

"Afraid of a little snow, Hansen?"

Holt struggled not to snap back at the high-ranking officer.

"Not at all, sir. But I refused to risk my men's lives."

Helgesen pinned Holt with an intense stare. "How was it a risk?"

"The snow above us was unstable. Still shifting and falling. And the drop off of the edge, well..." Holt lifted both hands. "None of us would have survived."

"Did you explain that to your commanding officer?"

"Yes, sir."

Helgesen's gaze didn't move from Holt's. "What was the response?"

"I didn't follow orders, I second-guessed them." *Might as well go all in.* "And we arrived at the checkpoint an hour and a half late as a result."

Helgesen leaned back in his big swivel chair. "Because, again, you were protecting your squad."

Holt nodded glumly.

"Hmm." Helgesen picked up what Holt had figured out were reports from his personnel file and not his OSS application. "In another maneuver at Camp Hale, your half of the platoon was again given a route to follow, in addition to strict orders regarding the use of your Army-issued equipment."

Holt wished the floor would simply open up so he could drop out of sight. What was the point of rehashing all of his failures when there was clearly no way he was going to pass this interview?

Holt didn't wait for the question.

"We were told to pitch our tents in straight lines instead of searching out protected spots, and we all did that the first night of the march. But—I assume you have been in Alpine winter conditions at ten-thousand feet, sir, so you know—there is no way that keeps the men warm."

Helgesen didn't acknowledge Holt's assumption, he merely steepled his fingers. "Go on."

"So on the second night I said we should forgo the lines and pitch our tents where they were protected from the wind."

"Tell me about the fire."

"Again, sir, trying to light our camp stoves in the thin air at high altitudes is very difficult," Holt explained. "Plus they don't give off much warmth. And at twenty or thirty below zero, the men need warmth."

Helgesen looked startled, as if something Holt said was new information to him. "And the shared fire provided warmth."

Holt nodded. "And heated our rations faster."

"What about the threat of being seen by the enemy?"

"That was never part of our objective," Holt countered. "We were told to test the equipment—which we did, and the equipment failed—and to reach the checkpoint as quickly as possible."

"So you traversed the ravine by rope to reach your objective faster."

"The fourth flag was right in front of us, sir. Straight across the ravine." Holt pointed with both hands. "Skiing a mile-and-a-half to get to it was a waste of both time and energy."

Major Helgesen leaned forward again and squinted at the paper. "Had you begun your ropes training yet?"

"No, sir. Not as a unit," Holt qualified. "But I've had extensive personal experience with the search and rescue teams."

"The report says you risked the lives of the men on your team." Helgesen looked up at Holt, who was beginning to tremble with anger. "How do you answer that?"

"I would never, *ever*, put my men at risk," he growled. "The process was simple. I went first. Anyone who did not want to follow could have skied around the ravine."

"Did anyone refuse to cross?"

"No, sir."

"Was anyone injured?"

"No, sir."

The major's eyes narrowed. "How much did you beat the other team by?"

"An hour and a half."

"And then you were demoted."

"Yes." Holt determinedly swallowed his frustration. "Sir."

Helgesen nodded. He straightened the pile of papers and laid them inside a file folder, which he closed. Then he added Holt's folder to a short stack of folders on his right.

Only then did he look at Holt again. "Here's what I see, Private. I see an older man who admittedly has quite a bit of experience with search and rescue, and puts that knowledge to use in order to keep his squad safe."

Holt sat still and silent.

"In fact, I see a man for whom the integrity of the team wins out over the execution of orders."

Holt folded his arms, tensing for what he expected was coming.

"I also see a man who evaluates his orders and bases his decisions on the outcome, not necessarily the process."

Holt had to admit that was a fair evaluation.

"You have good instincts, Hansen. There's no doubt about that."

"Thank you, sir."

"And your ability to solve problems and find alternate solutions is impressive."

Holt was waiting for the *but*…

"But—"

There it was.

"—the problem that I can clearly see is that there will be times when your orders must be followed *exactly* to the letter in order for a specific mission to succeed, do you understand that?"

Holy stopped breathing.

There will be times?

"Even if that means one or more of your team members are sacrificed." Major Helgesen clasped his hands on his desktop again. "Can you do that, Hansen? I need your answer, and I need it now."

Holt felt the blood drain from his face. "One sacrifice for the good of many."

"We face that possibility every single day in the OSS. Can you tell me honestly that you will vow to follow your orders in such a situation?"

Even if that sacrifice is me.

In a blinding rush all of that OSS paperwork made sense.

Holt nodded slowly. "I understand, sir. And while I will do everything in my power to protect those men with whom I serve, if that protection endangers the mission, I will make the sacrifice."

The major allowed a grim smile. "You do understand that those men you will serve with also make the same commitment."

Men I will serve with?

This interview had taken a surreal and unexpected turn.

"Y-yes, sir."

"Good." Helgesen stood so Holt jumped to his feet. The major held out his hand. "Welcome to the OSS, *Corporal* Hansen."

When Holt shook his head and began to object, Major Helgesen interrupted him. "I'm reinstating your first stripe, which I believe was unfairly taken away from you."

"Uh, thank you, sir."

"And I'm promoting you to Private First Class for your ingenuity and leadership traversing the ravine."

Holt was gobsmacked. "Thank you. Again."

The major grinned. "So the next step is Corporal, and that's the rank you now hold as you enter the OSS. Congratulations."

Chapter Ten

Holt trudged back to his barracks through the typically damp autumn afternoon wondering if he was dreaming. The interview with Major Helgesen was the polar opposite of what he expected. Not only was he accepted into the OSS, but he was suddenly promoted three levels.

Wait until I tell Raleigh.

When Holt climbed the stairs to the second floor, Roald was waiting for him. "You've been gone a long time. How did it go?"

Holt was almost afraid to say anything out loud, in case he had been hallucinating. He took off his jacket as he walked to his bunk and then plunked down on the narrow mattress.

Roald sat next to him, frowning. "Are you all right?"

Holt nodded. "I think so."

Sergeant Dagestad came thundering up the stairs. "Hansen!"

Holt jumped to his feet, narrowly missing braining himself on the upper bunk. "Yes, sir?"

Dagestad stomped toward him, his expression enigmatic. "I don't know how the hell you pulled this off." He thrust a small envelope toward Holt, and though his brows were lowered, a smile tugged the corners of his mouth and his eyes twinkled. "But here are your stripes."

Holt accepted the proof that what just transpired in Helgesen's office was real. "Thank you, sir."

The sergeant spun with a low grunt and headed back down

the stairs.

Every man in the half-filled barracks turned and stared at Holt.

"Stripes?" Roald asked. "What happened?"

Holt sat back down, unsure his legs would keep him vertical. "I met with Helgesen, and he rehashed my record…"

When he paused, Roald prompted him to continue. "And?"

Some of the men moved closer to Holt's bunk.

"And," Holt continued, "He made me a Private First Class again for teaching my team how to use ropes to cross the ravine safely."

Roald smiled. "That's great!"

Holt's platoon mates closed in, obviously curious about what was in the envelope.

Holt opened the envelope and dumped the stack of double striped insignias into his palm. Only when he felt them did he trust they were his.

"Those are corporal's stripes." Roald stared at Holt. "What does that mean?"

Holt started to laugh.

This really happened.

His gazed passed over the other men. "It means I'm entering the OSS as a non-commissioned officer!"

*****

As Holt expected, Wilhelm Steen would not let Holt's good fortune pass without loudly voiced sneers and not-so-subtle insults.

"Ignore him," Roald growled as the nearly one hundred volunteers who were selected for the OSS filed into an auditorium for their first instructions. "He's a corporal now, too, so he's just acting like a spoiled child."

Holt sighed heavily as they took their seats. "Hopefully he'll be in another unit, and I won't have to put up with him anymore."

Major Helgesen took the podium and the men in the audience fell silent.

"Welcome, men. You are now members of the Office of Strategic Services. I command the Operational Group Administrative Headquarters for all of the operational groups— OGs for short—which are units of twenty-eight men and four officers."

Smaller than a platoon.

Interesting.

"The plan for each of these units is to parachute deep behind enemy lines on any front, and to carry out work which is designed to accomplish three objectives," Helgesen continued. "First is to organize the nationals into guerrilla forces and lead them against the enemy."

That will be helping the Resistance in Norway.

"Second is to disrupt any enemy activity as much as possible."

Holt glanced at Roald and mouthed, "Blow stuff up."

Roald grinned.

"And third, we expect you to send back, by whatever means possible, any and all intelligence that you can gather." Helgesen paused and looked at the soldiers. "Are there any questions thus far?"

The men looked at each other and no one expressed any confusion. Everything was pretty straightforward.

"You will operate both in and out of uniform, depending on your assignments. But if you are captured, the chances are *fifty to one* that you will be not treated as a prisoner of war under the Geneva Convention," Major Helgesen warned. "The work is highly confidential, and highly dangerous. Knowing all of this do you still want to volunteer?"

Holt drew a deep breath. The prospect was thrilling and terrifying at the same time. But he had not felt this alive for three years.

He turned to Roald. "I'm good. You?"

The younger man's expression was solemn as he nodded.

"Yes."

Four soldiers rose to their feet and made their way out of the auditorium, each either red-faced or pale.

Major Helgesen looked pleased. "It is far, far better to return to your platoons now, than to go into our specific training and quit later—or fail."

One more man hopped up and sprinted from the room.

"Anyone else?" the major asked. When no one else stood, he stepped from behind the podium, his voice carrying over the men remaining. "Welcome to the OSS. Go back to your barracks and pack your gear. Tomorrow morning at six, we'll truck to the train station and head north into Scotland."

*****

The train ride from Perham Downs in southern England to Inverness in northern Scotland took eighteen hours. Adding in the hour and a half it took to get from the camp to the station and wait for the train to start moving, it was one-thirty in the morning when the tired soldiers chugged to a stop in Inverness.

Amazingly, Army personnel carriers were waiting for them.

"It's twenty miles to the Powers Hunting lodge where the Norwegian Operational Group will be training," Helgesen told the men as they crowded into the three open-backed vehicles. "Make yourselves as comfortable as you can."

"It's a lot colder here than Perham," Holt stated the obvious as he pulled his jacket's collar tighter around his neck. "Feels like we're back at Hale."

"Almost," Roald tempered his agreement. "But there's sure plenty of snow."

A full moon lit the rolling snow-covered landscape in pale blue while the Scottish Highland mountains loomed black and bleak on either side of the road. Wisps of clouds moved across the night sky like gauzy ribbons.

The trucks rumbled across wooden bridges stretched over

tumbling rivers, whose turbulence glowed white in the moonlight.

Can't wait to see this in daylight.

*****

The soldiers didn't hit the hay until three o'clock in the morning, so reveille was delayed until nine.

"Don't get used to it," Captain Winters said jovially to the assembled soldiers. "I plan to make you all miserable from here on out."

Holt pressed his lips together.

And I believe he plans to enjoy it.

"As I call your names, please step forward." Captain Winters shouted twenty-eight names and the men stepped forward. "Your unit will be referred to as Company A. Your commanding officer is Lieutenant Moland."

The designated lieutenant raised his hand and motioned for the men to follow him.

Captain Winters called out twenty-eight more names, whose unit would be known as Company B, and sent those men off with a Second Lieutenant named Valen.

Holt groaned inwardly. While he and Roald still remained together, Wilhelm Steen and Bjorn Lind were also in the last group

"Lieutenant Bull is your commanding officer, and obviously you are Company C." Captain Winters smiled his oddly satisfied smile and addressed the lieutenant. "I'll leave you to it. Lieutenant."

Lieutenant Bull faced the remaining twenty-eight men. "Form up!"

The soldiers moved into four straight rows of seven and stood at attention.

Bull looked pleased. "As you know, we all are part of Norwegian special operations. We call it NORSO. And as you've been told, our ultimate goal is to liberate Norway. In order to do that, we plan to drop operatives—that's you men—into Norway without being noticed by the Nazis. Are you with me so far?"

"Yes, sir!" the soldiers chorused.

"Good. And so you don't plummet to your deaths when we drop you, we're eventually going to teach you how to parachute out of airplanes."

Holt's first thought was that might be fun.

His second thought was if the impact would kill his hip.

I guess I'll find out.

"For now, we need to make sure you men are in shape and acclimated to the cold once again. Get suited up and bring your skis. We're going on a hike. Dismissed."

December 1943

Holt waded into the frigid water of the running Scottish river, brown and dense from the surrounding peat that it gathered along its way, and clamped his teeth together to keep them from clattering. The water came up to his shoulders at the deepest point, and he struggled to keep his footing.

This chilling cold was worse than any he experienced at Camp Hale. Once his clothes were wet they clung to every inch of his body, pressing the freezing air against his skin until he was numbed by the frost that formed over his uniform.

The pack marches led by Lieutenant Bull were twenty miles long, going up and down the Highland mountains, with skis and without depending on the terrain. At night the soldiers crawled through fields of wet heather, trying not to be seen by patrolling "sentries."

And Holt spent every single night in the hot showers before downing aspirin like it was candy.

In between their long overland marches the three companies ran maneuvers. The companies took turns going into the woods at the top of a hill and creating a secured defensive position, or digging in at the bottom of the hill and then storming the company at the top. The third company was tasked with infiltrating a location and destroying something there.

That was Holt's favorite.

Because the soldiers would be surreptitiously deployed either alone, in pairs, or at most a group of three, there was no heavy artillery for them to count on. The only weapons and firepower they would have was what the OSS could drop in with them.

Holt loved that challenge. He was always trying to figure out how to stretch his ammunition, or find ways to increase the destruction one grenade could cause by blowing up something that would fling rocks or maybe start a fire.

"Corporal Hansen?"

Holt faced the corporal from C Company command who stopped him as he entered the mess for supper. "Yes?"

"Lieutenant Bull wants to see you after you eat. He'll be in the company command tent."

"Got it." When the man walked away, Holt turned to Roald. "Wonder what I did wrong now."

"Maybe you messed up and did something right," Roald teased.

When Holt went to the company command post after supper, Wilhelm Steen followed him into the tent.

"Good evening, Corporals. We are going on a spontaneous night compass run. I'm splitting Company C into two groups of fourteen and you two will each be leading them." Lieutenant Bull handed Holt and Wilhelm each a map and a list of soldiers. "Study your routes. We march out at nine tonight."

"Is this a competition?" Steen asked.

Bull shook his head. "No, Corporal. I wanted smaller groups so more of the men can participate in actively finding the way. Next time we'll do four groups of seven."

That made sense to Holt. But his map didn't.

"I don't remember this stream." Holt pointed at the map. "How deep is it, does anyone know?"

"Only about a foot," Bull's assistant Sergeant Major Michaels answered. "I went around the course earlier this afternoon."

"It should be fine," Bull stated. "There's another thing you both need to know—we're only allowing one pinhole flashlight per group for map reading. Absolutely no other lights. No matches, no smoking. Understood?"

"Yes, sir," the pair answered in tandem.

"Don't worry about packing your equipment, either. This run shouldn't take more that an hour and a half. Two at the most." Bull grinned. "So go gather your men and be back here ready to set off before nine. Dismissed."

*****

The night's compass run through the Scottish countryside began under a half moon, but by the time Holt's group reached the stream in question the sky had clouded over.

Holt stopped his group. "I can't see the water yet, but I can hear it. And it sure sounds like more than a foot deep."

Jensen concurred. "And we don't have our ropes this time."

Holt spoke to the man currently holding the map and giving directions. "Olsen, are you sure we're crossing at the right spot?"

Olsen switched on his pinhole flashlight. "If we are, there should be three standing stones on a rise to our left."

"How far?" Jensen asked.

"Thirty paces."

"Everyone stay put. I'll go." Holt turned to his left and counted his strides out loud. By the time he got to twelve, the ground was angling up. Five more paces and he could see the outline of the stones ahead against the clouds above.

"The stones are there." He pivoted one-hundred-and-eighty degrees and retraced his steps. He almost collided with Olsen. "I walked true, there and back. Can I look at the map?"

Olsen handed Holt the map and light. Holt examined it and

Olsen had them exactly where they were supposed to be.

"Okay, men. We're wading across. Follow me." He handed Olsen the map and light and walked straight toward the sound of water.

When Holt reached the edge he waded into the murky running water, which reached his thighs on the second step. He turned around and scrambled up the bank.

"A foot deep my ass!" he bellowed.

"What should we do?" Jensen asked.

Holt decided not to answer and see if his men could work it out. "You tell me."

"We don't have ropes, but we have belts," one of the younger guys pointed out. "Let's make a rope of belts to cross with."

The weather took a brief moment of pity of the group and allowed a sliver of moonlight to illuminate the scene. The opposite bank was only about four yards away, but it was an obstacle course of branches and vines.

Once their belts were buckled end-to-end, Holt stepped back into the water. "Watch your step! The bottom is rocky and slippery!"

The water reached Holt's armpits and some of the shorter guys struggled to keep their footing. When Holt managed to climb to a safe spot on the opposite bank, he dug in his feet and pulled the men across.

After the last man crossed, the group headed back to the command tent. He passed Wilhelm on the way—obviously the other group got back faster and didn't have to swim across a river on their route.

"Hey, Hansen! You're soaked." Wilhelm laughed. "What did—"

Holt strode past him. "Fuck off, Steen!"

Holt threw back the flap and stormed inside, right up to Sergeant Major Michaels in a cold and dripping wet mess of a temper.

"Hey, watch it! You're getting me wet!" Michaels yelped.

"Not as wet as me and my men!" Holt shouted. "Where do

you get off telling me that rampaging torrent was only a foot deep?"

Lieutenant Bull's stern gaze moved from Holt to Michaels and back to Holt. "How deep was it?"

Holt forced his glare to soften when he addressed his commanding officer. "Over five feet. Running fast. Rocky-bottomed. And with a nearly un-climbable far bank."

Bull's eyes narrowed. "How wide?"

"About four yards."

"Why did you go in, then?" Michaels asked like it was Holt's fault the men were soaked and freezing.

Holt rounded on him. "We didn't have any lights remember? I could have *lost* men out there! And it would have been *my* neck on the line!"

"Are your men all right?" Bull demanded.

"Other than being soaking wet and freezing?" Holt pulled a shivering breath. "Yes. Sir."

"Are you sure you crossed at the right place?" Michaels pressed.

Holt thrust the map in the sergeant major's face. "Thirty paces from the standing stones. I marked it off myself."

Bull grunted. "If it was that bad, how did you all make it across?"

"One of my men suggested we buckle our belts together, sir, since we didn't have any equipment with us."

Lieutenant Bull cocked his head. "*You* didn't suggest it?"

Holt blinked. "I, uh, I asked the men to work out the solution. And they did."

"Good," Bull approved. "That was good. Now go get changed. We'll see you in the morning."

Holt shot Michaels one last glare before pulling back the tent flap and facing the thirteen intense faces of his waiting men.

"You told him good," Jensen murmured.

Olsen agreed. "I'd follow you anywhere, Hansen."

From the other side of the flap, Michaels grumbled, "Well it only looked about a foot deep to me."

Fucking idiot.

Chapter Eleven

Raleigh sat in the church pew on Christmas Eve with her hands folded and her head down, hoping to discourage anyone from trying talk to her. If one more person asked her about Holt, she was going to lose her fragile composure and fall completely to pieces.

That was best done in the privacy of her own home with a few beers and a pillow to wail into.

Two years ago this very month the Japanese attacked Pearl Harbor and set every single American's world on edge. Raleigh had no way of knowing then that the events which followed would not only awaken their country to renewed patriotism and a sense of belonging, but they would also awaken Holt from a two year mourning period to a renewed sense of purpose.

The blessing of that was that he'd finally come to realize he was in love with her. But after he enlisted. And after his path toward war was solidified.

Loving Holt was always a risk, but Raleigh couldn't help herself. She fell hard and fast, and now all she could do was wait and pray.

Which was why she was in church tonight.

That, and the knowledge that Holt was probably at a chapel service earlier this same night and thinking of her.

After their five days spent together four months ago, the fact that she and Holt were now an item was out in the open. Berlin residents expressed their happiness that Holt seemed to be moving forward after the tragic death of his wife, and they seemed just as happy that Raleigh was the one to bring him back to the world of the living.

As a relatively new resident of Berlin, Raleigh appreciated the consensus that she deserved a man like Holt Hansen. That vote of confidence made her feel like she had been accepted by the little community, and after years of running and hiding she felt like she had found her forever home here.

The problem was that every single day, either in the salon or when she was out running errands, at least one person would ask her how Holt was doing.

She always said he was fine, and then added some tidbit like he was hiking or skiing twenty miles a day with a full pack in preparation for their assignment. And then she'd listen to the polite reply with a forced smile and tried to never let on how deeply and desperately she missed him.

Please bring him home to me, Father. Alive and whole.

Raleigh lifted her eyes to the cross on the wall at the front of the now nearly-empty church.

Please don't let us have found love only to take it away.

*****

In spite of the boisterous Christmas revelry of the NORSO group, Holt was lonely. And while his mind replayed his holidays with Nora, he found that his more recent memories with Raleigh were taking precedence.

Two years ago, when Pearl Harbor was attacked, Holt and Raleigh attended the somber Christmas Eve service together at the Lutheran Church, then went back to her house for a late night supper. Over beers and in front of a cozy, crackling fire, they pondered together the fate of the world, and how their newly declared wars would affect the United States of America.

That Christmas Eve, Holt felt something was different from the previous year. He was healing, and he knew it. Not just physically, but in his soul.

He still wanted to enlist. He still wanted to fight. For the two years after the war in Europe began and Nora was killed, enlisting was at the forefront of his thoughts. He wanted to serve his country, sure. But at that point he didn't care if he died doing it. He actually relished the idea.

But not now.

Now he had Raleigh to come home to, and an uncharted new life to begin. He couldn't help but worry if those plans would interfere with his determination to do whatever was required of him by the OSS.

He already knew that he might have to sacrifice one or more of his men if their situation went south, if doing so assured their objective was achieved. And he was reminded that every OSS recruit had to make the same commitment.

I could be the sacrifice.

After wrestling with that reality, Holt poured out his feelings in a letter to Raleigh on New Year's Eve. He told her everything he was thinking, as he always had. And as his sentences took shape, so did his resolve.

> *Both of our lives, and our future together, are entirely in God's hands. For that reason I will act as I must, and do what I must do, in spite of the risks involved. Please pray that God will protect me and bring me home to marry you.*

Holt folded the letter and stuffed in the envelope. Stepping out of the empty barracks into the cold and moonless night, he walked through the snow to the command post to mail it. Before he reached the office, cheers and guns fired into the air marked the beginning of a new year.

January 1944

Holt didn't hear back from Raleigh until nearly the end of January. In between exhausting maneuvers and training exercises that pushed him close to his breaking point, Holt wondered if he had said something to her to make her change her mind about him.

Should he write her again and take some of his words back?

But which words would those be?

Holt had been nothing but honest, because he didn't know how else to be. He'd just have to wait it out.

Today at mail call when his name was announced, Holt pressed forward toward the sergeant passing out the letters and claimed his. He blew a sigh of relief when he saw Raleigh's distinctive blue ink and feminine writing on the envelope.

This letter was thicker than usual. Holt wondered if that had delayed its arrival, but the postmark was only a week earlier. Raleigh really did wait weeks to write him back, and now she clearly had a lot to say.

Holt didn't want to read the letter in the barracks with all the other men, so he sought out a spot behind one of the camp's buildings that was out of the wind. He sat in the snow, leaned against the stone wall, and pulled off one mitten with his teeth. With a nagging sense of foreboding he carefully tore the envelope open and pulled out the folded sheets.

My dearest Holt,

Thank you so much for your heartfelt letter. I apologize for taking so long to respond, there is so much I want to say to you that it took me a while to get it all organized.

First of all, nothing you said to me was a surprise...

Holt's shoulders relaxed at those words. Only then did he realize how tense they had been.

...because I know you so well. I agree with everything you said and, above all else, you and your safety have always been and will continue to be in my prayers every single night ~ right after my prayer that this war will be quickly won and all you men can come home to us.

That is not why it took me so long to write.

I do have something else to tell you, and now that we have confirmed our intent to become engaged when you return after the war, it is important that I do this before we go any further. This letter will be long. Please be patient and read it all the way through.

Holt flipped the page over, noting how many were to follow, and that the writing covered both the front and backs of the pages. The first words made his pulse surge.

I am not a virgin. But that's not the worst of it.

It was my mother's second husband ~ whom I will never call any sort of father ~ who took care of that soon after I turned sixteen. He was rough and cruel and I was terrified.

Holt's hands began to shake. He gripped the pages tightly to stop the trembling while he read Raleigh's account with growing rage.

Then next day at school I went to see the nurse because I couldn't sit on the classroom chairs without crying. I told her what happened and she called the sheriff. So, even though I was completely mortified, I had to tell him everything that the man had done to me.

The sheriff went to our house and talked to the man,

who denied ever touching me. He lied and said that I was in the woods with two boys after dark the night before, so whatever happened to me was my own fault. The sheriff believed him, so nothing happened to him.

When I got home from school my mother met me at the front door. She slapped me across the face hard enough to leave a bruise, and warned me to never, ever tell such tales to anyone ever again.

I went upstairs to my room and bawled into my pillow. I was so badly hurt, and when I risked telling the very people who should have protected me, it was made clear to me that they wouldn't save me. I was alone.

Holt growled out loud. How could a mother treat her daughter in such a way? And what sort of man rapes his stepdaughter?

Over the next two years, that man repeatedly forced himself on me. In the meantime, my mother's health was failing. I am certain it was because she knew of her husband's behavior and her guilt was eating her alive. In any case, she died about three weeks before my high school graduation.

Long before that, I had been making plans to escape.

One thing Holt knew about Raleigh was that she never cowered in the face of adversity. The fact that she was always willing to step into the unknown and take risks was the one thing about her that scared him.

I already knew that the man hid money from my mother in the basement, and I searched for weeks until I found it. After my mother died I packed a suitcase and hid that in the basement as well. All I needed was a good mid-western cyclone and I would leave Kansas forever.

A storm moved in two days before my graduation ~ the worst in a decade, they said. I knew I had to leave and risk not getting my diploma, but I couldn't stay in that house a minute longer. The storm hit at sundown and grew worse over the next couple of hours.

The man had been drinking much of the afternoon, and whenever he got up to use the bathroom I secretly refilled his drink. By eight that night he was sound asleep in his chair with the radio on, and he didn't hear the warning sirens.

I went into the basement and wedged a chair against the door so it wouldn't open. Then I hid in the corner of the basement and prayed.

Holt drew a deep breath as he realized exactly what Raleigh had done. Yet, he couldn't fault her. The law had abandoned her first.

No one else was going to take care of her.

The winds howled ferociously, like I'd never heard before, and the noise went on for hours. The house above me shook and groaned like it was being torn from its foundation, but thankfully the floor above me remained intact.

I had no idea what time it was when the winds finally stilled. When it did, I packed all of the man's money into my suitcase and climbed the stairs. When I removed the chair and opened the door I could see that one wall of our house was completely torn away.

It was still dark and raining a little when I walked out of the house through that terrible opening. I never looked to see if the man was still there.

So he wasn't slumped outside the door she had blocked, that was good. Maybe he got out. Just because Raleigh didn't drag him to safety didn't mean she killed him, even if he had died in the storm.

I went to the bus station and bought a ticket for Iowa City where one of my cousins lived. I enrolled in Beauty School there and stayed in that town until a coworker told me that the shop in Berlin was for sale. So four years ago, I bought the shop in Berlin and moved there.

After what happened to me, I vowed to myself that if I ever knew anyone who needed help, I would do whatever I could for them. That's why I signed up to bring you lasagna after you got out of the hospital.

Even though we hadn't met yet, I'd heard all about you and the accident from the ladies who came to me to get their hair done. And because I knew you needed me, I kept coming back.

You are probably wondering why I never told you this before. To be honest, when we met you were the one hurting. Our conversations revolved around you and your recovery, about your joining the search and rescue team, about you hunting again, and then about you enlisting.

Until you realized how much I meant to you, there weren't any conversations about me and my past. But now there need to be, and that's why I'm writing this difficult letter.

Holt's hands fell to his lap, stung by Raleigh's revelation. As he thought back to their long talks, though, he had to admit she was right. It was always about him.

He stared at the neatly inked words on the stationery and they blurred a little.

This explained why Raleigh never went anywhere else for Thanksgiving or Christmas, and why no one came to visit her. Holt was vaguely aware that she spent all her holidays with him, and never took vacations to visit anyone, but he had been so wrapped up in his own grief that he never really thought about why that was.

And because Raleigh was such a strong woman, she never seemed to mark her lack of family or visitors. Another reason the subject never came up.

Holt wiped his eyes and refocused his attention on the startling and very revealing words on the pages.

> *As I got you to know you Holt, I understood that, just like you are doing with America, you would always protect me against 'any and all threats.' You are a protector by nature.*

> *That is initially why I was so attracted to you. You would have believed my story all those years ago. You would have saved me from that horrid man. And you would have seen justice done.*

Damned right he would have. And given that repugnant asshole a taste of his own violent medicine in the process.

> *It nearly destroyed you, Holt, when you weren't able to protect Nora from that drunk driver. But now you are moving through your grief to renew your life. You are protecting your country and your purpose is reborn.*

Holt's hands lowered again, this time in awe. Raleigh's assessment of his mental and emotional state was dead-on accurate. He began to think she knew him better than Nora ever had.

> *I have no idea if that man is still alive. But he has never found me, so maybe he died that night. Either way,*

it was worth the risk of walking away from my life ~ and taking that man's secret savings with me ~ to end up in Berlin, Wisconsin with you.

Please write back and tell me if you can accept me as I am ~ damaged, yes. But healed.

All my love,
Ralls

Holt clambered to his feet and jogged back to his barracks in the half-a-foot of snow covering the grounds. He ran up the stairs, strode past the bunks to his, flashed a reassuring smile at an obviously curious Roald reading on the top bunk, and dug in his locker for paper and pen.

Once settled on his mattress, Holt began to write in a dark and intense script.

My dearest darling Raleigh ~

I don't care that you're not a virgin! Not the tiniest bit. My only regret after reading your letter is that I wasn't there to take your side and see justice done. That said, I can't fault you for doing anything that you did to get away.

In fact, I'm proud of you for finding a justifiable path out of your terrible situation...

February 1944

NORSO was on the move again—this time to Manchester, England for the British paratrooper school. To qualify to be a British paratrooper, every soldier had to complete four tower jumps, and one jump from a helium balloon, before jumping from a real plane.

Holt and Roald stood at the bottom of the forty-foot-plus wooden structure, topped by crisscrossed telephone poles with angled cables hanging from pulleys, and listened to the British officer proudly explain how the tower worked.

"See the ladder?" He pointed helpfully to the wooden slats that went straight up the side. "We recommend that as you climb to the platform on top, you do not look down. Soldiers have frozen in fear when they did, and the only way to come down at that point is the same way you went up."

He gave them a grim smile. "We don't like having to stop our training and have all the other men climb down because you lost your nerve. However, it is one way in which we can weed out our candidates."

Holt thought that actually made sense.

"Instructors are waiting at the top to harness you to the cables. Next, you'll take the exit position in the doorframe." The officer crouched with one foot in front of the other and grasped imaginary harness straps. "When you hear the exit command the instructor will slap your leg and then you launch yourself forward, off the platform."

A few of the men groaned.

"I knew there would be parachuting, but this..." A man behind Holt cleared his throat. "This seems scarier."

The Brit didn't acknowledge the comment if he heard it. "Once you slide down about twenty-five feet, you will bounce back up ten because of the harness and cable combine—which simulates the jerk of your parachute opening. After that, you will ride down the cable into that huge pile of sawdust over there."

Again, he pointed helpfully to the landing spot about thirty yards away.

Holt took a quick moment to look at the men around him. Expressions ranged from cocky confidence to nervous bravado to downright terror.

Bjorn Lind looked like he was ready to tackle the tower. So did Roald.

Wilhelm Steen looked like he'd already shit his pants and

was pretending it didn't smell.

"Line up men. Let's go."

The guys fell in line at the bottom of the ladder. Holt stood behind Wilhelm, but didn't say anything to him. When the man ahead of him was eight feet or so off the ground, the instructor motioned for Wilhelm to begin his ascent.

Once Steen was eight feet up, Holt took his first step.

The first ten feet were easy. Then next ten made everything feel real. Halfway up the next ten, Wilhelm stopped.

"You okay, Steen?" Holt asked softly.

"Yeah. Sure. I just got a splinter from this fucking ladder."

Holt heard the tremor underlying the bravado. "We're more than halfway. Just don't look down."

Wilhelm didn't answer.

And he didn't move.

"Look up, Wilhelm," Holt urged gently. "Grab the next rung and move one foot."

"Leave me alone, Gramps," he growled.

"I can't, son. Because I'm behind you and you have to go first."

Wilhelm slowly raised his right arm. Then he slid his left boot up to the next rung.

"Good. Now pull yourself up so your boots are on the *same* step."

When he did, Holt followed close behind. "Okay, now do that again. One arm, and one foot."

Wilhelm raised his right arm again, and his left boot. After a brief pause he pulled himself up and his right boot rested next to his left boot.

Holt moved up as well. "Everyone thinks you have to climb a ladder like it's stairs. That's not true. It's much easier this way. One rung at a time."

Wilhelm reached up again without being prompted. And again he moved his left leg to join his right.

Holt followed Wilhelm in silence, figuring that if he kept yammering at the kid that his help might backfire. When they reached the top, Steen didn't look at him or talk to him.

The first guys up were already in harnesses and crouching in the four doorways. When one instructor shouted go, the others slapped the guys' legs and they jumped into forty feet of air with a variety of enthusiasm.

Wilhelm looked like he was going to vomit.

Holt leaned sideways so his shoulder pressed against Steen's. "We'll go at the same time. Just do what I do."

Wilhelm shook his head. "I can't."

Holt stepped around in front of him so Steen had to look at him. "Yes, Wilhelm. You can. All those guys going ahead of us are fine. We're tied to the cable. We can't fall."

Steen looked away, clearly not convinced.

"Follow me, then. How else you going to get down?" Holt prodded. "And what? You going to let an old man like me beat you?"

Steen's eyes shot back to Holt's and his face reddened in anger. "Shut up."

"Hey, listen." Holt leaned forward and lowered his voice. "You don't do this now, and you're done. No more OSS. Plus there's no guarantee that you'll go back to the Ninety-Ninth if that happens. The Army will send you wherever they feel like it."

Wilhelm's eyes narrowed.

"Come on." Holt clapped Steen's shoulder. "Let's go take a ride."

Chapter Twelve

Holt hit the sawdust feet first as instructed, and then tumbled face first into the dusty, gritty pile. He wasn't the only one who landed that way by a long shot—they all hit the pile with a variety of hilarious gymnastic maneuvers, and not one of them managed to keep his footing in the shifting woodchips.

As he climbed to his feet, dusting sawdust from his uniform and spitting bits of wood from his mouth, he waved to the tower that he was fine. Then he stepped away from the pile and looked up at Wilhelm, now crouching in the jump's doorway.

"It's fun!" Holt shouted. "Even if the landing's a mess!"

Holt decided on top of the tower to jump before Steen did, figuring that watching the older man he derisively called 'gramps' complete the jump would poke Steen's pride enough that he'd jump without hesitation.

Plus it forced Holt not to hesitate either, thus preventing his own strong sense of self-preservation from kicking in.

Wilhelm jumped.

The cable zinged as his harness carried him down, jerked him back, and dropped him in the sawdust. Wilhelm scrambled to his feet, his expression unexpectedly awestruck.

He waved to the tower and shouted, "That was great! Can we do it again?"

Holt guffawed. "I believe that's the plan!"

Not all of the soldiers had the same reaction, unfortunately.

One guy from their operational group froze in the doorway and refused to jump, so his days in the OSS were finished.

Wilhelm didn't say anything to Holt to thank him for his help, but Holt really didn't expect him to. The soldier was still young and immature, and didn't fully understand that asking for help wasn't necessarily a sign of weakness. More often it signified strength.

Holt chuckled.

I could probably use a dose of that myself.

*****

In addition to practicing the mechanics of jumping off the tower, the soldiers needed to learn how to pack their own parachutes.

Each man was responsible for personally packing every chute for his own jumps, including their reserve chutes, so even though the task was monotonous and dull every soldier paid close attention.

And no one complained about the endless practice. Leaping from the tower and riding a cable to the ground was one thing. Jumping out of an airplane thousands of feet above the earth was an entirely different prospect.

After a full week of tower jumping, the NORSO soldiers were moved to a two-hundred-and-fifty-foot tall 'uncontrolled descent' steel tower, also with four arms. In this case, the students were harnessed into an open parachute while on the ground. The outer edges of the shoot were then connected to a large iron ring, which hauled the soldier to the top of the tower.

On this unusually sunny English afternoon, Holt swung in his parachute harness, dangling like a rag doll under his open chute, and watched the grassy meadow retreat from under his feet. He'd been watching the other guys being dropped from the top for the last half hour and reminded himself that none of them had died in the process.

Maybe this will turn out to be fun, too.

With a metallic clank, his ascent halted.

The instructor called through a loudspeaker, "Number two?"

"Yes!" Holt shouted back, suddenly nervous. "Throw the damned switch!"

"A simple yes will do, Corporal."

The ring traveled up ten more feet. Holt counted off the five seconds before he was released. They were the longest five seconds of his life.

When the parachute was released from the ring, Holt went into a gut twisting freefall for the first fifty feet or so, until the flapping silk canopy above him caught the air with a soft whoosh. After the expected jerk of his abruptly slowed return to earth, he floated the remaining two hundred feet in a silent, gliding descent.

Transfixed by the experience, Holt remembered his instructions just in time—feet together, or broken ankles. His stumbling landing was adequate, and his ankles remained intact, but he felt like he should probably pay closer attention in the future.

March 1944

The first jump which the soldiers made that counted toward their five jumps to graduate from paratrooper school was the leap from a helium balloon.

The balloon in question hovered over another grassy meadow—which seemed to make up ninety percent of the English countryside—and was hooked to a pair of steel cables to keep it from being blown away.

"How high is it?" Roald asked as the operational group stared up at the silvery gray specter swaying in the strong breeze.

"Not bad," Steen answered. "Only five hundred meters."

Holt laughed. "That's over fifteen hundred feet. More than a quarter mile."

"What?" Bjorn Lind paled. "Then this is a serious jump!"

"It has to be high enough for our chutes to open." Roald shrugged. "Better higher than too low."

"And with the leg bags, we'll weigh more and fall faster," Holt added.

The leg bags were another step up in their training. They were filled with things like ammunition, explosives, and food rations—supplies which would be needed when the soldiers jumped behind enemy lines.

"Remember, men," Captain Winters told his group. "Pull the cord attached to the leg bag first so it will land first, at least fifteen feet below you. That will lighten your load and make your own landing that much easier."

The helium balloon was pulled down to the ground by a huge winch. Four soldiers climbed into the woven wicker basket, whose edges had been cut down for easier exits. The cable was loosened and the balloon handler—a British lieutenant—monitored the whining cable as the balloon rose silently into the sky.

As the balloon floated back up to the maximum height allowed by its tether, the soldiers alternated between staring at the ever-distant ground, and the scenery which their new vantage point presented. The balloon's ascent was so quiet that Holt could hear the men's conversations from the ground.

"If we jump in pairs, we need to remember not to talk to each other on the way down—if we are close to each other, that is," Holt observed. "Our chutes won't make any noise either."

Captain Winters turned around and looked at him. "That's a good point, Hansen. I'll make sure all the guys hear it."

Holt gave a little nod. "Thank you, sir."

Roald and Holt were next. They climbed into the balloon's basket together. Wilhelm and Bjorn were behind them in the line.

Wilhelm paused, then hopped inside. Bjorn scrambled in after him.

The lieutenant fired the furnace and the balloon lifted off.

As the quartet watched the ground fall away, Steen nudged

Holt. "Let me know if you get scared, Gramps."

Holt's first thought was that the younger man was needling him again. But when he turned a grim face to Steen, his irritation disappeared when he saw Wilhelm smile a little.

"We're members of the same OG," Steen said with a casual one-shouldered shrug. "We need to make sure we can all complete the task at hand."

Holt smiled back. "Well said."

Maybe the little shit was learning something after all.

The balloon stopped moving with a little jolt. "Okay, men. Who's going first?"

"Me!" Wilhelm grabbed the basket's stiff frame and lifted his legs over the edge so he was sitting on the rim. "Do I just push off?"

"Yep." The lieutenant rested his hand on Steen's back. "Or I can push you."

"No need!" And with that, Wilhelm disappeared.

The other three guys bent over to watch his chute open, and didn't turn away until it crumpled to the ground, downwind of a scrambling Steen. Wilhelm let out a triumphant whoop. Then he looked up at the balloon and waved.

"Me next!" Bjorn climbed onto the basket's edge just like Wilhelm did. "Do I need to wait for him to get out of the way?"

The lieutenant chuckled. "If you're skilled enough to land on top of him, then I'll buy you all drinks tonight!"

Bjorn looked over his shoulder at the British officer. "Challenge accepted!" And he was gone.

Holt and Roald watched again as the chute opened and obscured their view of Bjorn.

"Damn," the lieutenant grumbled. "He might hit the spot."

The officer's pay was saved by a last minute gust of wind which pushed Bjorn ten yards west of both his leg bag and Wilhelm.

Roald straightened and looked at Holt. "You or me?"

The younger man looked nervous.

"You go," Holt said. "And give me a target to aim for."

Roald heaved a deep breath, bounced a nod, and climbed

onto the rim of the balloon's basket.

"Fooooor Norwaaaaaaaay!" he bellowed on the way down.

The lieutenant faced Holt. "How old are you?"

Holt tried not to appear irritated. "I turned forty last month."

The officer frowned. "Are you sure you want to do this?"

"I am. I missed the first war because I was too young." Holt grabbed the basket frame and put one leg over the edge. "And when I found out that if I spoke Norse I could enlist for this one, I…"

Holt lifted his other leg over, then grinned and winked at the lieutenant. "I literally jumped at the chance!"

A moment later he was falling.

Pull the leg cords first.

Air rushed up into his face as he did. The heavy bag jerked away from his leg and he grabbed his own parachute cord. He yanked it, hard.

The smooth flutter of silk from his back only lasted a couple of seconds before he was jerked by the shoulders in what felt like an upward thrust. Holt knew that he wasn't actually going up. He was just going down that much more slowly.

He could see his leg bag's parachute below him and he decided to try and steer himself toward it by pulling on his straps. That was marginally effective.

His leg bag's parachute crumpled and tossed itself to the side. The ground came rushing upward. Holt bent his knees and kept his feet together as he watched the blades of grass come into sharp focus.

His feet hit the ground, then his knees hit the ground, and he rolled onto his uninjured right hip.

I did it!

Holt understood exactly why Steen whooped triumphantly at this moment, and he let out a yell that dwarfed the younger man's.

*****

I don't know how to describe it Ralls. It was like flying. I felt like a hawk circling a field looking for mice. It was so quiet up there. I couldn't even hear the wind because I was moving with it.

And then, quicker than I could imagine, the ground started coming up to me. I bent my knees and kept my feet together, like they taught us, but I still fell and rolled on my side ~ my right side, of course. I've heard of guys landing on their feet and walking forward. I hope I get good enough to do that someday.

Now to reply to your last letter.

I am glad to hear that you decided not to move your shop and join the barber. Your ladies like their privacy, I think. Sometimes I feel like I'm intruding when I'm there. And if it wasn't for dear Miss Whitley and her flirtatious comments I might stop coming. How is she doing?

I have to admit that your letter caught me off guard a bit. Why were you surprised at my response to your past? Why would you ever think that I wouldn't accept you as you are?

Lord knows, and so do you, I'm no saint. And you have been so patient with me and understanding of my pain during these last four years or so.

I fell in love ~ finally! ~ with the Raleigh Burns who brought me the best lasagna I'd ever tasted and then stuck with me after that, even though I was not very good company most of the time at first.

As much as I have been shaped by the events of my past, so have you. We would not be the people we are today, otherwise. And as hard and painful as those events were, they did bring us together in the end. I am very grateful for that.

*****

I have one last thing to tell you, Holt. Burns was my mother's maiden name, not the name I was given at birth. I changed it when I moved to Iowa City, just in case the man tried to find me.

If I had the courage, I would go back to Kansas and see if he did die that night. Or if he was injured and died later. Or if he's still alive and in Kansas, wondering where his money went.

Oops ~ I guess I actually do have another thing to tell you. I left that house with nearly ten thousand dollars that night. It was enough for me to live on while I went to school, and later to buy both my little house in Berlin and the shop. And now I have a nice nest egg tucked away for my old age.

God forgive me, but I don't regret anything.

*****

The day after everyone in the group successfully completed the helium balloon jump, Captain Winters' operational group was taken into one of the airplane hangers. The plane waiting inside had a ladder leading up to the open door on its right side.

"Today we begin our training on how to jump out of a real airplane flying at real altitude." The captain then passed off control of the class to his British counterpart. "Captain Smythe?"

"Thank you. Let's begin by entering the aircraft. Everyone climb in and fill the benches from back to front." He turned to Winters. "The commanding officer goes in last and jumps out first."

Holt swore he saw Winters' face go a shade whiter.

Once the men were inside and seated, Captain Smythe went through the steps of the exercise. "First the airplane takes off, of course. Once it does, you need to stand up and hook up. Fasten your static line to the overhead cable. That will keep you from falling out of the open door at the wrong time."

He grabbed the cable with one hand. "After that, everyone stays put until the aircraft passes over the drop zone."

Smythe then pointed to a pair of lights at the front of the compartment. "The pilot will turn on this red light when we get near the drop zone."

When the light did not turn on, he banged his fist on the door to the cockpit. "*I said* the pilot will turn on this red light when we get near the drop zone!"

The red light obediently came on.

He faced the men again. "When the red light comes on, everyone is to stand up and face forward."

They did.

"Now, we do the final equipment check," Smythe stated. "Both the equipment that you are carrying, and the parachute on the back of the man in front of you. Let's go through those motions."

Holt leaned over and patted his leg where the leg bag would go. Then he pretended to check Roald's parachute.

"Sound off from back to front of the line that everything is okay."

The men shouted their okays, one at a time, from the back of the plane to the front.

"Good. Now everyone step forward and line up at the door."

Smythe raised his voice again. "When the green light comes on, that means we are in position."

The red light went off and the green light came on.

"After the green light comes on and you reach the front of the line, unhook your static line. The jump master will slap your leg and shout go!"

Smythe put his hands on his hips and stared the men down. "Go as soon as he says go. If you hesitate, we may not get enough men dropped. Understood?"

"Yes, sir!" the soldiers barked backing unison.

"This is *just* as important—do *not* go until he slaps your leg and says go. Understood?"

"Yes, sir!"

Smythe pointed back over his shoulder. "And if that little green light turns red?"

Holt ventured an answer. "Stay put."

The captain nodded. "Exactly. Do. Not. Go. Even if your leg has been slapped. Is that understood?"

"Yes, sir!"

Smythe folded his arm across his chest. "Good. Let's run through it again."

*****

They went through the sequence ten more times, each time with less prompting. By the tenth repetition the men inside the plane moved wordlessly and perfectly through all the steps, prompted only by blinking lights.

After Captain Smythe bestowed his approval and declared the training successfully completed, the men climbed back down the ladder and headed to the parachute packing shed.

Right away Holt noticed the difference in the parachutes that they were given this afternoon. "These are in really good condition."

"They are!" Roald held one up and looked at it in the sunlight streaming through the southern window. "They make the ones we've been practicing with look like rags."

"If they saved the good ones for the airplane jumps, I can't be mad about it," Wilhelm Steen added his two cents.

"What the hell?" Bjorn yelped. "The jumps from the helium balloon could have killed someone if the chute failed!"

Holt didn't argue with that. "Just focus on folding your parachute the way we've been taught. Don't get distracted now."

"Right," Steen agreed. "If it fails this time, you can remember to blame yourself right before you go splat."

Chapter Thirteen

April 1944

After packing and repacking their parachutes—the good ones—and taking more practice jumps off the steel tower and the helium balloon, it was time for the men in Captain Winters' operational group to go up in a military airplane and jump out of it.

Holt had to confess he was a bit leery of the jump, but after all their training he wasn't about to wash out now. He'd make a successful jump or die trying.

"Tell me we aren't going to die," Roald murmured as the plane taxied to takeoff. "You never lie so if you say it, we'll be fine."

Holt chuckled and looked at Roald.

His young friend was absolutely serious. Then he noticed that Wilhelm and Bjorn were watching him with the same intense expressions.

They are looking to me for assurance.

Because they trust me.

The realization was startling. And the accompanying responsibility was heavy.

Holt gripped Roald's knee and shook it a little. "Of course we aren't going to die. We've all trained for this until we could do it in our sleep. And I don't know about you guys, but I do!"

The three soldiers glanced at each other with a *that's true* sort of expression. Holt realized they needed more, though. A battle cry of sorts.

Holt let go of Roald's knee and held up a clenched fist.

"*Vikingregel!*" he grunted. Vikings reign!

The younger men smiled then, and held up their fists as well.

"*Vikingregel!*" they chorused.

The men behind the trio also shouted unexpectedly, "*Vikingregel!*"

A very good thing was happening, Holt realized. He stood and faced the men waiting to take their first real jump out of a real airplane. "Who are we?"

"*Vikinger!*" they barked back, grinning.

"What do we do?"

"*Regel!*"

"Say it!"

"*Vikingregel!*"

"Again!"

"*Vikingregel!*" The combined male voices thundered, filling the compartment with their sound.

Holt pointed at each man. "Never forget who you are. You all are modern day Vikings. Be proud and brave—and act accordingly."

*****

Five guys jumped before it was Holt's turn. He swung into position and unhooked his static line.

The jump master shouted, "Ready!"

The green light flashed on and Holt felt a hard slap against his leg. "Go!'

He did.

The wind hit his face like a wooden board as he tumbled out of the plane. He was so high up that nothing below him looked real.

Thankfully for this first run they didn't have the leg bags to distract them, so he counted to five and pulled his ripcord, praying that his chute opened as it should.

He heard a *crack* above him and his whole body was snapped upward like a whip. The dreaded opening shock was living up to its reputation. Holt was torn between loathing it with every fiber of his being, and praising it for proving his chute had opened just as it was supposed to.

Holt looked up at the silk canopy, arching in a perfect dome over his head with a bright spot where the sun was.

Beautiful.

He looked down again. Time to concentrate on landing.

There was no wind now. The drone of the airplane was fading. Instructors on the ground had loudspeakers so they could coach the neophytes as they landed.

"Number Four, remember to roll next time. That landing had all the grace of sliding into second base while stepping on a landmine!"

"Number Five, put your feet together!"

"Number Six!"

That's me.

"Try pulling your left strap."

Holt tugged on the designated strap and held it. For the last sixty feet he coasted closer to the big white X on the field.

The ground was suddenly rushing up at him with alarming speed. Holt remembered not to tense up. To bend his knees. Keep his feet together.

The blades of grass appeared in sharp focus. Holt's boots hit the ground. His parachute yanked him to his right as a gust of wind filled it.

Holt stumbled after his chute, trying to keep his balance and not fall to his knees. He wasn't successful.

But he was on the ground, and in one intact piece.

As he unhooked himself from the parachute, stood, and gathered the silk from the meadow he heard, "Number Seven, beautifully done."

He turned around to see Roald crouching near the X as his

chute fluttered gracefully to the ground. Holt smiled.

He needed that more than I did.

Multiple planes were dropping men all over the area, so the sky resembled an aerial mushroom farm. Holt and the others from his flight were to meet at the parking area about a hundred yards from the drop target. A personnel truck would take them back to the airport for a second jump.

"Jumping twice the first day will ensure that you all know you can do this." Captain Winters grinned at the group. "And after the second jump you can go back to the barracks and wash out your underwear."

The breezes on the ground cooperated this time, so on Holt's second jump he drifted in for a landing which wouldn't have popped a soap bubble.

"You can never be sure whether you're going to bounce halfway up again or ease in cotton soft," one of the instructors told him after he gathered his chute. "But you did real well today, old man."

Holt smiled. "Call me Gramps."

*****

The next week, after successfully completing three of the four airplane jumps required for their certification—two with the leg bags—the fourth and final jump was a night jump.

Unfortunately, the weather had turned quite foul that spring evening. Gray-bottomed thunderclouds built beautiful billowy towers into the sky, their heights lit in pink, orange, and purple by the escaping sun. In spite of that, the soldiers climbed into the plane an hour later and took their spots on the benches.

"This will be interesting," Bjorn grumbled. "Bound to be a bumpy ride."

"All the more reason to jump out," Holt quipped.

"You got that right," Wilhelm huffed.

Roald rechecked his harness. "Will we really go up?"

Holt shrugged. "If this was war and we had an objective to complete, would we go up then?"

Glances bounced among the men.

"I guess we would," one of them ventured.

"Yeah, and jumping away from the storm is probably easier than jumping into a battle," another observed.

Captain Winters climbed into the plane and took his seat. His uniform was covered in dark wet drops.

The jump master followed him and pounded on the cockpit door. "Let's go!"

The plane started moving and the jump master closed the door. Flashes of lightning illuminated its little window.

The engines turning the propellers droned as the aircraft took off, albeit unsteadily. As they approached the drop zone, the jump master opened the door to the cockpit.

"The captain thinks it's too rocky to send the guys out," he shouted over the combined din of thunder and engines. "But I think they'll be fine."

"I'm all for lightening my load, sir," the pilot responded as the plane bucked like a Colorado bronco.

"Then flip on the red light when we get close."

The pilot flipped the switch. "We're almost there now."

The jump master shut the cockpit door and opened the outside one. "Get ready, men!"

It was raining hard now, and the propellers were blasting the water right past the opened jump door. The soldiers stood and pressed forward.

Captain Winters bellowed over the cacophony, "Equipment check!"

One by one the *okays* were shouted from the back of the line to the front. Lightning flashed continuously, turning the men in Holt's view into pale blue statues in staccato bursts.

Holt raised a fist. "*Vikingregel!*"

Several men answered back.

Holt shouted again, "*Vikingregel!*"

This time the response was Viking worthy.

The green light went on.

The first man jumped.

When Holt got to the front of the line and unhooked his static line the plane dipped precariously. He wasn't sure if it was the sudden movement, the green light, or the jagged lightning that triggered his leap from the flying metal beast, but he went out without ever hearing *Go!* or feeling the slap on his leg.

Rain pelted his face and stung his eyes as he fell through the black storm toward an invisible target somewhere below. He counted to five, then pulled his ripcord. He never heard the snap of silk, but was yanked upward nonetheless.

Once he was out of the plane and held up by his parachute, he began to breathe again. He looked down, searching for the target. The lightning which was so recently his enemy now obligingly lit the ground and revealed the location of the landing spot.

Holt tugged on his straps, urging his chute to carry him in that direction. He seemed to be descending more slowly than usual.

The atmosphere's heavy because of the rain.

He came down gently, and managed to hit close to the trucks. It turned out to be his best jump of them all.

It's hard to describe the sensation, Ralls. Once you convince yourself to jump from a flying airplane into nothing, it's just falling without control, terrifying and extremely windy. The ground is so far below that it doesn't even look real.

But you have to remember to open your chute! I know that sounds silly, but it's true. You count to five, then pull your leg bag's cord first, if you have one, and then pull your own.

For a few seconds, nothing happens. Then you hear this loud crack when the chute opens, and then there is an upward jerk that feels like it'll break every bone in your body. It is as horrible as it sounds, and there is nothing you can do to make it easier.

But then, everything changes. There's no more wind making your eyes water, no more roaring in your ears. All of a sudden you are floating toward the earth, quietly and peacefully. And that's when you absolutely love what you're doing.

It's like flying, except you don't have to flap your wings ~ just coast on the wind.

When you get close to the ground, you relax, bend your knees, keep your feet together, and hope for a soft landing. You can never predict how you'll land, because a gust of wind can spring up and mess with you.

That happens more often than it doesn't in my limited experience, but I successfully completed my balloon jump, my three daytime airplane jumps, and my one nighttime airplane jump in the middle of a fierce English springtime thunderstorm.

I feel invincible.

May 1944

After graduating from paratrooper school, the NORSO group returned to the Powers Hunting Lodge outside Inverness to continue their specific training. One of the most important skills for a penetrating operative to learn was the ability to stealthily take out sentries.

At night.

Without being caught.

"We'll all have blanks in our rifles, of course," Lieutenant Bull said to the gathered NORSO soldiers. "Each company will take turns being the sentries and being the operatives."

Bull looked at his roster. "Hansen!"

"Which one?" Holt called out.

Bull looked back at his clipboard. "Corporal Holten Hansen."

Holt raised his hand.

"You're going to be a judge tonight. It will be your job to stick with Company A and evaluate their tactics against the target. Eilertsen!"

A burly merchant marine raised his hand. "Here!"

"You will judge Company C's defense of the target."

"Yes, sir."

"Go get ready," Bull barked. "Dismissed!"

*****

This will be interesting.

One thing Holt had noticed early on about the Norwegian guys who volunteered from the merchant marines is that they were a group of hard men—hard fighters, hard drinkers, and hard to control.

The goal on this muggy Scottish night was for the men of A Company to either get close enough to touch a sentry or to rush him before he could fire his rifle. If they did either one, that sentry was considered taken out.

Holt soon discovered that some of the merchant marines took the task way too seriously.

"Hey, you can't do that!" Holt grabbed a brick out of a squad leader's hand just as he was about to heave it. "These are *our* guys, remember!"

"We're supposed to act like it's real," the man grumbled.

"Yes. *Act*." Holt pointed away from the sentry. "Go back and regroup."

They did.

Then three of them hit Jensen while he was patrolling a

wooded area—one dropped out of a tree and the other two jumped him from opposite sides of the path.

"You got the points!" Holt yelped as he helped his beleaguered comrade up. "You're lucky you didn't break his back!"

The men shrugged, unconcerned.

Holt heard an odd sound. "Stay here."

He followed the faint creaking and cracking to a group of four guys trying to push over a dead tree with the intent of using it to knock out the sentry downhill.

"Stop! Now! I'll give you the points." Holt jammed his fists on his hips. "You know he can hear you up here, right?"

"He hasn't shot at us," one pointed out. "He probably thinks it's some kind of animal."

That was a good point, and Holt made a note to talk to his Company C guys about ignoring sounds. "Even so, you aren't supposed to actually kill another army soldier who's *on your side*."

When Holt made his report to Lieutenant Bull at the end of the exercise, the Scottish officer appeared conflicted. "On the one hand, they were probably going to succeed if this was actually war…"

Holt had to agree. "No doubt, sir."

"But on the other hand, we can't let them injure or kill their own soldiers during training." Bull tapped his chin. "I have an idea for tomorrow night. You can go on back to your company, and thank you, Corporal."

"Yes, sir."

The next night, Lieutenant Bull had Company C on the attack and Company B on defense as the sentries. Then he split Company A in half and had them attack and defend against each other.

Holt thought that plan was either risky or brilliant. "I guess we'll find out tomorrow."

Company C decided to set up an ambush on the road to take out the Company B sentries. While they were setting it up, two armored cars appeared which were not part of the exercise.

"What do we do?" Bjorn asked.

"Treat them like the enemy! *Vikingregel!*" Wilhelm shouted.

After "blasting" the armored cars with dummy grenades, the men inside climbed out and surrendered. When Lieutenant Bull heard about it he congratulated the men for thinking fast and acting appropriately in the situation.

"There's just one problem," he told Company C the next day as they gathered in a classroom and wondered to each other what was wrong. "In all the excitement, only six of you remembered to pull the pins from your grenades. The rest of you were no more effective than if you were throwing rocks."

Holt slumped in his seat, wondering if he was one who forgot.

Then Lieutenant Bull placed a grenade on the desk. He said nothing at first, and then he picked it up.

As the men watched, he pulled out the pin while holding the safety handle in place.

Every man in the room straightened in their chairs.

He set the grenade back on the desk and let the safety handle go and the grenade started to sputter. "That, gentlemen, is how you pull a pin on a hand grenade."

Without another word, he strode to the classroom door and left, closing it behind him.

WHAT THE HELL?

Before anyone could do more than dive for the floor under their seats, the grenade exploded with the pop of a firecracker, and filled the room with smoke.

Holt was furious. None of this was funny.

Lieutenant Bull calmly opened the door and walked back to the desk where the dummy grenade lay impotently on the desk, smoke still curling from a hole in the bottom where its cotton plug had blown out.

The room was deathly quiet.

Bull clasped his hands behind his back.

"Are there any questions gentlemen?

*****

Holt was still shaking as he stomped toward the mess hall.

"What the hell was he thinking?" Wilhelm blurted. "What was the point of that?"

"He was thinking that if he scared the shit out of us, we'd never forget to pull a pin again." Holt hated to admit it, but the terrifying lesson was likely to stick with all of them for the rest of their lives. "I can't say I agree with his tactics, though."

Wilhelm stopped walking and faced Holt. "How's your heart, Gramps?"

Holt huffed a laugh. "Beating harder than it has in a long time."

"Good. Keep it that way."

Roald pointed at the merchant marine guys from Company A who looked like they'd all been in a prize fight—and lost. "What happened to them?"

Sergeant Major Michaels walked past Holt's group on the way to the mess, looking smug. "Lieutenant Bull taught *them* a lesson, too, when he pitted them against each other."

Michaels turned back to face them. "Let's just say, they've learned their lesson. They won't be trying to *literally* take out men during practice maneuvers anymore."

Chapter Fourteen

May 1944

The NORSO guys were all called into the command post, one at a time, with no explanation beforehand. Those who went in first were tight-lipped about what went on when they came back out.

"Whatever it is, it's a secret and it's serious," Bjorn observed while they waited to be called.

"We are a secret operations group." Roald looked to Holt for confirmation. "This is probably the start of the 'secret' part."

Holt nodded. "That would be my guess."

Wilhelm stroked his chin. "What's the first secret for an operative, I wonder?"

Jensen was leaving the building after his interview and he overheard the question. He spoke over his shoulder as he walked away.

"Your identity."

Holt's turn came and he sat in front of Major Helgesen. There was nothing on the major's desk but his folded hands.

"How's it going, Corporal?"

"Good, sir."

"I understand you've excelled at all of the challenges we've put in front of you."

Holt felt his face heating. "I have applied myself and done

everything to the best of my ability."

The major nodded. "And you've helped those in your company do the same."

Holt realized with a jolt that he was being watched twenty-four hours a day and seven days a week. Had to be, if someone reported back how he helped Steen on the first jump tower.

"We might be training for covert work, sir, but none of us operates without the support of others."

"That is certainly true, Corporal." Helgesen unfolded his hands and leaned back in his chair. "And thinking ahead, what do you think is the most *important* part of supporting others in covert operations?"

Holt thought a moment. "I suppose it would be following orders and completing your task."

The major nodded. "That's certainly critical."

Holt narrowed his eyes. "But not the answer you were looking for."

Helgesen smiled softly.

Holt mentally skimmed over the various components which he assumed would be part of the work they were going to do, and just like a light bulb turning on in a dark room, Jensen's cryptic comment made sudden sense.

"The identity of the other operatives, sir."

Helgesen looked pleased. "Good. But not only the *other* operatives…"

And there it was. "My identity."

"Yes." Major Helgesen leaned forward again. "So everyone is getting a new one."

Holt frowned. "A new one?"

"Together we'll create a fictional name and life story for each of you, and give you papers in that name."

Holt's jaw dropped.

"You can choose a name, but we have to approve it of course. After we're finished creating this persona, you will commit it to memory and become that person for the rest of your time in the OSS. Do you understand?"

"Y-yes, sir"

"Once the war is over, you'll carry these details to the grave."

And hopefully that grave is many decades ahead of me.

"I understand, sir."

"And though it may seem unimportant today, you must *not* discuss any of this with the rest of the soldiers. You can never know when the memory of a minute detail might trip you up."

"Understood, sir."

And they will be watching us.

Major Helgesen stood so Holt jumped to his feet. "Report back tomorrow morning at eight with every set of your uniforms and a clear head. Dismissed."

Holt saluted. "Yes, sir.

*****

The next day the soldiers all changed into fatigues, removing the visible declaration of each man's rank. The point was to completely strip away every man's identity, including his name.

The most important link in the OSS's covert no-identity chain was a cover story. That could be any possible tale—except the truth, of course—about the what, when, where, how, and why of who the operative was.

The possibilities were staggering.

Who do I want to be?

Holt went into the makeshift dressing room with an armful of fatigues. After he changed he handed his corporal's uniforms, complete with stripes and a name patch, to a waiting sergeant.

"Will I ever see these again?" Holt asked.

"I can't answer that." The man slipped the clothes into a linen bag and wrote Holt's serial number on a label on the outside. "Good luck."

Holt walked to another waiting area where the soldiers were, once again, being called into small offices one at a time.

"Hansen?" The captain looked up from his clipboard.

"Holten?"

"Yes, sir." Holt followed him into the little room and closed the door.

"Have a seat." The captain who did not introduce himself and had no name on his uniform sat across a small table from Holt. "Do you know why you're here?"

Holt shook his head. "No, sir."

The captain smiled. "We are going to create your new identity. I'm going to help you come up with a plausible story—which is close enough to who you actually are—so that you won't blow your cover."

Holt chuckled and relaxed. "So I don't claim to be able to do something which I know nothing about."

The captain nodded. "Or be from a part of the country which you've never visited. Exactly. We aim for close, but completely untrue."

This was going to be interesting.

"Let's start with your name. Have you given that any thought?"

"I have. I know some guys get to keep their first names, but I think Holten is too unique for America," he offered. "So maybe Holden instead?"

The captain nodded. "That could work as long as the last name is nothing like Hansen." He put up a quelling hand. "I know Hansen is the most common name in Norway, so normally that would be a way to hide, but not in your case."

That made sense. "What about one of the most common names in America, then? Like Smith?"

The captain frowned a little. "No, when you're dropped into Norway, you'll still want to pass as Norwegian by heritage. What about using Hans as your first name?"

When I'm dropped?

A little thrill skittered up Holt's spine. "I like that."

"Any family names you could use?"

"My mother's maiden name is Ellefsen," Holt suggested. "I could be Hans Ellefsen."

"Perfect." The captain wrote that down. "Where was she

from?"

"Outside Bergen."

"We'll keep that. Where were you born?"

"Oshkosh, Wisconsin."

"We'll make that Iowa City, Iowa." He wrote without looking up. "How old do you want to be?"

Holt startled. "Can't I still be forty?"

"You can, but it's best if we change every thing, at least a little." The captain tapped the pen against his lips. "You were born in oh-four? Let's make you forty-four. That makes you less likely to be pegged as an active duty soldier."

Holt had a disconcerting moment where he wondered if he actually looked older than he was.

This is no time to be vain.

"And it's easy to remember," Holt added.

"Married?"

"Widowed." That came out easier than he expected it to.

The captain looked empathetic. "How'd she die?"

"Car accident."

Please don't ask if I was in the car.

He nodded and wrote that down. "Let's keep that, too. Now, college."

"I went to Oshkosh Normal School where my father taught."

"Did you graduate?"

"Barely." Holt winced. "A teaching career wasn't for me."

"What did you do?"

"I moved to Berlin, Wisconsin and hunted for pelts."

The captain looked surprised. "What kind?"

"Black bear, mostly. Also beaver and fox." Holt shrugged. "And occasionally a wolf."

"That's interesting, but awfully specific… Do you have any other skills? Something more generic?"

Holt thought a minute. "I did build my own house."

"Construction skills!" The captain looked very excited. "You did everything? Plumbing? Electrical? Roofing?"

Holt didn't think that was particularly special but he was glad the captain did. "Yes, sir."

The captain grinned. "All right, Hans Ellefsen. You are a forty-four-year-old widowed construction foreman from Iowa City. You have some college, but never graduated."

"Can I hunt on the side?" Holt asked.

"Sure, but let's say it's for food. Like deer." The captain made more notes. "Deer hunting is common, and that way your skills with firearms won't be a surprise."

One glaring detail was still missing. "So what am I doing in Norway?"

"If you are questioned, you won't pass as a Norwegian national, because your accent still twangs like an American." The captain looked up from his paper. "So you'll say you were looking for relatives, and were stranded after the German invasion and occupation."

The captain's expression shifted. "That actually did happen to a good number of American citizens."

That was a surprising piece of information. "Did I find the relatives?"

The captain shook his head. "No. If asked, the Ellefsens you found were not in any way related."

Holt sat quietly, pondering his new story and looking for holes. All in all, he thought he could remember it well, and none of it pointed back to his real life and identity.

"So what name do I use now?" he asked.

"You'll keep your real identity when you're training with the other guys in your Company, because that's how you know each other."

Of course. And that way they kept their new identities secret.

"But," the captain continued, "you'll use your new identity when you are working with the OSS training staff and sent away on maneuvers."

Holt frowned. "Sent away?"

"You'll be sent into Manchester, and maybe London, with challenges to complete. Practice objectives before you hit the real thing." The captain handed Holt a paper with the new details they just decided on. "Memorize these in the next half hour, then burn the paper. Is that clear?"

*****

Today we had the oddest experience ~ each of us was taken alone into a little room and, together with an unnamed officer, created an entirely new identity for ourselves.

Of course, I can't tell you anything about mine, just that I have one now. We'll all get a set of official papers with our new names, and when we drop into our target that is the man we will be. Everything that identifies me as me will be left behind.

My job now is to be so familiar with the man who I will become that I will never crack under interrogation.

This is the oddest sensation, Ralls. And I'll never be able to tell you about any of it. I'm to take that information literally 'to my grave.'

*****

The day after all of the NORSO soldiers received their secret new names and stories, they met the OSS covert training staff. The staff turned out to be made up of various professors, doctors, psychologists, psychiatrists, and experts in hands-on skills.

Their collective mission was to examine and test the men in every possible way to make certain each one was up to taking on the risks and stresses associated with living out a fake persona in a hostile environment.

And because the soldiers risked possible failure and subsequent discovery while in action, they all had to sign a dozen or so forms concerning who to contact, and what to do with the body, if they were killed.

"We're going to be tested morning, noon, afternoon, and night," Roald observed. "We can never let our guard down."

"And we must remember who knows us by our real names, and when to use our spy identities," Holt added. "That in itself is a test."

The soldiers then spent two full and exhausting days taking intellectual and psychological exams, both oral and written. They filled in blanks, picked numbers, chose pictures, pulled levers, pushed buttons, and wrote page after page on assigned topics.

On the third morning they were taken outside for a scavenger hunt—which took place over an obstacle course.

"Find these items and complete the course as you do so," their instructor barked. "The list is in random order, as are the items. Some are hidden, some are in plain sight but might not be what you're expecting. Do not touch them, just mark where they are using compass coordinates. Understood?"

"Yes, sir!" the soldiers barked back.

"You are to work alone and you are all working against the clock." He held up a stop watch. "Go!"

Holt unfolded his paper and read the entire list of ten items while some of the men—Wilhelm Steen and Bjorn Lind, included—bolted toward the course.

Something to help you break in unnoticed.

A useful tool.

The smallest disguise…

Holt folded his paper and walked toward the course, slipping into tracker mode. His gaze swept back and forth over the ground, looking for any sign of something out of place.

His reached the first obstacle—a narrow board over a wide, shallow stream—and balanced his way across. Something under the water caught his eye. He carefully leaned down to see what it was.

A lapel pin with the Nazi swastika glinted red and black in the shadow of a rock. Holt smiled.

He pulled out his compass and next to 'the smallest disguise' marked the location of the pin.

One down nine to go.

He kept moving, ignoring the other men scattered around him.

What is a useful tool?

Holt walked slowly, scanning the ground without success. He reached the next obstacle, a three-foot diameter drainage tube about twenty feet long, and slithered into it. At the halfway point, and not visible from the end, was a gap between two sections. In the gap sat a beeswax candle and a tin of chewing tobacco.

Holt wondered if those items were senseless decoys until their purpose hit him. If he melted the wax into the empty tin, he could make impressions of keys.

Something to help you break in unnoticed.

Holt couldn't see his compass in the dark, narrow tube, but as soon as he exited the other end he marked the coordinates on his list.

He continued through his list and traipsed through the course, hesitating when he found the screwdriver. That 'useful tool' seemed too easy, but he marked the coordinates anyway.

When he reached the last obstacle, and could see the end marked fifty yards ahead of him, he was supposed to make an animal from modeling clay. The golf-ball-sized lump of clay was mashed, but still held the hint of some four-legged creature which its previous competitor had made.

Holt picked up the clay and began to knead it. It had an odd texture, not like the clay he used in art class. Then he sniffed it.

Holy cow.

It's plastic explosive.

Holt quickly rolled the clay into a snake and coiled it on the child's table where he found it. Then he crossed out the screwdriver's coordinates on his list beside 'useful tool' and marked the table's position instead.

With his list in one hand and his compass in the other, he turned and sprinted toward the finish line.

*****

That afternoon the men were lined up outside a closed door in the classroom building.

"Each of you will have exactly five minutes to search the contents and condition of this room," the instructor stated. "After that, you will have exactly ten minutes to write as detailed a description as you can of its occupant. Any questions?"

Holt raised his hand. "Can we move things if we replace them as they were? For the next man?"

"Would you move things if you were working on an objective?" he countered.

"Yes." Holt had to admit. "But this is a test."

"Exactly." The instructor gave no other indication of an answer. Instead he opened the door and motioned the first man in line inside.

It took three hours for every man in Company A to take his turn in the room. Holt's turn was in the third hour, so he wondered if things had been moved.

Nothing to do but do what I can.

The room was messy, but the sort of messy he might encounter if the occupant left in a hurry. For example, every item was near where he would expect it to be stored, just not put away.

The occupant is normally a tidy individual.

They left the room suddenly—were they running to something? Or away from something?

Holt checked the closet. There were several empty wooden hangers all hanging askew. There was one white dress shirt still in a cleaning bag.

They valued their appearance.

Holt looked inside the neck of the shirt and read the size.

The individual was slight in stature.

He checked the size of the pressed dress pants. The man was taller than his waist size indicated.

Tall and thin.

There were three ties hanging on hooks. Holt was struck by the colors—or rather lack of them. Most men liked to add a little flair to their dark and conservative suits by wearing a striped tie, or a solid color.

This person does not want to be noticed.

Holt looked at his watch. Three minutes left. He crossed to the desk in the room and pulled open the drawers. He found exactly what he would expect: plain stationery, two plain fountain pens, a pencil, sharpener, and gum eraser, stamps for basic postage...

Holt noticed two inkpots. He screwed the top off of one and dipped a piece of twisted toilet paper into it.

Solid black.

He screwed the lid back on and put it back in place. Then he tested the other.

Blue.

The same blue that Raleigh used when she wrote to him.

Holt sniffed the stationery. The faintest whiff of perfume rewarded him. He smiled, knowing he'd cracked the assignment.

The room's occupant was a woman.

A woman passing as a man.

And she left in a hurry.

Chapter Fifteen

The roughest test of all, however, came late that same night when every man was dead tired from the packed day. As usual, the soldiers were called in one by one. This time they were taken back into the little rooms where they'd created their new identities and told to sit.

"Here is your situation," an instructor read from a script without looking down at Holt. "You have been caught red-handed while going through top secret files in the Nazi headquarters in Bergen. You cannot feign amnesia or insanity, and you cannot refuse to talk. You have precisely three minutes to prepare your explanation before the investigation board enters. Your final rating in your training is dependent on whether or not you can talk your way out."

With that, the instructor turned and left the little office, pulling the wooden door shut behind him with a loud clunk.

Holt drew a deep breath and closed his eyes.

I am Hans Ellefsen from Iowa City, Iowa. I came to Norway in late March of nineteen-forty to look for lost relatives when the war escalated.

I was stuck here when Germany attacked and occupied Norway on April ninth of nineteen-forty. Since the German munitions ship's explosion in Bergen in forty-four, I have been using my construction knowledge to help rebuild the town.

The door banged open and three men in Nazi uniforms

marched in and sat down across the little table from Holt. He hated to admit that even though he knew the men were Americans, the specter was disturbingly daunting.

"Mister—Ellefsen is it?" one man sneered at Holt in Norsk.

So that was how this would be.

"Yes."

"We have some questions to ask you."

*****

After his thorough interrogational shredding and completely disastrous interview, Holt was moved into another little room and left alone to ponder how he was going to explain it to Raleigh when he was booted from the OSS.

One of his favorite instructors—also a man of a more advanced age—opened the door and came inside. "How did you do?"

Holt wagged his head dejectedly. "I blew it. They tore my story apart in minutes."

"I'm sorry to hear that. You were really doing well up to now." The instructor took a seat next to Holt. "What happened?"

"They asked me about my wife."

The other man cocked his head. "Your wife?"

"When we were married, how long we were married, how long ago did she die…"

Holt was too embarrassed to say it out loud, but he forgot that, because he was supposed to be four years older than he actually was, he needed to work out new corresponding dates. Stumbling through those answers on the fly was his undoing.

Instead, he said honestly, "I forgot what year it was, you know? After Pearl Harbor and all the training at home and here… I've been working so hard that everything just ran together."

The instructor sighed. "I get it."

Holt looked sideways at him. "So what happens now?"

He shrugged. "Maybe they can send you back to your old outfit. Where are they?"

Holt opened his mouth to answer when a jolt sent a zing of adrenaline though his frame. This was part of the test. That's why the investigators asked so many questions about his wife. They saw that as his weakest area.

And rightly so as it turned out.

"They're still back in the U.S. as far as I know," Holt lied. "Camp Carson."

"They haven't deployed yet? Why not?"

Holt huffed. "You're asking me to explain the Army?"

"Well, I could probably arrange for some leave time, if you want to go home for a while."

Holt was momentarily tempted to accept that offer in case it was real. He missed Raleigh fiercely. He pulled a deep breath of regret.

"That's not necessary. The trip's too long."

"You don't have someone special back home that you'd like to see?" the instructor prodded.

Holt shook his head. "Nope."

"Suit yourself." The other man leaned back and folded his arms. "I'm just trying to help you out, because you were such a strong candidate up until today."

Holt wondered if he meant the compliment. "Thanks."

"Besides, I've heard that springtime in Wisconsin is supposed to be nice."

Holt smiled a little. "It might be. But in Iowa it's about plowing all that flat land and getting the crops planted. If it's the same to you, I'd rather stay here and be reassigned than ride a tractor all day."

"I can look into that for you."

"Thanks again." Holt decided it was time to call a spade a spade. "So are we done yet?"

The instructor's gaze cut to Holt's. "Done with what?"

"Done with all the test questions. I'm ready to hit the sack." Holt grinned. "Our OSS training resumes early tomorrow, right?"

Once Holt broke through the charade, the instructor admitted that interview with the three brutes in Nazi uniform was actually intended to break the soldier and destroy his confidence.

"Then it's my job to see how you all react when the tension eases," he explained. "Whether you talk too much when you relax. And mostly to see if you maintain your cover story."

Holt winced. "What if I blew this part as bad as I did in the interrogation?"

"If the rest of your work has been satisfactory—which yours has been—it wouldn't have made a big difference." The instructor looked pleased. "We aren't out to crucify anyone. We just want to shake you up enough so that you don't make the same mistakes ever again, especially when it counts."

"Understood."

"So what year *did* your wife die?"

Holt was sticking with that answer out of respect to Nora. "Five years ago. Nineteen-thirty-nine. The year before I came to Norway."

"How long were you married?"

Six years.

"Ten years. I was twenty-nine when we tied the knot."

The instructor's mouth curved at one edge. "Kids?"

"Sadly, no." This part was also true. "She had several miscarriages, so we stopped trying. That situation was just too hard on both of us."

The inspector's half-smile faded. He must have seen the truth in Holt's eyes. "I'm sorry, Hansen."

Holt resolutely wagged his head. "The name's Ellefsen, sir."

"Oh, right. Sorry." The half smile was back. "You can go."

Holt reached for the door handle and turned the knob.

"One last thing?"

Holt looked back over his shoulder.

"If you don't mind me asking, what was your wife's name?"

"That's nice of you, sir." Holt smiled at the other man. "It's Raleigh."

Then he opened the door, stepped out of the room, and closed the door behind him.

*****

That core-shattering test drove home the fact that Holt had to stay ready all day, every day, from here on out. He punched up his narrative with the facts and dates that were missing, and recited it silently to himself in the morning before leaving his cot, in the shower in the morning or at night, when he shaved, and before he ate in lieu of saying grace.

Forgive me, Father.

I need to help you keep me alive, and let you concentrate on those in more precarious positions at the moment.

The training staff for the OSS, now that they were getting into the real covert stuff, was always trying to trip the men up.

"A pat on the back feels like they're looking for a spot to stick in the blade," Roald complained.

Holt agreed. "And the fact that we can't talk to each other about anything that happens in the one-on-one tests really isolates us."

"I guess Steen and Lind did okay," Roald observed. "They're both still here."

"So is Jensen." Then a realization dawned. "But I haven't seen Olsen for a while."

"Neither have I." Roald looked sad. "I'd ask if he washed out, but I doubt I'd get a straight answer."

"No, I don't think you would." Holt lifted his lunch tray. "Come on. We have to be on the field in ten minutes."

When Company C was assembled, they were broken into four-man teams. Holt was with Jensen, Steen, and a different man named Olsen.

"Obviously they're keeping us from our closest friends," Steen observed. "I guess they don't want us to rely on anyone but ourselves."

Holt chuckled. "Why, Wilhelm. I thought we *were* close friends."

"Shut it, Gramps!" Steen snapped.

But his eyes twinkled.

"Each team has a different objective," Captain Winters said as he handed each team a map. "Once you reach your objective, you are to retrieve the item tagged with your map's color and return here. If you find a tag of another color, leave it be. Any questions?"

Wilhelm started off as orienteer for the purple group. After following his directions for a mile, however, the quartet came to a dead end.

"Let me see the map." Holt held out his hand and Steen gave him the map.

"North is clearly marked, see?" Steen pointed to the compass rose in the bottom left corner. "But we aren't in the right place..."

Holt squinted at the map, noting the topographical details.

"Hold on..." He turned the map ninety degrees to the right and the problem became suddenly clear. "Look at this. This creek actually runs east west, not north south."

"So the compass rose is skewed," Olsen sneered. "Sly bastards."

Jensen leaned over the map. "So we must actually be over here somewhere, close to that outcropping..."

Steen pointed at the slab of granite ten yards to their right. "You mean *that* outcropping?"

Holt chuckled. "Yep. Now let's figure out what direction we need to take to reach our objective."

He started to hand the map back to Wilhelm, but the younger man declined. "I didn't catch the problem. You did. You go ahead and lead us."

Holt refocused on the map. "We started here, and now we're here. We need to head south for half a mile, then west for a mile."

The soldiers turned around and headed back in the opposite direction. After about a quarter mile, Wilhelm stopped walking.

"Look."

Off to their right and tucked next to a rotting fencepost was a wooden gunpowder cask with a red *Danger!* placard nailed to the top.

"That must be the red team's objective," Jensen guessed.

Holt agreed. "So they're lost, too."

Steen frowned. "The objectives aren't just flags, then."

Holt shook his head. "Guess not. Let's keep going."

The purple team's objective was located near a small pond which they reached in another twenty minutes.

"Which side is the objective on?" Olsen asked.

Holt showed him the map. "Should be right here."

The four men looked at the motionless pool of greenish water surrounded by cattails and long grasses.

"Do we have to go in?" Steen did not look happy about that possibility.

"Let's start by walking around it," Holt suggested. "You and Olsen go left, Jensen and I'll go right. Shout if you find anything."

The two pairs headed off. When they rejoined each other on the opposite side they found a small wooden rowboat, with one oar, hidden in the reeds. The oar's handle was painted purple.

"Do we take the oar?" Jensen asked. "Or the whole boat?"

Holt looked at the little craft. "If I was on a real-life objective, the oar alone would do me no good."

"The boat it is, then." Steen squatted down and untied a rope from a stake, also hidden in the edgewater vegetation. He pulled the tiny craft out of the water and onto the grass.

Holt consulted their map.

"We're only a quarter mile from where we started." He looked up and scanned their wooded surroundings for a landmark.

"There!" He pointed east. "I can see the top of the flagpole. Let's go!"

The purple team trotted back to their starting point with two men on one side, two on the other, carrying the little wooden boat. They were the second of the seven teams to return.

"So, what challenges did you encounter?" Helgesen asked after they set down the boat.

"The compass rose on the map," Steen blurted. "It was off by ninety degrees."

"Good," Helgesen approved. "When did you discover it?"

"I, uh—"

"I was the one to realize that, sir," Holt interjected.

Helgesen shifted his attention to Holt. "And what brought that to your attention?"

"This stream here." Holt pointed at the map. "Runs east west, not north south."

"How do you know that?" the major pressed.

"From studying maps of the area, sir." Holt lifted one shoulder. "And I'm familiar with a lot of the surrounding area because of other maneuvers."

Helgesen faced Steen. "Did you examine the map before setting off?"

Wilhelm looked like he wanted to disappear. Just sink into the ground and not come up.

"Yes, sir," he grumbled. "But not as well as I should have, obviously."

Helgesen smiled grimly. "That's why we run you through this sort of training. When you are given a challenge, you need to examine the information given and not assume everything is kosher."

"Yes, sir," he mumbled.

The major addressed the two remaining team members who had been silent. "Why did you bring the boat and not just the oar?"

Jensen blinked. "Because, sir, a real-life objective, the oar alone would do us no good?"

"Good thinking." Helgesen nodded and turned to Olsen. "Did you find any other objectives on your way?"

"Yes, sir. We came across a cask of gunpowder for the red team."

Helgesen's brow plunged. "Gunpowder?"

"The cask had a red tag with the word *danger* on it," Holt offered.

The major handed the map to Holt. "Can you show me where it was on this map?"

That was odd.

"Sure. It's here." Holt pointed to the spot. "But can I ask why you're asking?"

Helgesen snorted. "Because we didn't put it there."

*****

So, Ralls, it turns out that our team found a cask of gunpowder near where we are training, and the Brits didn't hide it there. Some of their military police guys went to the surrounding farms and ending up routing out an actual Nazi sympathizer. He bragged that he was planning to blow up some of our training areas.

And before you write back and ask me Raleigh, the answer is yes ~ while we were training out there.

The part of all this that gets to me was how proud he was of his plan. But then, that's why he bragged about it. In the end, criminals think they're so brave or brilliant and they always want credit for their crimes.

The hardest part about that particular situation is that spies will want the same thing. We'll want to come home and brag about what we accomplished.

But we're forbidden to, at least for the first decade. The government wants to make sure that all those involved are safe from retribution ~ both us as foreign operatives, and those nationals at home who might have had to make hard decisions. Decisions which might have caused the death, or imprisonment, of their own countrymen.

War, it seems, is a very messy business, and that business lasts for a long time afterward.

*****

I never thought of you being in real danger while you were still in the middle of England, Holt. Now you've given me yet another thing to worry about ~ and to pray about.

Oh, my love. My darling soldier. I've hungered for your touch for such a very long, and very <u>lonely</u>, time. I can't wait until this war ends. You are on my mind every single day. But our time spent apart can change so much ~ please tell me that you're still mine.

*****

My dearest Raleigh! Of course I'm still yours, and you are still mine! You have no idea how much I need your love. Every night I pray that God will carry your love across land and sea, and speed your love straight to me.

When Holt returned to his barracks after posting his letters, the locker at the foot of his bed was suspiciously askew. When he unlocked it and flipped the top open, it was obvious the contents had been gone through quite thoroughly.

Roald walked up and sat on Holt's bunk. "Mine was broken into, as well."

"Was this an official job?" Holt asked while he straightened the lockers' contents. "Or was some student practicing his lock-picking skills?"

"Don't know, to be honest. Is anything missing?"

"No. I don't think so." Holt closed the lid, relocked the boxy container, and sat back on his heels. "But either way, it's unsettling. Either I'm being spied on by the instructors, or I could be robbed by an overeager classmate who is good at picking locks."

Roald scowled. "I guess the answer is to turn over anything valuable for safekeeping with our uniforms, and then make sure we don't leave anything incriminating in our lockers."

"Incriminating?" Holt cocked his head. "Like what?"

"I don't know. Maps? Photos? Letters that we received? Or half-written letters that the censors haven't redacted yet?" Roald pointed a stiff finger at Holt. "If part of your cover story is that you're a widower, and it would make sense to me that it is, then who are you writing to?"

Holt felt the blood drain from his face. "I told the instructor during that cover story test that my dead wife's name was Raleigh."

Roald nodded sagely. "I think you need to stop putting her name in anything. Can you address her letters to anybody else?"

The beauty shop.

Holt jumped up and headed back to company headquarters.

I need to rewrite that letter.

Chapter Sixteen

June, 1944

In an uncharacteristic move, Major Helgesen called all of the ninety-six remaining OSS recruits and officers from the Ninety-Ninth Battalion together at one time.

"Gentlemen, I have top-secret news. For the next few minutes I'm going to break all of your covers and talk to you as American soldiers, originally part of the Ninety-Ninth Battalion." He smiled a little. "The Viking battalion, as you are so fond of calling it."

"Something bad has happened," Holt murmured.

"Must have," Roald murmured back. "The only good news that would affect them—or us—was if the war was over."

"And that news wouldn't be top-secret. It'd be shouted from the rooftops."

"Agreed."

The group was small enough that the major didn't need a microphone to address them. "Earlier this month, on June sixth, to be exact, the allies invaded France, attacking the beaches on Normandy's coast."

Holt perked up. Maybe the news was good after all.

"Unfortunately…"

Aw, shit.

"The Allies sustained extremely heavy losses in the attack." Helgesen paused and seemed to be trying to hold on to his suddenly fragile composure. "There's no way to soften this blow…"

He drew a deep breath. "Six thousand soldiers were lost."

Six?

Six thousand?

Holt felt punched in the gut. He couldn't breathe.

A few of the men moaned. They easily could have lost brothers, cousins, or friends in that devastating battle.

"As a result…"

We better not have surrendered France.

"The eight hundred soldiers remaining in the Ninety-Ninth have been diverted from their original task of liberating Norway, and are on their way to France."

"To fight?" Holt blurted.

"Yes, soldier, to fight." Helgesen's brow twitched. "The irony of their situation is that once these 'Viking' soldiers are in France, they are forbidden from speaking Norwegian."

Wilhelm snorted his disbelief. "Why?"

Helgesen's gaze pinned Steen's. "Because, soldier, it sounds too much like German. We don't want any of our men shot by mistake."

"So they were recruited to liberate Norway because they're fluent in Norsk, and now they'll be fighting in France and forbidden to speak that language." Bjorn wagged his head. "That is the definition of irony."

"And disappointment." If Holt felt it here, then his former comrades must be feeling that same emotion even more strongly as they traveled south.

But he felt something else, too. "Permission to speak, Major?"

Helgesen nodded. "Go ahead."

Holt stood and stepped to the front of the assembled soldiers.

"Because we all volunteered to do strange things, like jumping from airplanes in the middle of the night and completely changing our identities under the threat of death…"

"We're crazy," one man muttered.

A couple more chuckled.

"Crazy? Probably." Holt smiled a little, then cleared his throat as his smile faded. "But the truth is that the eight dozen men in this room, men who signed up to save our parents' and grandparents' homeland—or even our own homeland like Roald Rygg here—are the only ones left to do so."

Holt paused a moment to let that reality sink in before he continued.

"We—the men sitting in this room—are now the defense and the salvation of Norway. And for the sake of our former comrades in arms, those brave men who survived Camp Hale with us, and are now denied the very thing they hoped for, every single one of us needs to understand that we are not playing a game."

No one spoke as Holt looked at a sea of somber faces.

"Is it a lot to take on? Sure it is." Holt was absolutely serious in his message, his tone, and his expression. "But remember that in February, just over three months ago, a team of four saboteurs sank a ferry near Telemark so that Hitler cannot make bigger bombs and attack more places. True?"

Several heads bobbed.

"Well, the truth is, there are twenty-four 'teams of four' sitting in this room right now."

Several men straightened and more glanced at their comrades beside them.

"If we apply ourselves to our training, and then take our training to Norway…" Holt's vision blurred a little but he didn't rub his eyes. "Then these twenty-four teams, working together with the men and women in their Resistance, can have a real impact. We can oust the Germans."

"*Hell*, yeah." The comment was quiet but definitive.

Jensen stood up in the back. "*Vikingregel*, men. Remember?"

A low rumble moved through the men.

Bjorn climbed to his feet. "Yes. *Vikingregel*."

"*Vikingregel*," Wilhelm Steen echoed as he stood.

Soon every soldier in the room was on his feet.

"*Vikingregel. Vikingregel. Vikingregel!*"

Major Helgesen waved his hands and the men quieted. "Your commitment today says everything about the sort of men you are. And you, Hansen—" He face Holt and grinned. "I'm going to have you make every one of my motivational speeches from now on!"

****

I've never felt prouder to be where I am, darling, I have to be honest about that. And I truly believe every single word that I said, too.

Heroes usually don't work alone, true. But at the same time, they seldom work with crowds. It only takes a handful of men to sink a ship. Or blow up a bridge. Or sail a fishing boat to Scotland.

We will all be heroes someday soon. Whether we remain grouped, or paired, or work alone with our national counterparts, every one of us will have an impact on our ultimate goal.

And I will be eternally grateful for this opportunity.

*****

Raleigh read Holt's letter and immediately noticed that it was different from all of his previous ones. For starters, it came to the beauty salon in her shop's name and not to her house.

Secondly, he didn't address her by name anywhere in the

document. Were these things for his protection, or hers?

Probably both.

When he wrote to her that he had an alternative identity, Raleigh completely understood that he couldn't say anything at all about what that identity entailed. But with this letter she realized that her existence—or at least her name—were not part of the identity which he chose.

That realization constricted her chest. She struggled to take a deep breath and forced her lungs to fill. Even though she knew Holt was still her future husband, to be wiped out of his false life was more unsettling than she would have expected.

It was as if she had ceased to exist.

Raleigh stuffed Holt's letter into her handbag and switched off the shop's lights. She stepped outside and locked the door while she decided what to do.

Walking straight home won the contest. That way, she could think about the letter and what it meant without interruption. She didn't want to run into anyone at the moment and have to act like everything was peachy when she felt so knocked sideways.

Raleigh let herself into her house, but didn't turn any lights on. She could see well enough in the late summer's dusk to walk into her kitchen, get a glass from the cabinet, and retrieve a bottle of Leinenkugel's from the fridge.

She poured the beer into the glass and then walked back to the living room. She kicked off her shoes and curled on the sofa to talk some sense into herself.

She told herself that secret or not, she still existed, whole and hearty, and that being left out of a false narrative was for her and Holt's own good. In fact, if she *was* a secret, that meant she was an important part of his life.

His real life.

And in his real life, she mattered. A lot, obviously.

All right, then. What should she do now?

Write back to him in the same way. Don't mention his name. Don't reveal details that might go up against that false

identity. Details like the name of the town, or its location—
she would stop using a return address. Don't use names for
people Holt knew, and instead use terms like the grocer or the
tavern keeper. Holt would know who she meant.

Raleigh finished her beer and switched the lights on. She
got her plain paper and blue-inked fountain pen and sat down
to write her first covert letter.

> *My dearest man, I see the changes in your*
> *correspondence and I understand the reasons ~ or*
> *believe that I do ~ so I will mimic them. Someday we'll*
> *see each other again and you can confirm your reasons.*
>
> *For now, know that I remain both unchanged, and*
> *that much prouder of you. God speed, my love.*

September 1944

After the devastation in Normandy, the soldiers' OSS
training stepped up in intensity.

During their first hour of radio training every day, the
soldiers memorized, and then practiced sending and receiving
messages in Morse code. The goal was to be able to send and
receive at least five words a minute.

That was the easy part.

The second hour dealt with cryptography—figuring out a
coded message and coding an appropriate response. Mastering
cryptography depended on having a set of keywords, which
could be changed as often as necessary to prevent the enemy
from intercepting, decoding, and utilizing the information.

"Properly used, these codes are as unbreakable codes as any
codes can be," their instructor informed them. "Try again."

Holt applied himself to the skill and learned the training
codes in three days, intrigued by the ability to concurrently hide
and reveal information. It was a cross between learning a new

language and putting together a jigsaw puzzle.

Knowing that the codes worked was the only thing that pushed him forward when he tried to figure out frustrating messages filled with intentional mistakes.

"I'd compare today to doing calculus, reading a blueprint for a train terminal, and picking the winning horse at the Derby—all at the same time," Holt grumbled after a particularly rough session.

"At least our instructor isn't a shouter," Roald countered. "He's surprisingly patient for a Brit."

Wilhelm and Bjorn caught up with the pair as they headed to the mess hall.

"I think my brain overheated today," Wilhelm whined. "Bjorn said there was actual steam coming out of my ears."

Bjorn dragged an earnest forefinger in an X over his chest. "God's honest truth."

"So in addition to sending these messages in Morse code, I would imagine they could be sent normally by radio, right?" Holt posited. "I mean, if we wanted to tell someone that there was an entrenched enemy unit half a mile ahead on the right, we could say 'the shepherds will be in the pasture until the sun sets' couldn't we?"

Wilhelm shrugged. "Don't see why not."

*****

The students' intensified classes included instruction on how to carry secret documents—and the best way to take them from someone else.

How to tap a phone, and how to know if a phone line was tapped. How to rig up a dictaphone from a regular telephone, and how to plant one that would not be discovered.

How to steal anything the soldier could lift. How to open letters and reseal them so the breach was not detectable.

How to tail someone through hell and high water, and how

to get rid of someone if they discovered they were being tailed

There was an extensive, and somewhat disturbing, course on body searches, followed by an even longer one about how to hide something on—or *in*—the soldier's own body.

The men learned how to interrogate a person, and how to trick that person into unwittingly revealing things. At the same time, they practiced maintaining their covers while learning hundreds of ways their cover could be broken,

Of course, the basics also included how to break into practically anything, anywhere, and how to get out again, leaving the place looking untouched.

Of course I can't give you any specifics, darling, but today we had to search a room to find an object, and then conceal another object in the same room for the next man. It was actually fun trying to be as sly as possible and trip up our comrades.

So many of our new skills are surprisingly simple, they are just things the ordinary person doesn't think about when they aren't in the situation in which we might find ourselves one day.

We just have to keep practicing so we have them so deeply ingrained that we will remember what to do without having to think about it.

December 1944

After celebrating an American Thanksgiving at the training center near Manchester, the NORSO guys in OSS training were given their graduation assignment.

The men were being sent into Manchester in pairs with instructions to bring back, by whatever means necessary, the proof that they had entered a government building, military warehouse, or wartime manufacturer.

They were then expected to select and return with an item which proved the depth of their penetration into the building. If they were caught, they were to talk their way out of the situation.

If they weren't back to the training center in twenty-four hours, their British instructors would check with the local police.

"Please understand that being arrested and detained is the worst possible outcome," Major Helgesen warned the men. "We would rather you came back empty-handed first. At least that way you would be alive and available for another mission."

That made sense.

"You'll be dressed in civilian clothes for this maneuver, of course. Go to the uniform dispensary and get outfitted. You'll be randomly paired and dropped off tomorrow after breakfast. Dismissed."

Holt and Roald trudged toward the dispensary with Wilhelm and Bjorn not far behind them as usual.

"Random pairings, my ass," Holt scoffed. "I know exactly what they'll do."

"Pair us with guys we don't know well," Roald responded. "That makes the most sense, because once we're dropped into Norway, everyone we work with will be a complete stranger."

"Sending us in pairs on our first real test will help some of the guys with nerves, I suppose."

"Good point, but…" Roald glanced Holt's way. "Would you rather be alone?"

He shrugged. "To be honest, I don't know. I guess we'll see how it turns out."

*****

"Ellefsen! Jarland!"

Holt stood and walked to the front of the city bus, which was used to disguise the drops, followed by a strapping guy who barely looked twenty-one.

Captain Winters handed Holt a map of Manchester with various targets circled. "Pick your target and completely destroy this map."

"Yes, sir."

The bus slowed to a stop near the Irwell River and the driver opened the door.

"Go."

Holt hurried out, followed by the younger soldier. The bus's door clunked closed. With a puff of diesel smoke and a rumble of the engine, the big vehicle eased away from the curb and continued down the road.

Holt faced his partner in spying and stuck out his hand. "Hans Ellefsen."

The young man grinned and shook Holt's hand. "Hans Jarland."

Holt chuckled. "That'll be easy to remember."

He unfolded the map. "Any preference for a target?"

Hans looked at the street sign. "First we have to figure out where we are."

Holt squinted at the map.

I'm going to have to get glasses.

"Here." Holt pointed to the spot. "Looks like we're close to the place where they make the English rations."

"You mean the starvation rations?" Hans leaned over and looked at the map. "Maybe we could go in as inspectors."

"We could say we're civilian contractors looking for an English source for NORSO supplies," Holt suggested. "For when those guys invade Norway."

"Right. Because the idea of liberating Norway isn't a secret in England." Hans traced their route to the cannery with his finger. "What do we do once we're in there?"

Holt thought a moment. "I say we fake some sort of sabotage so the cannery knows they were vulnerable."

Hans nodded. "Good idea. Let's go."

Holt took a last look at the map and used the compass in his pocket watch to orient himself. Then he ripped the map into several pieces. "I'd set this on fire if I could."

Hans took one of the pieces, crumbled it, and threw it in the river. Holt mimicked his actions but tucked a rock inside some of the pieces. After they watch the last bit of the map sink or float away on the current, the two men sauntered off in the direction of the cannery.

*****

Holt strode up to the reception desk in the cannery's business office after examining the board listing the officers inside. "Hans Ellefsen to see Mister Carnes-Wight.

The pretty young secretary looked up at him. "Is he expecting you?"

Hans stepped forward and flashed a very charming smile.

He has dimples.

Holt resisted rolling his eyes.

"No, I'm afraid he isn't." Hans' expression turned impishly apologetic. "I hope that won't be a problem."

Her lashes fluttered. "You're Americans."

"Yes. Hans Jarland." Hans held out his hand. "And you are?"

"Suzanne. Um, Browne." She accepted Hans' proffered hand and stared up into his eyes.

"We're looking for a supplier for rations," Holt interjected, sounding optimistic. "We were hoping to speak with Mister Carnes-Wight and perhaps get a tour of the plant."

Suzanne dragged her gaze away from Hans. "Let me see if he's available."

Hans let go of her hand and she lifted the heavy black telephone receiver from its cradle.

"Hello sir," she said a moment after dialing. "There are two American gentlemen here wondering if you were available to discuss possible orders for rations."

She paused. "Yes, I'll tell them." Then she laid the receiver back in its spot.

She smiled at Hans. "He'll be down in a few minutes."

Hans laid his hand over his heart and bowed a little. "Thank you *so* much Suzanne. You're an absolute gem."

As her cheeks pinkened adorably, Holt realized that having a young and charming partner wasn't such a bad thing after all.

*****

Mister Carnes-Wight never asked the men for identification, he simply took the pair of Hanses at their word. As he walked them through the plant, Holt decided to push the point about the so-called starvation rations.

"Lost weight, you say?" Carnes-Wight looked like he was trying to act surprised. "Well, we are a country in their fifth year at war..."

"I understand, sir. But when our boys invade Norway, they'll need more calories to keep warm in that frozen environment." Holt stroked his chin. "Could we possibly taste some of what you have to offer?"

"Yes, certainly!" The man looked pleased that he wasn't being shut down—yet. "Let's go to the kitchens."

Holt and Hans exchanged a satisfied glance. The kitchen was exactly as deep as any saboteur would need to go.

The men had decided on their walk to the plant that Hans would drop the evidence of their visit—the tiny Nazi lapel pin which had been part of one of their earlier tests. It was Holt's job to select and steal a piece of evidence.

Once inside the kitchen, Holt's gaze moved over every piece of equipment and supplies as Carnes-Wight explained how the rations were made, and offered suggestions for how calories might cheaply be added. He and Hans sampled some of the less-than-tasty options, and Holt silently thanked God he would be dropped into Norway with American food.

"And here is how the food is canned," their host said. "The lids are marked in code so we know what is inside each tin, you see."

Holt picked up one of the pre-printed lids. "What will be in this tin?"

"That one will be beef jelly and carrots."

Holt pointed at another lid. "And that one?"

When Carnes-Wight turned to look, Holt dropped the lid into his pocket.

Then he winked at Hans, who winked back.

Chapter Seventeen

January 1945

After passing their final test, the NORSO troops were sent back to parachute school for a refresher course. This particular training school was situated on the outskirts of Altringham, a small town about eighty miles northwest of London, near the regular British airborne school.

Their bus from Manchester carried the American soldiers through the village and out to the school, a lovely old estate complete with lawns, gardens, and a small lake. Captain Peter Leghorn was the chief instructor there, and it was soon evident that his attitude toward American military personnel in general, and OSS personnel in particular, was less than positive.

Unlike the American training, the British students who came here were only taught the absolute basics—enough to make one operational jump, and land behind the enemy lines alive. So after one day of somewhat casual instruction, the NORSO guys were back to jumping from a plane.

Holt was horrified. "Thank God we all had more extensive training last year."

Wilhelm looked understandably nervous. "I hope I remember everything."

"You will," Holt assured the younger man, sounding like he had more confidence than he did.

Right after they arrived at Tatton Park the first plane passed overhead. It was an ancient Whittley bomber, ideal for training purposes because of its low speed. When the first man dropped out of the bottom of the plane, not out the side like American drops, his chute opened gracefully while he swung peacefully back-and-forth underneath it.

Holt looked at his cohorts, surprised. Where was the vicious jerk that defined all of their previous training jumps?

"In Britain we pack our chutes so that there is no shock to the jumper," Captain Leghorn explained, his disdain for the American practices clear. "We want *our* men to feel comfortable in their trip back to earth, ensuring that they land with a clear head and a strong body."

Holt couldn't argue with that, especially after jumping with the British-packed chute.

I wonder if there's a way to pack my American chute like that.

February 1945

"I feel like a ping-pong ball," Holt teased as the NORSO guys boarded a train out of London headed for the Scottish highlands. "I think I've seen more of England and Scotland than most of the residents on this island!"

There was a strong opinion held by those in charge of the British military that the Nazi high command might hole up in the Norwegian mountains and make a last stand. So the soldiers preparing to be dropped into Norway were now resuming their long-neglected ski and mountain training.

Directing and supplying the Norwegian resistance was supposed to be a joint affair, but the British were clearly determined to keep control. And so back in Scotland the Intelligence officers assigned to the Norway unit were a pair of likable Scots in suitable regalia.

"I am Major Peter Douglas of the Seaforth Highlanders," the

first officer stated in a thick brogue. "And this is Captain Hamish Frazier-Campbell of the Argyll and Sutherland Highlanders. We will be running your show from here on out."

Running was definitely the word for it.

Holt was exhausted by the long, cold ski-marches through the snowy Scottish mountains—not nearly as tall as the Rockies around Camp Hale, but every bit as challenging. The worst part was that his hip was aching again with the return to the damp cold and the physical strain.

Even though the Scottish officers in charge of them were part of the British Office, the men's heritage and their roots fomented a bit of anti-English sentiment now and again.

"The Brits dinna like the idea of American troops going in t' Norway," Major Douglas admitted one night over beers. "And they are pretty vocal aboot it when ye're no' around."

Holt scowled. "Do they want to do it themselves?"

"Nah. They're just arguing with the Norwegian Army command." Douglas took a long pull on his beer before he continued. "Seems those guys are afeared the appearance of Allied soldiers will touch off a Resistance uprising, aye? And they dinna think they can support it."

Holt was confused. "Aren't *we* the ones who are supporting it? The Resistance, I mean."

"Aye." Douglas wagged his head. "I don't say they're bein' sensible. The Norwegians are afraid of it, the English want to be the ones to do it, since King Haakon is living there, and all. But the Americans raised up a battalion of Norwegian guys to get it done."

"That's a lot of elbowing for top dog." Holt chuckled and held up his beer glass. "To the soldiers of NORSO, whoever the hell is in charge!"

"Hear, hear!" Douglas tapped his beer against Holt's and both men drained their glasses.

*****

In between ski-marches and practice with ropes, the NORSO guys spent hours pouring over maps of Norway's train tracks, bridges, tunnels, and towns.

They were tested by drawing their own maps and accurately marking the location of any town or tunnel that was named, along with mileage estimates from place to place and the best means of transportation to get there. And because ninety percent of Norway's population resided on the country's extensive coastline, the best transportation was often boat.

"The Shetland Bus, a system of volunteer fishermen and their non-descript boats, will be available to you, but you can't count on them all the time," the instructor warned. "Rely on your Resistance partners and trust their judgment. They've been doing this for almost five years now. They have a lot of the problems worked out."

All of the photos and maps which the Army had called for when the Ninety-Ninth Battalion was formed had found their way here to the NORSO training center in Scotland, and were added to reconnaissance aerial photos and other Army intelligence.

Holt paid particular attention to Bergen, the city his mother would be most familiar with, and the shocking photos of the aftermath of a German munitions ship exploding in the harbor. The medieval fortress was badly damaged, and the devastation to the civilians' homes was unimaginable. Not to mention the loss of fifteen hundred lives.

Holt had to wonder if any of his Ellefsen relatives had been in Bergen that day and might have died there.

I hope I can be of use there.

March 1945

The NORSO soldiers were assigned to be dropped into Norway in two groups. Holt was assigned to the first group, as were Roald, Wilhelm, and Bjorn. The second group would follow six days later and provide reinforcements, which may well be needed depending on how the first drop went.

"You will all parachute into the mountains northeast of Trondheim, and land on a frozen lake," Major Douglas informed them. "Once there, ye'll be met by Norwegian Resistance, and take yer orders from them. Questions?"

No one raised a hand.

"Good. There'll be eight plane loads of men and supplies. Each unit will be self-sufficient, capable of independent operation in the field, on skis, for forty days without help."

He smiled a little. "Yer initial job will be to break up the Nordland Railway system wherever possible. Ye'll blow up bridges, tunnels, and tracks. Besides messing up the Germans' transportation abilities, ye're to do whatever damage ye can to the Germans' lines of communication."

Several of the men punched each other's arms, grinning. Holt chuckled.

Tell a man to blow things up, and he's immediately on board.

"Now do ye have any questions?"

"I do." Wilhelm Steen stood up. "When do we leave?"

*****

Once again, the soldiers were called into an officer's presence, one at a time. When they cam out, every single one of them was ashen and somber.

"What do you suppose is happening?" Roald whispered.

"Hansen?"

Holt shrugged. "I guess I'll find out."

Holt went into the office and sat facing a British colonel whom he'd never met before.

"Good afternoon, Corporal. I'm here to give you one last—and critically important—detail before we drop you into German-occupied Norway." He reached into an open drawer and took out a small white box, which he placed in front of Holt. "Open it very carefully."

Holt did. There were two tablets inside, each slightly smaller in diameter than a dime. One was white, the other brown. Holt looked up at the colonel, curious as to what these were.

"The white tablet is a powerful sedative," he began. "It can be swallowed as is, or dissolved in water. Half of it will put you to sleep, all of it will knock you—or someone else—out cold."

That could be useful.

"And the brown one?" Holt asked.

"Do you see that's it's marked with an L?"

"Yes, sir."

"That is a lethal tablet." The colonel folded his hands and stared hard at Holt. "That tablet is rubber coated. If you need to dispose of it, you can swallow it and nothing will happen to you."

Holt nodded and hoped he'd never need to test the integrity of that rubber coating.

"However, if you bite that tablet, you will be unconscious in seconds." The colonel looked grim. "And you'll never wake up on this planet again."

Now Holt knew why every man leaving this interview looked shaken. "Why would I bite it? Sir."

"Remember when, earlier in your training, you were asked about sacrificing a man to save a unit?"

Including myself.

"Yes, sir." Holt drew a shaky breath. "I understand."

"You are a spy, dropping into enemy territory. Lord willing, you won't be discovered. But if you are, and you can't talk your way out of the situation, then you must do whatever is required to protect your unit and your mission."

Protect my unit and my mission.

Holt nodded and put the lid back on the little box. "Yes, sir."

"Keep them handy, Corporal. Tape them somewhere on your person, and keep track of them. You'll be held strictly accountable for them."

The colonel slid a clipboard across the desk. "Please sign

this affidavit that you received both of these tablets today."

As Holt signed and dated the form he asked, "Do we know when we will be leaving?"

"Best guess is towards the end of March. But I wanted to give every man time to consider the severity of the situation before sending you off."

The colonel retrieved the clipboard and his eyes met Holt's again. "It's easy to say you're willing to die in the excitement of an imminent mission. But after you walk around with that lethal pill taped to your side for two or three weeks, the reality sinks in."

So men could change their minds about going? Wash out of the program at this late date? Would anyone do that?

"Dismissed."

Startled out of his musings, Holt rose, saluted, and left the office.

This interview changed everything.

He knew he ran the risk of injury or death once he enlisted. That was part of the deal. And with all his OSS training, he knew the stakes were high.

But like the other guys training with him, he felt like he would be in less danger, because there was no actual fighting in Norway.

No one was likely to shoot a cannon at him. Drop a bomb on him. Even lob a grenade at him. So the idea that he might die by necessity and at his own hand was core-shattering to put it mildly.

Could he do it?

Only under one condition. In light of the risk he had just accepted, he had to write to Raleigh—tonight—and break off their relationship. That way, his concern for her would not cloud his decision-making process in the critical moment.

That was the right thing to do.

*****

Dearest Soldier,

I received your letter. You have an interesting perspective on what you think that I need, but unfortunately it is not a correct one. Let me explain:

I know you are compelled to protect whatever or whomever you love—that compulsion defines the man that you are. Though I've only know you for six years, I suspect you were always like that.

But you could not protect your wife from the man who drove his car into yours, and that still eats at you.

Now you are protecting our country and ~ according to your letters ~ the soldiers who are training beside you. So when your training turned down a more dangerous path, you decided that you should protect me. You want to save me from experiencing the loss of you.

The problem with that is that I am willing to take that risk. I am willing to risk that loss.

And I will not allow you to deny me anything because you are scared on my behalf. I am a strong woman, you know what I have been through, and at thirty-four years of age I know what I want.

So here I stand. I am still yours. You can <u>not</u> shoo me away, no matter what you say or how hard you try. You can <u>not</u> stop me from loving you. Nothing can.

So please, stop trying.

*****

Dearest heart,

I am defeated in my endeavor to keep you safe. It's clear that you are a strong-willed woman, and nothing I can say will sway your determination. Therefore, I must surrender to your conditions.

Wait for me, my love. I will not be able to write to you once we leave here, and we are expecting to be sent to our destination any day now. We are all packed up and ready, and are practicing codes to pass the time.

Please wait for me. It can't be much longer now until this thing is finished. Soon I'll be coming home. And I do need your love. God speed your love to me.

March 24, 1945

Holt looked at his watch for the hundredth time. It was just past midnight. Further up his wrist, where he could feel it but not see it, was the strip of adhesive tape holding the dreaded *L* tablet.

A sergeant bundled against the blustery Scottish weather stuck his head in the waiting room and shouted, "Fifteen minutes, men!"

Holt pulled a dark patterned camouflaged British parachute smock over his white snow-camouflage army uniform. The parachutes for the night drop were dark in color, to avoid being seen by German lookouts.

They were dropping into a remote area, so hopefully their arrival in Norway would go unnoticed.

He was as ready for this as he could be.

The sergeant appeared again. "All set?"

The eighteen American soldiers scheduled for this drop under the command of Major William Colby all nodded.

"Let's go!"

The men followed the sergeant toward the sound of the British plane, warming up on the runway. Its roaring motors made conversation impossible. Even so, the sergeant tried.

All Holt heard was, "—ood weather!"

About fifty yards from the shed they had been waiting in, Holt could see the outline of the huge bomber.

God be with me, and with my men.

The men climbed into the belly of the aircraft, filed down the benches to their spots, and hooked up their static lines. They had all been through this routine dozens of times, so when the time came, they wouldn't have to think about it.

Holt certainly wasn't.

He was looking at the men in his group, grateful that Roald was with him. Wilhelm and Bjorn were in this group, too.

Through their time training in England and Scotland, Wilhelm had dropped his open hostility toward Holt and the two men had reached a truce based on necessity. They needed to have each other's backs now as comrades in arms.

The realization that he'd bite his L tablet to save Wilhelm and Bjorn rattled Holt for a moment.

Who would have guessed?

The door slammed shut and the plane rolled forward. The bomber rumbled down what felt like an endless runway before lifting into the air, thankfully cutting the noise in half.

It seemed like every man inside heaved a sigh of relief.

"Here we go," Wilhelm offered. "*Vikingregel!*"

The response was half-hearted.

There was no heat inside the bomber, so the men were in freezing conditions for the flight which was just over two hours long. All of it, until they made a sudden turn east and headed inland, was over the icy North Sea.

An hour in to the transport, the jump master opened the first of four thermoses and poured hot chocolate for the guys. That warmth helped sooth Holt's nerves a little.

Before he was ready for it, and long after he wished it would happen, the little red light went on.

This is it.

Holt stood along with everyone else.

The men went through the parachute check automatically.

When it was complete, they tightened the line next to the bomber's bottom bay door which the jump master opened.

Freezing air blew upward as the plane's motors cut out and the plane went into a silent downward line glide.

A tiny light shone upward, marking the location of their landing party.

The first jumper, Major Colby, grabbed the edges of the hole and sat on the edge with his legs dangling into nothing.

The green light went on.

The major unhooked his static line and dropped through the opening.

Holt was next. He sat, unhooked his line, and waited for the signal.

The jump master shouted in Holt's ear, "Go! Give them hell."

And then Holt dropped through the hole in the plane's floor into a freezing black void.

Chapter Eighteen

Holt counted to five before pulling the cord on his parachute and looking up frantically to see if it opened—or if he was about to go splat on a frozen lake. He could barely see it in the dark, but did feel the slight tug and lessening of wind as the silk canopy of his British-packed chute caught the air.

No jerk, no loud crack of fabric.

Definitely better than the American method.

In the drifting silence, Holt looked around and tried to make out the lay of the mountainous landscape. A sliver of a moon and the stars helped as his eyes adjusted to the frigid darkness. Their dim light reflected off the snow-covered slopes and Holt could make out the flat frozen surface of Lake Jaevsjo below.

Above him, Holt heard the return of the bomber's engines as their transport began its return to Scotland.

At about five hundred feet above the lake, Holt finally saw the little landing fires of their welcoming committee. He tugged on his straps to aim his chute that way, thankful that there was no wind pushing him off course tonight.

He bent his knees, pressed his feet together, and concentrated on the frozen lake that was rapidly coming up to meet him.

The jolt of the unforgiving surface jarred his frame—and especially his left hip.

Holt allowed his knees to give way and he rolled onto the

ice. Stinging snow crystals flew into his eyes and mouth.

When he came to a stop, he flopped on his back for a moment to get his bearings. His hip throbbed but he knew it couldn't break again.

He repeated his litany in his head.

Aspirin and sleep and I'll be fine.

All around him other soldiers were hitting the ice, many muttering choice swear words. Holt climbed to his feet and rolled up his parachute.

"Welcome friends!" A bundled-up Norseman skied towards the slightly scattered group. "You are the third group to land."

"Only the third?" Major Colby sounded concerned. "There were supposed to be eight drops tonight. We were the sixth plane to take off."

That was not good news.

"Do you have a radio signal?" Holt asked, kicking into search and rescue mode.

"Yes, but it's weak."

"Go ask if any other soldiers have been seen anywhere else." Holt looked at Colby. "Maybe they were dropped nearby."

Another pair of Norwegians skied up to them.

"Did you hear any other planes besides the three?" the first man asked them.

"No." One of the men looked at Colby. "Which is strange because we expected more of you."

Their apparent leader nodded. "Go and see if you can make a radio connection. Ask if the men have landed anywhere around us."

"Yes, sir."

As the men skied back to the edge of the lake, their leader introduced himself. "I am Arvid. We have set up camp in the woods. We must get you and your supplies tucked away there now."

*****

The equipment drops were scattered all over the lake. Several of the containers hit the ice and broke open because their chutes hadn't been hooked up by the air crews loading the planes. Other containers hit the hillside and were buried in the snow.

There was nothing else to do, but to gather the packages and their dark colored parachutes—at least from the ones that *had* a parachute—and pull them into the forest and out of sight.

"Even in an inactive sector like this," Arvid explained, "the Germans are certain to know that the planes flew overhead. There is a very good chance they will make observational flights tomorrow to see what they can find."

"What about our tracks on the lake?" Holt asked.

"We will put a tent out tomorrow and will have several volunteers do some ice fishing."

Good enough.

"Let's get to it, men!" Colby barked. The sooner this is all cleared, the sooner we can get some sleep!"

Holt pulled his scarf up over his face and stuffed his parachute back into its pack. Silk was warm and he'd wrap himself in it when he finally laid down to rest.

As trained, the men worked silently and efficiently. The temperature on this slab of ice was easily fifteen or twenty degrees below zero. Thankfully the equipment dropped with the soldiers was thoroughly tested at Camp Hale in similar conditions.

Now all we have to do is find it.

*****

A fourth plane successfully dropped the soldiers on the lake about two hours later, just past four o'clock in the morning, while Colby's men were setting up the tents they managed to find.

"When we were about to take off, we heard that three of the

planes were heading back without dropping anyone," Colonel Boland, the group's commanding officer, told Major Colby. "And one plane completely missed the coordinates and dropped the men east of the lake—in Sweden."

"We'll sort it out in the morning," Colby replied doggedly. "For now we have to get everything off the ice and hidden in the woods."

Holt and Roald pitched a two-man tent and crawled inside, with both men using their parachutes for extra protection against the frozen ground and seeping cold.

"Well, we are in Norway," Roald said softly.

"Yes we are. Are you glad to be home?" Holt realized he didn't know where Roald's home actually was. "Where is that, exactly."

"Stavanger. Pretty far south from here." Roald shifted a little. "And not quite so cold as here."

Holt had managed to dig out a few aspirin tablets before they pitched the tent, and swallowed them with a cup of the melted snow from the bucket which the resistance troops had sitting by the fire. Now he laid on his right side and tried to get a couple hours of sleep before their first day of spy soldiering began.

He wished he could write to Raleigh, but that was impossible now. He thought about writing letters and saving them, sort of like a journal. But he knew that if he was caught by the Germans that such documentation would be his death sentence.

He felt for the *L* tablet, still taped securely to his forearm.

Please protect me, Lord. And those I am with.

*****

The next morning it was decided that Colonel Boland would take his men across the lake to Sweden to retrieve the lost group. Once found and joined together, they would move on to the operational area and accomplish what they were assigned to do.

"Our orders are to wait here for the next drop of personnel,"

Colby stated. "That is scheduled for six days from now, but at least we are well-supplied at the moment."

So for the next six days, the frustrated NORSO soldiers hunkered down in the woods, waiting to hear that the others were on their way. They gathered firewood during the day, and sat in a bored circle around the fires at night when the smoke was invisible.

When the expected drop was announced over the resistance radio, the men cheered and looked to the night sky in relieved anticipation. But the weather this far north was skittish, and though the day was perfect earlier, with nightfall the lake became shrouded in fog.

Holt heard the planes' engines, and his mood lifted immediately. "Here they come!"

There were two planes that night that dropped nothing but cargo. A third plane turned around without doing anything.

The next day the NORSO guys waiting so impatiently were told that the third plane crashed on Orkney Island, killing everyone on board except the co-pilot.

"He reported that two of the bomber's four motors failed," Major Colby told his somber soldiers. "So our orders are to wait here for another drop."

Damn.

The men had no choice but to remain in place, dug in with their supplies, and pass the time impotently.

Meanwhile, only Arvid stayed with the Americans for the duration. The other three men were replaced one by one, assuring that there were always four Norwegians present to assist the NORSO soldiers.

"They have families and business to see to," the Resistance leader explained. "If they are gone for too long, it is harder for them to make legitimate excuses."

"What about you?" Roald asked. "How do you live?"

"The Resistance pays me." Arvid smiled a little. "You are aware that King Haakon escaped with the treasury, so there is not a shortage of money."

The currently departing volunteer—Holt forgot this one's

name—waved a cheerful goodbye and gave the Americans a thumbs up before skiing off.

"This waiting and doing nothing is not helping them men's moods," Holt grumbled. "I feel like every day that goes by here is one day that the war will last longer."

"You're not that big of a threat, Gramps." Wilhelm chuckled. "I doubt the Nazis are quaking in their spit-shined boots right now."

Holt knew Steen was teasing him out of respect more than disdain, so he gave it right back. "No, they're planning your welcome party, son. How's your German?"

April 7, 1945

Another six days and the end of March passed before the army tried again. This time they sent four planes, but the unforgiving sub-Arctic weather fought back with everything it had, throwing wind, sleet, and hail at the aircraft.

Tragically, one bomber came in too low, hit a cliff within earshot, and exploded. The light from the flames lit the misty midnight sky in a terrible tribute to the men who died aboard.

Holt stood in shock, staring at the orange glow before it slowly faded.

What about the other three planes?

They simply never came. That left Major Colby in the field with two officers and eighteen men, and less than half of his supplies.

Meanwhile, twelve days had been completely wasted.

"Twelve days with the Germans sneaking out of the trap we were to set," Colby growled. "Well I, for one, am tired of waiting for the army to get its collective shit together."

Holt shouted, "Yes, SIR!"

Colby smiled. "I don't know about you men, but I feel like the reputation of America depends on us pulling this thing out of the ice, and pulling it out now."

Several other soldiers shouted their agreement.

"So…" Colby continued. "We are going to scrap our original plans and fight our own war. We'll attack the Nordland Railroad without waiting for help. We'll head west to Jørstad and south to Steinkjer, on our way to Trondheim, and blast as we go!"

"YES!" the men shouted. "*Vikingregel!*"

*****

The men loaded up their rucksacks with food rations and ammunition in addition to their sleeping bags and personal items—and their rubberized wallets with their official cover story credentials, of course.

Then they retrieved skis from one of the dropped containers, making certain the pair they picked out was not damaged in the fiasco.

"Anything else?" Holt asked Major Colby.

Colby shook his head. "I doubt we'll need snowshoes at this point. But make sure every man has climbing equipment."

"Yes, sir!"

The repacked rucksacks rivaled the ninety-pound versions the men trained with at Camp Hale, but almost two years had passed since then. As a result their progress was slow the first day, as the men remembered how to ski under such heavy and awkward loads.

The distance from Lake Jaevsjo to Jørstad was twenty miles as the crow flew. But, with Arvid as their guide, these heavily-laden 'crows' ski-hiked up and down the uneven terrain, traversed frozen lakes, and stumbled with their skis resting on their shoulders through thick forests—and only covered half that distance by nightfall.

"Dig in men," Colby ordered. "We leave again at dawn."

Holt searched for a protected cranny and tucked in out of the wind. The soldiers left their tents behind at the drop site now that their plan was to stay on the move.

Roald tucked in next to him. "We'll have all day tomorrow, so we should reach Jørstad when it's still light. I wonder what we'll do then?"

Holt pulled out a tin of cold rations and opened it. "I don't know, but it's going to be an interesting ride from here on out."

April 8, 1945

There wasn't anything for the soldiers to do in tiny Jørstad that would significantly impact the Germans, so they left the villagers in peace. After sleeping in the woods outside of the village, and studying the maps with Arvid, the Americans headed south along the edge of Lake Snasa on their own.

Their objective, Steinkjer and the Nordland Railway, was twenty-five miles south and had no discernable civilization along the way.

Three hours after setting off, Norway's capricious weather mood turned nasty, and her ever-present western wind hit the men with a vicious sleet storm. The spitting spray of frozen water covered their clothing, their equipment, and the snow with sheets of ice.

Such harsh conditions made it nearly impossible for their skis to take hold, so the effort required to simply move forward was exhausting.

"At least we won't have to worry about being discovered," Holt muttered to the wind. "No one in their right mind would be out in this damned weather."

After scraping along for another miserable hour, Roald stopped and shouted, "SUMMER HUT!"

The line of twenty-one men halted. Roald scrambled his way up to Major Colby at the front of the line. Holt followed.

"That house up there. It's a summer hut. No one will be there at this time of year," Roald explained to the major. He pointed at the modest cabin with a traditional sod roof poking out of the layer of sleet and snow. "We can shelter there for the rest of the day and ski out again tomorrow."

"We could make a fire and dry our clothes," Holt added the self-serving incentive to the suggestion. His hip throbbed so badly in the freezing and damp chill that he knew he was limping in his skis. He desperately needed to get warm.

Colby nodded, clearly relieved at the prospect of getting his men out of the storm. "Let's do it."

An hour later a roaring fire burned in the cabin's stone fireplace. Soldiers, stripped to their skivvies, hung their wet uniforms over a myriad of ropes strung throughout the two-roomed hut like a web made by a drunken spider.

Holt snagged a spot near the fire and let its heat seep into his aching hip.

Roald sat on his other side and offered him a cup of icy water. "For your aspirin."

That simple act of kindness prompted such emotion that it threatened to be too much for Holt to hide. He nodded his thanks and pulled the little aspirin tin from his rucksack.

"What's the plan for Steinkjer?" he asked Colby after surreptitiously swallowing a few aspirin tablets.

"Disrupt the railroad." Colby grinned. "But we have a highway bridge to blow up on our way there."

April 10, 1945

"Hand me the clay." Roald held out his hand and Holt laid the lump of plastic explosive in his palm.

Roald pressed and tied the clay to the joint in the bridge, and then climbed to the next bolted joint. Holt followed and stuck the detonator into the clay before he attached the wired fuse.

Dressed in their mostly-dry white uniforms, the men used their ropes to swing under the bridge and into its center, out of sight from most angles. Four teams of two were climbing through the wooden struts and placing the explosives.

The rest of the men were on lookout on both sides of the

bridge over the narrow waterway connecting Lake Fossem to the north and Lake Reins to the south—both currently frozen over.

When they finished, the NORSO team gathered on the western bank of Lake Reins and took cover.

"Ready men?" Colby asked. "Our first official act of sabotage in Norway!"

The major pressed the detonator, sending an electrical charge through the fuse to the detonators.

The explosion was deafening.

The men were pelted with debris falling from the air. Chunks of concrete and wood clanked against helmets and rocks, and the acrid smell of the explosive filled the air.

Holt held his hands over his ears until the rainfall of detritus ended, then he lowered his arms and looked over the boulder he was using for cover.

The center of the bridge was now a gaping, jagged, and impassable mess.

"Let's move men!" Colby ordered. "The Germans in Steinkjer will have heard that and will certainly come looking for whoever blew the bridge."

The soldiers hurried west and up into the rocky, wooded mountains bordering Lake Reins. From their sheltered vantage point near the top they used binoculars to watch the Germans below.

Though they couldn't hear anything from that high up, Holt recognized the flapping arms and stomping strides of angry and frustrated men.

He smiled.

Take that, you Nazi bastards.

April 11, 1945

After another cold night in the mountains, Major Colby went alone into Steinkjer to find the Resistance contact whose name Arvid had given him. He returned to the team, now hidden in the woods on the edge of the town.

"Our man in the underground has railroad contacts. He says there is a freight train coming from Grong that's scheduled to enter Steinkjer at two-fifty-five this afternoon." Colby smiled a little at the assembled soldiers. "They want us to blow up the track so they can seize the contents of the freight cars."

"So that's the plan?" Holt asked.

Colby nodded. "We are going to blow up the track and the engines, if we can. And take out any Germans who disembark."

Holt blinked. This was the first time that any of the men would actually be shooting at another human with the intent and the power to kill.

He hoped that they were all ready to do so.

And that he was.

"Then the locals are going to ransack the freight cars and take whatever they can use?" Roald clarified.

"Exactly." The major pulled out a map and the NORSO guys gathered around.

"We are here." He pointed to a spot on the north side of town. "They want us to stop the train here. At the south end of Lake Rungstad."

That location was across the river and three miles north of where the soldiers were at that moment.

"Our man said they have locations in the mountains where they can stash the goods." Colby looked up from the map and addressed the gathered group. "Let's move. We can plan along the way."

*****

Holt and Roald were assigned to be guards. If any Germans in uniform exited the train, they were to be shot on sight.

"We are Americans, we at war with Germany, and we have invaded German-occupied territory," Colby reminded the dozen men assigned guard duty. "Shoot to kill, gentlemen."

This is it. This is real.

The day could not make up its mind whether to give the sun full reign, or to let scattered heavy-bottomed clouds dominate. As long as the clouds didn't dump on them, Holt was fine either way.

Holt stood fifty yards to the east of the track with his rifle loaded and ready. Six members of their group, including Wilhelm and Bjorn, were placing plastic explosives and detonators along the track. The locals were waiting in the woods with wheelbarrows, small carts, and horses hitched to wagons of all sizes, ready to pilfer whatever they could use from the cargo cars.

The train blew its whistle when it passed through Asp, two miles to the north.

The Americans who were still near the track bolted to safety. Bjorn unrolled the fuse far enough for the Americans to be out of the blast. Holt and the other guards dropped on their bellies in the snow, camouflaged by their white winter wear.

The next four minutes were interminable. Holt checked the second hand on his watch several times to make sure time was actually passing.

And then the engine of the train chugged into view.

The explosives covered twenty-five yards of the track, and the moment the engine reached the marker which the soldiers had placed, Wilhelm depressed the fuse box.

Multiple explosives went off like deafening machine gun fire, if machine guns fired grenades instead of bullets. The first cars in the train popped upward, then tumbled into each other before falling to both sides of the track with screams of sliding and twisting metal. The cars behind them crashed and bent and scrambled to get out of the way.

Several minutes passed before the smoke cleared and the jumble of train cars shuddered to a quiet halt.

Two guys got up and sprinted for the train's two engines, lobbing grenades to assure that neither would be salvageable.

The locals cautiously came out of the woods.

Holt's gaze swept the area, searching for movement of any

sort. At first, there was none.

Then a uniformed German soldier staggered out of the debris and shot his Luger at the slowly approaching crowd. Holt took aim and fired. The man hit the snow face first.

Another man in German attire was climbing out of the roof of a box car. Holt took him out with one shot as well.

My first kill.

And my second.

Major Colby dropped to the snow next to Holt. "You're a damn fine shot, Ellefsen."

Holt smiled a little at the pseudonym.

"When I'm not plowing the fields of Iowa, I hunt bear in northern Wisconsin." He glanced sideways at the major. "If your aim isn't true there, you're facing a much bigger, angrier, and meaner enemy than any puny German, sir."

Colby chuckled. "Understood."

Chapter Nineteen

The soldiers spent that night outside Steinkjer, where they were housed in the relative luxury of a barn on a farm owned by a Resistance member. In addition to their cold rations, they were served a thin fish soup by their grateful host.

"At least it's hot," Holt observed.

"Agreed," Wilhelm admitted. "It doesn't look like the Germans have left them much in the way of food."

"Obviously." Roald waved his spoon at their surroundings. "You will notice that there are no dairy cows in this dairy barn."

"And the hay is old." Holt sniffed and spat the dust from his nose and throat. "But it will be warmer and softer than the ground, so I'm not complaining about any of that."

When their meal was concluded, Major Colby gathered the men in the unlit space.

"The Nordland Railway has a series of train bridges along its route from Steinkjer to Trondheim," the major said. "But our group's main target is the bridge at Tangenvegen."

"Just the one?" Bjorn asked.

Holt couldn't see his face very well in the dark barn, but Lind's tone made his opinion clear. "If we blow up every bridge or destroy too much track, then Norway will be immobilized when they're finally liberated," he explained.

Colby agreed. "It's better for us to focus our destruction at points which are most destructive to German movement, like we did today, and not leave our friends helpless in the aftermath."

The next day's hike from Steinkjer to Tangenvegen took the NORSO group twenty miles through some of the roughest and most inhospitable terrain that the men had ever encountered, even in Colorado—four feet of snow topped with six inches of thawing and refreezing ice.

Maneuvering over that precarious footing on skis, while carrying rucksacks full of grenades, plastic explosives and detonators, plus rations, sleeping bags, and a Tommy gun slung across the chest was no joke.

Midnight came and went before the soldiers set up camp in the rugged mountain peaks outside Tangenvegen. Though they were only three miles from their target, the chances of them being discovered up here were slim, considering their rough surroundings.

Holt curled into a ball on his right side, cocooned in his sleeping bag and parachute, and tried to give his exhaustion the upper hand over the pain in his hip. In the midst of his unrelenting and frigid discomfort, Holt wondered for the first time since starting this whole Viking Battalion and OSS journey if he had made a wise decision when he enlisted.

He was forty-one years old, for God's sake, with metal plates holding his hip together. And he was trying to fall asleep on top of a sheet of ice in the mountains of German-occupied Norway during a world-wide war.

What the hell had he been thinking?

And then Raleigh's face drifted into his drowsy thoughts. Framed by her impossible to control red hair and her blue eyes, she smiled lovingly at him and murmured, "I'm so proud of you."

Holt's core warmed and he knew he had done the right thing. It was the only choice he could have made, and lived with himself afterwards.

"I love you, Ralls," he whispered. "Wait for me. I will be coming home soon."

April 13, 1945

Arvid had given Major Colby the name of some underground members who were willing to help in the destruction of the Tangen Bridge, so it was time to ferret them out. The first order of business was to find a way down the mountain's steep and seemingly impassable slope.

"It's impossible to go down this way," Wilhelm complained. "We'd break our skis—and our legs!"

Colby tapped Holt, Roald, Wilhelm and Bjorn for patrol. "See if you can find another way down."

When the quartet skied away from the sheer incline, Holt led them toward a runoff that was marked on their map. "If water found a way down, maybe we can, too."

An ice-clogged waterfall had formed in a deep, rock-lined gorge about half-a-mile to the east of their camp. The water had frozen in stages, forming huge steps, like a giant's staircase, and ended in a frozen lake below.

"What do you think?" Holt asked Wilhelm.

Steen shrugged. "If we sat on our skis, and took one drop at a time, I think we could do it."

Holt turned to Roald. "Do you agree?"

The Norseman nodded. "I do. It sounds crazy, but I think it's worth a try."

The patrol skied back to camp and reported to Colby.

"How big are these 'steps'?" he asked.

"Six to eight feet," Holt estimated. "We could use our ropes, if the first drops turn out to be too dangerous."

"Good. Let's go."

The first two drops ended up requiring the use of ropes to keep the men from tumbling down the rest of the ice in a free fall to the lake, but after that the drops grew smaller each time—until the last one was only three feet.

"We need to get off the lake and into the woods before we're seen. Follow me." Major Colby skied toward the dense forest to their east.

The men followed and tucked into the trees. Colby pulled

out his map and the men pulled out their compasses.

"We are here." Colby pointed to an area north of the town. "And the bridge is here, three miles straight south. We have to pass through the center of Tangenvegen to reach it."

Major Colby looked at the gathered soldiers. "I need a volunteer to go into town and find our main contact. He owns a print shop here, next to the Helgåa River."

"I'll go," Roald stated. "I am Norwegian, and so I will not draw attention."

"Good. Take off your whites."

While Roald complied, Colby continued his orders. "When you find Sven, stick to your cover story. Tell him Arvid sent you, and tell him where we are. Ask him to bring a couple of men out here to make our plans for blowing up the bridge."

"Yes, sir." Roald stood in his plain gray woolen sweater and olive drab pants. "I'll be back as soon as I can."

"If you aren't back in two hours, we'll come looking for you."

Roald grinned. "I'll be back. Do not worry."

*****

True to his word, Roald returned in less than two hours, and an hour later Sven showed up with two other men. After brief introduction, involving first names only—real or fake was not important—the group got down to the business of planning a coordinated attack.

"We want to create a distraction," Sven began. "One which will aid our cause."

"We will attack after dark." A man named Josef pointed at the city map. "If we have a team of, say, four or five of your men going along this road snipping wires and smashing public telephones, that will impede the Germans' communications enough to buy us time."

"Then the rest of your men can set the charges under the

bridge here, while the Germans go out to see why their electricity is out over here," Sven continued.

Holt looked to Roald and nodded. "This will work."

"What will your men be doing?" Colby asked.

Sven grinned. "Misdirection. The Nazi bastards won't know a thing until the bridge blows up in their faces."

The major seemed to accept that answer. "We will trust you to make that happen, then. And we will begin our part at midnight tonight."

The trio of Norwegians stood and offered their hands. As Holt shook one of them, the man who had been silent through the meeting looked him in the eye.

"We waited so long." His voice held an undisguised tremor. "We thought the Americans had forgotten us."

"It took us a long time to get here, and not all of us made it." Holt's throat tightened. He cleared it before he could speak again. "But we are here now. And we will not leave until the Germans are defeated."

"Thank you." The man squeezed Holt's hand, hard. "Thank you my friend."

*****

The team assigned to cutting wires and destroying public phones started precisely at midnight. Holt saw streets go dark as the men progressed through the town.

Holt and the others left their skis behind and jogged the three miles to the bridge. Because it was hard to blow up steel—often it just bent out of shape—they planted enough explosives along the three-hundred-foot bridge to blow up four bridges that size.

Once the explosives were in place, and all the NORSO operatives had retreated to a safe distance, the fuse wires were connected.

A momentary flash so bright that lightning paled by comparison accompanied an abrupt blast. The sound was so loud and the explosion so powerful that Holt felt it against his chest. The roar of the explosion's impact echoed back and forth between the surrounding mountain peaks for several terrible seconds.

Smoke billowed around them, acrid and metallic. When Holt could see the bridge's location again, the structure which moments ago had stretched across the river had now completely vanished.

If he had not seen the bridge himself, Holt would have doubted it ever existed.

April 18, 1945

Bolstered by their success, the NORSO group unanimously agreed to head south to the major city of Trondheim. The sixty-mile journey took five days to complete through the rough and remote terrain, partly because the spring thaw was making the snow sticky and skiing over it was increasingly difficult.

Sometimes the men took their skis off and tried to walk, but the snow was too deep for them to move without extensive effort. So—the skis went back on.

There were no villages of any size along the way to find shelter, either. The fugitive soldiers were forced to ski from tree to tree as innumerable German planes crisscrossed overhead, searching for the culprits who blew up the Tangen Bridge.

The NORSO group stayed low and kept moving until they closed in on the coastal town of Værnes, which Norway had surrendered to the German Luftwaffe in nineteen-forty. Still twenty miles north of Trondheim, the soldiers hid in the high and heavily wooded hills to the east of the town and observed the air force activity below.

"The locals were hired to build this airport, which is the German bomber base for attacks on the Russian border in northern Norway," Colby explained. "The last intelligence reports claimed two-hundred aircraft are stationed here."

Holt peered through his binoculars from high up on the mountainside. "Do we want to sabotage anything?"

Roald sat next to Holt looking through his own binoculars.

"That's a big job. We don't have enough firepower left to do anything but hit a few planes."

"And the risk to our numbers isn't worth the minimal effect we would have," Colby stated. "We'll go on to Trondheim and hook up with the Resistance there, as we originally planned."

Once the men connected with the Trondheim underground headquarters, located in a big, sturdy, and most importantly warm barn on a secluded hillside overlooking the massive Trondheim Fjord, they were enthusiastically welcomed.

"We heard about the Tangen Bridge, and two other incidents right before that." The big ruddy Norseman who seemed to be in charge clapped his hands and grinned. "I'm Ole. What can we help you with here in Trondheim?"

Colby sighed and looked his group of exhausted, filthy, and starving troops. "My men have slept on ice, eaten cold rations from cans, and not had a shower for the past three weeks."

Ole nodded his understanding. "First a hot meal. Then the showers. I will find mattresses for all of you."

Holt felt a grateful surge of warmth tingle through his frame. "A thousand thanks, Ole."

"Thank you for coming to help us," Ole countered. "What else do you need?"

Once again Colby examined his men's condition. "If we are to blend in walking through the city, we'll need civilian clothes."

"Consider it done." Ole beckoned to three women who were standing off to the side. "Go bring whatever you can. Ask your neighbors. Borrow from dry cleaners and tailors if necessary."

"Yes, sir." The three women turned and headed to the door.

One woman stopped and looked back at Holt. "Now that you are here, we will be safer. Thank you."

Holt smiled at her, not at all sure she was right.

*****

Holt had never tasted better moose stew in his life. And no warm shower had ever been so luxurious. Now stretched out on a straw-filled mattress in the hayloft of the barn his hip didn't even hurt enough to think about.

Thank you, Lord, for such rich blessings.

Colby sent a Morse code message back to OSS Headquarters in Scotland telling them where his group was, and stating that they 'reached underground headquarters, where the men are resting and were fed.'

Because they had been moving through such a remote and sparsely populated of Norway, their OSS training had not come into play at all yet, while their Camp Hale training—bolstered by their continued training in the Scottish Highlands—proved indispensable up until now.

But when the operatives entered the German stronghold of Trondheim, that was bound to change.

Major Colby called the men together the next morning after a breakfast of rough bread, no butter, and dried fish.

"Ole gave me this map." Colby spread it out in the center of the loft floorboards. "The Resistance has marked the locations of Nazi offices, warehouses, repair services, and other points of interest. Once we are appropriately dressed, we will spread out through the city and see what sort of mayhem we might be able to cause."

"Boat repair." Roald tapped the map. "I will place explosives that will detonate once the engines have reached a high enough temperature to light the fuse."

Holt saw the words *submarine bunker*. "I'll take that area. I am a construction foreman, so my being there would make sense."

And blowing that up would be amazing.

The other members of the group chose areas to explore, some alone and others in pairs. Throughout that day the women returned in stages with civilian clothing, and fourteen of the twenty-one soldiers—including Holt—managed to put together complete outfits which would allow them to walk the streets of Trondheim unnoticed.

"The seven of you who don't have a change of clothes are assigned to patrol outside the city limits and look for another bridge to blow, or a stretch of train tracks to destroy," Major Colby ordered. "All operations commence tomorrow morning. For now, enjoy your rest."

April 20, 1945

Holt spotted the submarine bunkers from several blocks away. The hideous gray concrete behemoths rose six or seven stories above street level, and had hundred-yard-long piers extending into Trondheim Fjord from either side. The concrete portion of the structures covered a city block each.

Or more.

Holt blew a soft whistle of disbelief as he approached the bunkers. German soldiers scrambled along the piers, shouting commands to each other. Holt walked the nearby streets, trying to get a glimpse of what was inside, but the angle was difficult.

He finally decided to just walk down the road alongside the fjord, straining to see into the opening of the concrete cavern.

His curiosity was rewarded when an enormous German submarine exited the bunker, most of its bulk submerged. The slippery gray tube glided past Holt like a gigantic deadly whale of unthinkable proportions. It sank underwater slowly, until all that remained above the waterline was the watercraft's control room and gunnery.

With a swirl of seawater and a wet, sucking sound, the sub disappeared as it continued forward, until there was no evidence it had ever been there.

Holy mother of God.

Holt looked back at the inconceivably large bunker. Judging by what he could see, the walls were at least twenty feet thick, maybe even thirty, and made of solid concrete.

Any idea he might have had about trying to blow up the bunker disappeared. These hideous reminders of Norway's

German occupation would still be in place a hundred years from now. Probably longer than that, if he was honest.

The Romans gave the world classic architecture that was still standing after two thousand years.

The Germans left us this.

Holt turned to retrace his steps when he saw two officers in Nazi uniforms aggressively questioning a young man in waterproof boots, dungarees, and a traditional Norwegian sweater.

Shit.

Holt strode toward the trio, a plan quickly stitching itself together with every determined step.

"Helmut! What are you doing?" he called out, hoping that whatever Wilhelm's cover story had been, the young man was bright enough to go along with whatever Holt came up with now on the fly.

"We caught him trying to get inside the bunker." The officer with a death grip on Wilhelm's arm sneered at Holt. "And who are you?"

Wilhelm stood up straight, but he was pale and obviously scared.

Holt shook his head and assumed the demeanor of an exasperated mentor.

"Helmut, how many times must I explain this to you? Eh?" He cuffed Wilhelm's head, hard. "There are protocols for these things, yes? You cannot just barge your way in."

Holt turned to address the officer who spoke to him. "My apologies, General—"

"Captain," the officer corrected. "Captain Mueller."

"My mistake." Holt smiled a little. "My name is Hans Ellefsen, and this ignorant pup is my assistant—" *Pay attention, Wilhelm.* "Helmut Lind."

The officer's expression hardened. "You are not a natural Norwegian."

"You have a good ear for accents, Captain, though the fact that I am so easily recognized does hurt my pride a bit." Holt kept his tone light and congenial. "I am an American from the great state of Iowa."

"What are you doing here?" the other officer growled.

Holt affected an apologetic mien. "I got stuck. We both did, actually."

"Stuck?" Both men frowned. "How?"

"We had just arrived in the country before Germany occupied Norway," Wilhelm offered carefully. "Five years ago."

"Yes, I'm afraid our timing was unfortunate," Holt jumped in. "Our ship from New York docked in Bergen on March thirty-first, nineteen forty."

Captain Mueller jerked Wilhelm's arm. "Are you from Iowa, too?"

Wilhelm shook his head. "No, sir." *Good boy.* "We met on the ship. I'm from North Dakota."

"What business did you have in Norway?"

"Speaking for myself," Holt said, drawing the captain's attention back to himself. "My father passed away in the autumn of thirty-nine after living sixty-five years in America. When the European war escalated, I came to Norway to look for his parents' graves and perhaps ferret out some cousins to take back to America with me."

"And?" the captain pressed.

"I found the graves, but not any Ellefsens of close relation, I am sad to say."

One skeptical brow lifted. "What have you been doing since then?"

Holt shrugged. "I am a construction foreman. Someone always needs something built when a country is at war."

Mueller looked surprised. "You built for the Germans?"

"I built for anyone who would pay me," Holt said casually. "Until the tragic explosion of the German munitions ship in Bergen, that is."

The captain and his partner blanched. Clearly that was a sensitive and unpleasant subject.

"For the last year I have been overseeing several rebuilding projects in Bergen," Holt continued. "And that is where I ran into Helmut again, and took him on as my assistant."

Before either officer could ask another question, Holt pushed the conversation in the direction that he wanted it to go.

"And that brings us to why we were hoping to see more of your submarine bunker. The German Command along with the mayor in Bergen wondered if they should construct something similar in Bergen Harbor, in the event another catastrophe might occur."

Holt faced Wilhelm again and chastised his comrade. "All was well until this young fool ran off on his own and tried to take over. I certainly hope you have learned your lesson, boy!"

For a moment the two officers seemed confused as to what to do next, so Holt jumped back into the void.

"If you could escort us to the commandant of the bunker, we would be very grateful."

Mueller scowled at the pair. "Let the boy go, but put out the order that if he is seen again in Trondheim, he should be shot."

Wilhelm looked at Holt, his eyes wide. "And—Hans?"

"I am afraid that Hans' story is a bit too perfect. I'm taking him to headquarters."

Chapter Twenty

Holt gave an unconcerned shrug. "As you wish, Captain."

Then he faced Wilhelm. "Go back to the inn where we stayed and gather our things. I will meet you at the train station. Buy two tickets to Bergen."

Wilhelm nodded. "I will."

Holt returned his attention to Captain Mueller. "Lead on."

As the trio walked through the streets of Trondheim, Holt prayed that Wilhelm picked up the codes in his message. The 'inn' of course was the barn. 'Train station' meant to move the group. Naming a town to the south meant go north.

The city was warmer than the north-facing hillside where the barn was located. Trondheim's streets were clear with only gray-crusted, icy mounds along the edges to prove they were ever snow-filled. Sunshine heated Holt's shoulders when the captain's path led them out of the city buildings' shadows.

The walk to the Nazi headquarters was just under a mile. Holt followed Mueller up the steps of the swastika-bannered two-story granite structure and through a pair of tall wooden doors. The dimness inside took a moment to adjust to after the bright sunshine outside.

Mueller stopped at the receptionist's desk. "Inform Major Franzen that I need him in interrogation immediately."

Holt's composure took an internal shift. Stay calm, he reminded himself.

Your story is sound.

Don't give them any reason to doubt it.

Holt followed Mueller into a small office that was startlingly like the ones in Scotland where the OSS trainees were practice-grilled. Holt sat in the chair with his back to the door, and waited while Mueller sat in one of the two chairs facing him across a battered gray metal table.

Holt remained silent with a pleasant look on his face. He stroked his three-week-old beard in a manner which he hoped appeared absent minded. Patient.

Unconcerned.

After a quarter of an hour spent in silence, with Holt examining his fingernails, and occasionally smiling a little at Mueller, the captain planted his palms on the table, pushed to his feet, and left without a glance or a whisper.

Now what?

Holt drew a deep breath and, assuming he was being covertly spied upon, clasped his hands in front of him and settled in the metal chair. Nothing to do but wait.

*****

Holt's head snapped up when the door opened behind him. He'd actually dozed off and had no idea how much time had passed. Only that he was thirsty.

Mueller walked around the desk and reclaimed his seat. His expression was blank.

No help there.

"Could I trouble you for a glass of water?" Holt asked politely.

Mueller glared at him. "No."

Holt shrugged. "It's just as well, I guess. I doubt a trip to the lavatory would be allowed."

Mueller's eyes narrowed, but he said nothing.

Holt risked looking at his watch. Two hours had passed since he arrived at the Nazi headquarters. "I hope we don't miss the train to Bergen."

Mueller grunted. "That is not my concern."

"No, I don't suppose it is." Holt flashed a rueful smile and shifted in the cold, hard chair that was sending daggers through his left hip.

At least half an hour later—Holt did not dare look at his watch again—the door behind him burst open.

Mueller jumped to his feet and saluted.

Holt didn't move.

The major, whose uniform was not labeled with a name, stepped alongside the table, saluted back, and took the second chair facing Holt.

Holt held out his hand. "Good day, Major. I am Hans Ellefsen."

As Holt expected, the major did not shake his hand. But by speaking first, in a pleasant and polite tone, Holt had the initial upper hand in the interview.

He withdrew his hand and asked, "How may I help you?"

"What were you doing at the submarine bunker?"

Straight to the point, then.

Holt repeated his story about being a construction foreman, coming to Norway to look for relatives—with unfortunate timing—and his work in Bergen after the explosion.

"Are you married?"

Holt was surprised that the interview went in that direction, even though his training always did. "I am a widow, sir."

"How did your wife die?" the major pressed.

"Car accident. Drunk driver." Holt pulled a deep breath, deciding to make this interview as real as he could. "I was driving."

The major was clearly unmoved. "When did this happen?"

"Nineteen-thirty-five," Holt replied with his new math. "Almost ten years ago."

The major leaned back and crossed his arms over his chest. "Why do I not believe you, Mister Ellefsen?"

Holt lifted his hands. "I have no idea. This is all the truth."

"I think you are an American operative."

Holt frowned. "What is an operative?"

The major's fist hit the metal table with a resounding bang. "Don't play stupid with us, Ellefsen!"

Holt straightened in his seat and faced the officer. "Do you believe me to be working with American military of some kind?"

The major looked smug. "Prove to me that you are not."

Holt reached into his jacket and pulled out his American passport with its March of nineteen-forty stamp from the port in Bergen.

"Look at this." He pointed to the birth date. "I am forty-five years old. When I came to Norway, I was already forty. And America was not in the war."

The major shrugged. "Documents can be faked."

Holt initiated the plan which had formed in his mind while he waited alone and in silence. This was his best shot. He prayed it would work.

"Here is something that can *not* be faked." Holt stood up and unbuckled his belt.

Captain Mueller looked startled. "What are you doing?"

"I am proving…" Holt unzipped his trousers. "That I am not fit…"

He lowered his pants and briefs as low as he could without exposing his genitals. "To be in anyone's…"

He lifted the tail of his shirt to his waist. "Army."

Both Germans stared at the mess of scars on Holt's left hip.

"Underneath these scars, gentlemen, are three metal plates holding my hip together," he growled. "My hip was shattered when my car was hit by the drunk driver and my wife was killed."

Hold it together.

"If either of you think any army, no matter *how* desperate, would accept such an old man with such a debilitating injury, then I must question your sanity."

The major was clearly trying to retake the interview. "How can we know you are telling the truth?"

Relief surged through Holt's veins.

I've got this one.

"That is easy." Holt dropped the hem of his shirt. "Take me to the hospital and x-ray me."

*****

Holt stared at the black and white film, still surprised that the Germans would go to such lengths to try and disprove his story, but thankful that he thought of dropping his pants in the interview.

Three rectangular metal plates showed up bright white on the image, and the lighter gray paths of the healed fractures added their own weight. Holt was vindicated. He put his clothes back on, deciding how best to end this thing.

One path would be to ask to be let into the bunker as his original story claimed.

But it cannot be blown up, so that's an unnecessary risk.

The wiser path was to simply ask directions to the train station.

"I will find my assistant and return to Bergen tonight," he stated, adding, "If I'm not too late."

He was released with a stern warning from the nameless major to never return to Trondheim on penalty of death.

Holt went inside the train station, knowing he was being followed. He made a show of looking for Wilhelm without success, and then bought a single ticket to Bergen.

He waited until the train was ready to leave, then employed his 'lose your tail' OSS tactics to look like he was on board the train—when in reality he slipped out the other side, dodged his way through the waiting trains, and bolted in the opposite direction.

Holt hid under a bridge until dark and then, using his compass for guidance, zig-zagged his way back to the barn.

"Your group left here about eight hours ago," he was told.

"Heading north?" Holt confirmed.

"Yes. Follow the coast."

Thank you, Wilhelm.

North in this case was actually east as the road back to the airbase curved around the fjord. Holt collected his gear, ate a quick meal, and left the barn at nine o'clock.

Three exhausting hours later, he found the NORSO guys camped in the hills above the hamlet of Hommelvik.

Wilhelm was on guard duty and the first to greet him.

The younger man nearly tackled Holt. "Thank God! You got away!"

The commotion roused the rest of the group. Some rolled over and went back to sleep, but Roald, Bjorn, and Wilhelm huddled together with Major Colby to hear Holt's story.

He told them about sticking to his cover story, and presenting his 'Hans Ellefsen' passport as proof.

"But the bastard was still unconvinced," Holt admitted.

"So how did you convince him?" Colby asked.

Holt hesitated, taking a stalling sip of the tea Wilhelm made for him. There was really no reason to keep his hip-shattering injuries from the army brass at this point. They certainly weren't going to discharge him in the middle of covert operations in Norway.

Especially since he'd been capable enough to make it this long and this far.

"It seems," Holt began, "that I lied to the Army Recruiters."

Roald, Wilhelm, and Bjorn exchanged unsettled glances.

Major Colby looked confused. "Lied? About what?"

Holt met the major's gaze. "You know that part during enlistment when they ask if you have any physical defects that could prevent you from completing the Alpine training and mountain battles?"

Colby nodded. "Of course."

"Well, I said I didn't. And as it turns out, I've made it through just fine." Holt cleared his throat. "But at *that* time, I really wasn't certain I would."

The major face was a portrait of confusion. "What physical defect do you think you have?"

At this moment, Holt was very glad that the true account of how he lost his wife was part of his cover story, because he could tell Colby exactly what happened.

"When the drunk driver hit my car and killed my wife, he hit the driver's side of the vehicle." Holt had to clear his throat again and doubted this story would ever be easier to tell, no matter how long he lived to tell it. "My left hip was shattered, and is now held together with three metal plates."

Colby stared at him. "You're telling me you have three metal plates in your hip?"

"We've seen the scars, sir," Wilhelm spoke up. "They aren't pretty."

"Well…" Colby wagged his head. "How has that affected your performance?"

Holt opened his mouth to answer honestly, but he was interrupted by Roald.

"It has not, sir. I met Holt the day I boarded the bus to join the Ninety-Ninth, and I have never seen him flinch, not even once, from any bit of training or maneuvers in the last two-and-a-half years."

"In fact, he has excelled." Wilhelm looked contrite. "He saved my ass today. And it wasn't the first time he did, by a long shot."

Holt smiled his thanks to the younger men, then addressed Major Colby. "To be honest, sir, the cold can make it throb something fierce."

Colby narrowed his eyes. "I imagine so. But I couldn't name a moment when I've seen you slow down."

Holt felt his face heating." Thank. you, sir."

"So, go back to the Nazis," Colby prompted.

"Right. They accused me of being an operative with fake papers." One corner of Holts' mouth curved up. "So I stood up, dropped my trousers, and showed them the scars."

Four men's eyes rounded and four jaws fell slack.

Holt chuckled. "I didn't drop them *all* the way—though the thought was tempting."

"And the scars convinced them?" Wilhelm asked.

"Nope. But the x-rays at the hospital did." Holt shrugged. "I asked for a copy, but they refused to take another."

"Let me get this straight." Colby flashed a wry smile. "As proof that you weren't Army material, you took off your pants and demanded an x-ray?"

"And I pointed out that my passport says I'm forty-five years old," Holt added, knowing that Colby would understand he wasn't really that age. "With all of that combined, they were convinced I was not a military operative."

"Then you just walked out of the hospital?" Wilhelm prodded.

Holt faced him. "Yep. And I walked straight to the train station and bought a ticket to Bergen. Then I used my OSS training to disappear after I boarded the train."

"Well I'll be damned." Colby slapped his thigh and coughed a laugh. "Ellefsen, you're one for the books, and that's the God's honest truth!"

April 22, 1945

The next day the NORSO guys compared notes from their day of reconnaissance in Trondheim.

"I really hoped that the submarine bunkers would be a good target," Holt admitted. "But those things are not going to be coming down at any time in this millennium."

"We considered the Nazi Headquarters," another pair of spies offered. "But to be honest, I'm afraid the people of Trondheim would pay a hefty price if we hit that."

Several of the soldiers nodded their agreement.

"I think that if we keep our sabotage limited to things like bridges and train tracks, we'll have a bigger impact without implicating the locals," a second lieutenant added.

"Let's be honest," Holt interjected. "The Germans know well that the Norwegian Resistance is active, but we don't want to incriminate them with our actions."

"Speaking of which..." Major Colby's mouth twisted unpleasantly. "Twice daily railway service out of Steinkjer has resumed."

"That only took ten days," Bjorn grumbled.

"But it confirms the high priority the Germans place on transportation," Roald observed. "Maybe that's where we should continue to hit them.

"More train tracks, then?" Wilhelm asked.

The roar of bombers overhead quieted the men as they watched the planes through their tree cover.

"No," Holt stated when the sound of engines faded. "Let's hit the airbase."

*****

The soldiers spent the rest of the day on top of their little mountain, dressed in white again, and laying in the melting snow. They watched the airbase through telescopes and binoculars, evaluating the traffic and devising various strategies and plans—including where to go after attacking the air base.

"See how the runway sticks out over the water? I think we could row a boat up under that area in the dark and place our charges without being seen." Holt turned to Wilhelm. "What do you think?"

"I think you're probably right," Wilhelm answered, still staring through his binoculars. "And if we place the explosives close to the bank, we should have enough firepower left to break off everything that's sticking out over the water."

"And we can row back to wherever we launched the boat from before we detonate," Holt added.

Wilhelm dropped his binoculars and faced Holt. "And because the runway is in a bay, we can be miles from the airbase when we hit it."

"That will work. Let's go tell Colby." Holt slid backward and climbed to his feet. "Now we just have to figure out where to hide afterwards."

Major Colby was impressed with the plan. He pulled out the topographical map and the three men bent over it.

"Here." Colby pointed to a small beach north and west of the protruding runway. "This is at the base of a mountain. We can hide up there in the woods through the next day, and then head north again when it's dark."

"We'll have to sink the rowboat," Holt observed. "Or it'll lead right to us."

"The water's too clear," Colby countered. "I think the better plan would be to chop it up and spread the pieces in the woods."

"Are we agreed?" Wilhelm asked.

Colby nodded. "Gather the men."

April 23, 1945

In the morning the NORSO group collected all of their explosives and ammunition, evaluating what would be the most effective use of their dwindled supply.

"The remaining plastic explosives could be placed under the bridge here." Colby drew a line across the runway. "Do we have enough fuse line to reach the shore here?"

"How far is that, Major?" Bjorn asked.

"Looks like seven hundred yards to the closest point, but that's not a safe enough distance." Colby measured from the runway to the selected beach. "And that's two thousand yards."

Roald made a face. "We only have eight hundred yards of fuse left."

The men were quiet for a minute, then Wilhelm spoke up.

"We have lots of grenades. What if we stuck the grenades to the bottom of the runway with the plastic explosives, and then tied the pins to a rope?"

"Or a quarter of rope," Holt picked up the thought. "We can untwist the cords so it's lighter."

"So we pull the pins remotely?" Bjorn clarified. "Would that work?"

"It should if the cords go through a pulley," Colby theorized.

"So, we hang two pulleys and string six cords through each," Wilhelm planned out loud. "That's twelve grenades setting off the remainder of our explosives."

"That will be one hell of an explosion, men." Colby grinned. "And right now, I can't think of a better plan!"

April 25, 1945

The next day the soldiers hiked fifteen miles through the mountains, circling around the airbase and the bay, and ultimately heading west to the rise above the designated beach. The day after that was spent untwisting lengths of rope and tying them together.

Wilhelm and Bjorn were in charge of the pulley mechanisms. Holt and Roald went in search of a rowboat.

Along the way they debated the merits of buying a boat, stealing a boat, or asking if someone from the underground would give them one.

"They're not getting it back," Holt pointed out. "And if questioned about what happened to their boat, the owner would be in an awkward position."

"True," Roald agreed. "But the same logic applies to buying a boat. Being asked who he sold it to would be just as problematic."

Holt grinned. "Stealing it is."

Walking along the water's edge made the men targets visible from the airbase, so they stuck to the woods and fields. They reached a large marsh where an unnamed river flowed under a small bridge into the fjord.

"If I was hiding a boat..." Holt mused as he stepped carefully through the brackish water filled with dead and newly sprouting grasses. "I'd do it—here!"

Roald splashed toward him. "Did you find something?"

"Yep." A rowboat barely big enough for two was tied to a post pounded into the soft ground. "It's small, though. Should we keep looking?"

Roald looked over his shoulder. "We could go upriver a ways and see if we find anything else, and come back for this one if we don't."

"If it's still here." Holt considered the cloudy day and brisk wind. "But I wouldn't set out on the fjord on a day like today if I didn't have to, and especially not in such a little craft."

The men trudged along the bank of the narrow, twisting creek, away from the fjord. A mile in, they were about to turn back when Roald spotted a rowboat tied to a tree ten yards or so from the edge. The soldiers climbed the slope and untied the boat.

"Might as well test it out," Holt suggested. "There's no point in dragging it over land."

The pair climbed in and rowed back down the river until they reached the first boat—which *was* still there. At that point they disembarked, lifted both of the little vessels out of the water, and then carried them back to camp.

April 26, 1945

With all the mechanics of the remote detonation created, tested, tweaked, and solidified, the NORSO guys only had to wait for nightfall to set their plan in motion.

At moonrise, half of the NORSO group hiked around the bay to a spit of land that was closest to the end of the runway. The ever-present western wind blew into the men's faces on the exposed spit and pulled the relatively temperate day's temperature down to near freezing.

Four men rowed out and spent the next hour setting the twelve grenades securely into the plastic explosives at the base of the runway. They tied a length of the narrowest rope to each pin and left it dangling.

When they finished, they rowed back and the second team of four rowed out to anchor the pulleys. Once the pulleys were in place, they men tied six of the loose cords to one jump ring, and tied a rope to each of the two jump rings. Each of those ropes was threaded through one of the two newly-anchored pulleys to be the pull-cords.

The men got back into the rowboats and carried the slack ends of the pull-cord back to the men waiting on the shore.

Holt accepted the end of one of the pull-cords and climbed into the rowboat.

"Here's where it gets dicey," he said as he gingerly held the detonating rope.

Roald got into the boat after him and picked up the oars. "Easy does it."

Wilhelm and Bjorn climbed into the second, smaller rowboat. Wilhelm picked up the oars while Bjorn held the end of the second pull-cord.

The two little boats pushed off. The other eight men began their hike back to camp.

"There is no rush," Holt murmured. "Take your time."

The two boats moved quietly in the dark, bobbing along on the wind-ruffled water. The oars made no sound as Roald and Wilhelm stroked with easy rhythms.

It took an hour to reach the beach across from the runway. The landing party was waiting for them, aided by the glowing lights of the air base from behind the rowboats. Holt and Bjorn held the end of the pull-cords while another team of four men carried the rowboats up the hill to be destroyed and the pieces dispersed.

Major Colby motioned for Holt and Roald plus Bjorn and Wilhelm to follow him. The five men hiked another half a mile to the place where the slope met the beach. By this time, the rest of the NORSO group should be safely ensconced in the woods above—and have a bird's eye view of what they all hoped was about to happen.

Colby faced the men. "The key here is going to be yanking that rope hard enough to pull the pins on the grenades, so we'll need two men on each rope."

Holt tied one rope around his waist and Roald wrapped the

rope around his own waist in front of Holt. Bjorn and Wilhelm followed suit with the second rope.

"Ready? Let's blow up that runway, men. On my count." Colby pulled an audible breath. "Three. Two. One!"

Holt threw his weight into the rope with Roald straining in front of him. He managed one step backward. Then another. Then a third.

PULL, DAMN IT.

On the fifth step he felt it. A slight, sudden give.

The pins are out.

"Five seconds!" he warned in a loud whisper.

"Ditto!" Bjorn responded in kind.

Three.

Two.

One.

Chapter Twenty-One

The explosion was glorious.

And loud.

And Holt felt the impact of the blast against his entire upright frame.

As the uncountable flashes of light faded and smoke billowed upward—a surging and silvery cloud in the dim moonlight—activity on the air base also exploded.

Every possible light on the base flickered on. Shouts carried over the water in frantic, angry, guttural German. Klieg lights switched on and began to warm up.

"Go!" Colby ordered.

Holt and Bjorn got out of their ropes and tossed the loose ends into the fjord. Then the men turned around and scrambled up the side of the mountain to get well out of sight before the klieg lights gained full strength and began scouring the base's mountainous surroundings for the culprits.

The scramble was tough, but there was no time to stop and rest. Holt gasped for breath in the cold, damp wind and his recently disclosed bolted-together left hip felt like it had finally had enough and might give out. Holt stubbornly willed it not to.

Raleigh's earnest face swam through his thoughts.

You can do this.

And he answered in his mind, *yes I can.*

When Holt topped the mountain, he dropped to his belly.

Klieg lights now swished back and forth, lighting the trees around him from their halfway point upwards. He belly-crawled to his comrades, also lying on the forest floor and watching the scene below over the mountain's edge.

"Oh brother, that was awesome!" Jensen pounded Holt's back. "The blast sliced the whole end off the runway and dumped it right in the fjord!"

Holt looked down for himself.

Where once a proud concrete runway dared to jut out over the Trondheim Fjord, now the ambient light from the swirling German searchlights revealed a jagged stump presiding over a pile of rubble peeking out of the waves.

Holt grinned.

Take that that too, you Nazi bastards.

April 29, 1945

The march back north to Steinkjer took three days of—once again—keeping to the trees and taking cover at the sound of airplane engines. But this time there was no sleet storm, and the men carried their skis as often as they wore them.

Colby met up with their Resistance contact again, and reported back to the NORSO group that the man was thrilled that the Americans had returned, and that they planned to disrupt the repaired railroad once again.

"We're out of explosives, so we'll take a different approach," the major told his men. "This time we'll fan out along the track, say every five hundred yards give or take, and use two grenades each to blow up our point on the track. That will tear up almost two miles of track and require multiple repairs."

"Do we need to worry about being heard?" Holt asked. "One set of grenades could alert the Krauts."

"Not if we coordinate," Colby replied. "I'll stand in the middle and send up a green flare at midnight. If you don't see the flare, listen for other explosions and pull your pins immediately. Are there any questions?"

"I assume we all head back to camp afterwards?" Wilhelm asked. "Traveling through the forest and keeping out of sight, of course."

"Yes, soldier."

When the moon was solidly up, the men hiked a mile farther north of the spot along Lake Snasa where they first blew up the track, then split into two groups and started pacing off the yards in either direction. Holt stopped when he was three-quarters of a mile along the way and let his comrades continue on.

In order to maximize damage to the track, the men were instructed to find a fishplate—the spot where two lengths of rail were joined with a metal plate with four bolts—and tuck both grenades next to a single joint. The resulting dual explosions would damage both rails and at least two ties, and might even twist the opposite rail enough to make its replacement necessary as well.

Grenades, however, required a certain amount of finesse. Once the pins were pulled, the soldier had exactly five seconds to retreat to a safe distance before they exploded.

When the flare appeared, Holt needed to pull the pins from both secured grenades at the same time, turn, and run for the woods like hell's own demons were chasing him.

At eleven-fifty-nine on his watch, the flare soared overhead.

Holt pulled the pins from his grenades and bolted toward the woods, diving on his belly and rolling under the trees. Four seconds passed while he ran for cover, then forty grenades went off in a drum roll of explosions

Boom-Boom-Boom-Boom!

The staccato explosions echoed off the surrounding mountains, doubling the noise. Flashes along the track lit up the night in a bright river of destruction.

Holt watched from the woods, smiling to himself, and completely satisfied at that moment with his situation in life.

April 30, 1945

Back in Steinkjer the next evening, while the soldiers hid and dozed in the hayloft of their host's barn, the man who owned the barn ran inside, shouting, "I have news!"

Holt drew his weapon and peered over the edge of the loft, afraid this could be a trap.

Clearly frustrated that no one was jumping up to ask what his news was, the man groaned in frustration.

"Listen to me! Hitler is dead!"

Still skeptical, the soldiers glanced at each other with cautious hope.

Major Colby stepped forward and called down, "Who killed him?"

"He shot himself! And Eva Braun!" the man bellowed. "And he even shot his dog!"

Colby motioned to the radioman. "Let me send a message."

The NORSO guys clustered around the radio as Major Colby sent an obscure message in Morse code, asking if Adolf Hitler was indeed dead.

The men waited in silence for the answer.

When the *dits* and *dahs* began to click, Holt said the letters out loud. There were only three.

"Y. E. S."

For a moment no one spoke.

Then a cheer as deafening as the previous night's explosions filled the hayloft with the shared relief and joy of twenty-one exhausted, filthy, and hungry OSS operatives.

*****

Hitler is dead.

Holt turned onto his back in the hay that night and pondered what that would mean to the war—and to the world.

"It has to end the war, doesn't it?" he whispered to Roald so he wouldn't waking the snoring men nearby. "Their *Fuhrer*, their leader, has taken the consummate coward's way out. Who would have expected that?"

"None of us, I'll wager." Roald sighed. "I guess we wait here for further orders?"

And wait they did.

After seven long, boring, and tense days following Hitler's suicide, the OSS troops' radio came to life again. As their radioman translated the code into words, the soldiers watched over his shoulder.

"The Germans surrendered unilaterally in Paris. The war with Germany is over." The radioman looked at Colby, his expression unreadable. "Report to Oslo immediately."

Colby looked like he'd been punched. "Report to *Oslo?* Do they have any idea how far that is?"

"Three hundred and seventy miles from here," one brave soldier offered.

Colby pointed a stiff finger at the radio operator. "Reply that we have no more explosives or grenades, and are armed with only our rifles and pistols."

The radioman did as ordered. The group sat in tense silence waiting for a response. When it came, Holt felt his chest constrict.

"You are no longer an operative group. Report to Oslo."

Holt thought Major Colby might actually have a stroke, he looked so angry. "Tell them," he growled, "that we are completely out of rations."

The radioman looked stricken as he translated the next *dits* and *dahs* into words.

Report to Oslo.

Holt looked at Roald. "Well this will be interesting."

Roald swore bitterly.

He wasn't the only one.

May 7, 1945

When Raleigh and the residents of Berlin heard the unbelievable news that Adolf Hitler had committed suicide, they all said the same thing: this had to end the war in Europe.

Didn't it?

Raleigh kept the radio on in her shop, listening for any further word. She ate her lunches and suppers in the diner, where the radio also played non-stop, wanting to be with other people when the word of the Germans' anticipated defeat was announced.

Questions about Holt had ceased six weeks ago after she told everyone he was being dropped into Norway and she would hear nothing more from him until he either made it back to Scotland, or the war was over.

Today, the announcement they had all been waiting for was broadcast at last. "The Germans surrendered unilaterally in Paris. The war with Germany is over."

The crowd in the diner reacted with shouts, cheers, and tears. Wiping tears of relief, Raleigh took the last bite of her hamburger and slipped out before anyone could press her about what would happen to Holt next.

I wish I knew.

As she walked past her shop—which she quickly decided would remain closed for the rest of the day—and headed home, Raleigh prayed once again that Holt was safe and well.

Please send him home to me soon.

May 10, 1945

After another three-day march, where the men subsisted on Norwegian oatmeal which they begged for from the residents of Steinkjer, the NORSO guys were back in Trondheim. This time, however, they did not sneak in.

When the already-spent group of soldiers stumbled through

the streets they were hailed as heroes, much to Holt's surprise. People who recognized them as American soldiers waved and cheered for them. Somebody even started playing *The Star Spangled Banner* on a fiddle.

That was very unexpected.

One man ran forward and held out a newspaper with a glowing headline declaring that the Americans helped defeat Germany abroad, and how both the German's airbase runway in Trondheim and the Tangen Bridge were blown up by American operatives helping the resistance.

"Since we're heroes…" Holt rubbed his belly. "Think they'll feed us?"

"One can hope," Roald muttered.

The group walked past the Nazi Headquarters, where Norwegians were stripping the Nazi officers of their weapons and handcuffing them. Holt caught the eye of Captain Mueller who had recently pulled him in for questioning. Mueller was in cuffs.

Holt smiled and gave a two-finger salute as Mueller glared at him.

The major who assisted in the interrogation stood proudly to the side. When Holt reached him, he stopped and faced the German officer.

"Hello, again. Remember me?"

The major's eye's widened briefly, but he gave no other indication that he heard or understood Holt.

Holt grinned. "We Americans are tougher than you Krauts gave us credit for. Enjoy your defeat."

With another two-fingered salute, Holt strode away feeling extremely satisfied.

*****

The residents of Trondheim did feed and shelter the NORSO guys overnight, though Colby was careful not to deplete the

Norwegians meager personal stores.

"Any of you guys hunt?" he asked the group.

Five hands went up, including Holt's.

Colby nodded. "Plan on it as we work our way south. We'll need the protein. We'll hop on trains when we can, but for the majority of our journey south we'll be on skis or boots."

Colby spread out a new map of Norway which he procured from a local. "We're here, and Oslo is straight south of us. As you can see, there are a few villages scattered along the way where we might be able to shelter in a barn overnight, but since the majority of Norway's population lives along the coast, we'll be on our own most of the time."

"What's our daily goal?" Holt asked. "How many miles?"

"If we can cover fifteen miles a day, we'll get there in three weeks," Colby stated. "And if we can grab a train for any part of the way, even better."

The soldiers made sure their rifles and handguns were loaded, and packed the bread and oats the locals gave them in their rucksacks. Holt wished there had been another chance for a shower in Trondheim, but made do with a cold-water wipe down as did the rest of the men.

The group set out on foot, their skis slung across their backs, and their determination to reach Oslo as quickly as possible firmly in place.

May 21, 1945

Holt slowly raised his rifle to his shoulder and looked down the sight at the red deer a hundred yards away on the forest's edge and feeding on the tips of grasses poking out of the melting snow. He relaxed, drew a breath, held it, and squeezed the trigger.

The shot cracked against surrounding rock, echoing back to him as the deer jerked and dropped to the meadow's floor.

Thank you, God.

Ten days into their journey, Holt was starving. Even though it would take a full day to clean, cook, and dry the deer meat, it would be worth the delay to have something besides a lonely cup of oatmeal to keep up his energy.

Holt sprinted toward the downed animal and slit its throat to ensure the little doe didn't suffer.

Three other soldiers ran through the forest to meet him.

"You got it!" Wilhelm slapped Holt's shoulder. "We'll help you dress it."

The men set about slicing open the carcass, removing the inedible parts and leaving them in the field for scavengers. Then they hauled their bounty back to their camp.

The soldiers there were already stoking the fire.

"We heard the shot," Roald explained with a grin. "And we took the optimistic actions."

The men worked together to skin and butcher the deer meat. Then they ran sharpened branches through several chunks and spitted them over the large fire. They also sliced thin strips of the meat and hung them on impromptu drying racks at the fire's edges to make jerky.

Holt stayed by the fire, overseeing the roasting of the meat. He felt light-headed with hunger and swore that his belly button was touching his spine.

Ten nights spent sleeping on the ground following ten days of hiking through the mountainous Norwegian wilderness had just about done him in. The men had not come across any trains, and the only signs of humanity were the summer cottages of shepherds, currently empty and devoid of supplies.

His hip throbbed without ceasing and he had run out of aspirin. Standing by the heat offered some relief, and that was worth it even if it meant he had to be on his feet the whole time.

"Let me help you with that." Roald grabbed one end of a spit and together with Holt the pair turned the meat. "It's starting to smell really good."

Holt's mouth had been watering for the last hour. "This will be the best meal of my entire life, I think."

The men turned the second spit.

"Fresh roasted meat and a day without hiking." Roald clapped his hands clean and looked up at the sky. "And if those clouds behave and don't dump on us, it will be a perfect trifecta."

Holt took that opportunity to sit still—just for a few minutes. He wondered how Raleigh was doing. She knew the war was over, of course, and had to be wondering where he was. It made him a little crazy to know he had no way to write to her until he reached Oslo and reconnected with the Army.

And maybe not even until they returned to the OSS Headquarters in Scotland.

Which he assumed they would be doing after reaching Oslo, since NORSO was no longer an operational group.

Stick with me, Ralls.

I'll be coming home to you.

I promise.

*****

The deer meat fed the twenty-one men that day and the next, with enough dried strips for them each to pack a few in their rucksacks. According to the map they were halfway to Oslo, near the hamlet of Koppang. As the ragged group of NORSO soldiers trudged into the village, they were met with shocked stares and not a little fear.

"We are American soldiers," Major Colby hurried to explain. "We are on our way from Trondheim to Oslo. Might we sleep in a barn or stable tonight?"

One man stepped forward. "We all have empty barns. The Germans took everything."

"We are not asking for anything but protection from the weather," Holt offered, pointing at the lowering clouds gathering above. "We will be on our way in the morning."

A few heads bobbed as the men consulted each other.

"Come this way," the first man offered. "The Skagi place is

half a mile down the road and no one is there at this time."

The soldiers followed the man—who introduced himself as Gunnar—as he talked with increasing energy about the end of the war and his appreciation for the Americans' role in defeating Germany. By the time they reached the abandoned Skagi property, Gunnar was positively beaming.

"Make yourself comfortable. There is still wood for a fire stacked by the house." Gunnar planted his fists on his hips. "I will come back after my supper and check on you, if that is acceptable?"

Major Colby smiled. "Yes, of course. Thank you."

Holt wondered if the major's thoughts echoed his own *we don't have any supper.*

"Would you mind if we hunted?" Holt blurted. "For rabbit?"

Gunnar looked apologetic. "You can try, of course, but even with their ability to breed so quickly, I am afraid our own hunger has depleted their numbers."

Holt touched his forehead in a sign of respect. "Thank you, sir."

After Gunnar strode off toward the little town, the soldiers claimed spots for their sleeping bags. Holt, Roald, and a few other men loaded their rifles and spread out into the woods while the men who stayed behind collected the wood and started a fire.

A crack of thunder warned the soldiers of their impending fate, so after half an hour of combing the surrounding woods without success, Holt and Roald turned back. As they approached the barn, Holt smelled something more than wood smoke.

"Fish, I bet," Roald guessed. "Some of the guys probably went fishing in the river."

Roald's words proved true, though the catch was meager. In spite of the rumbling in his belly, Holt passed on his portion. He was hungry but still strong. And he had a strip of the deer jerky to chew on.

Not all of his comrades could say the same.

The skies opened up and poured on the town. Holt figured their hosts would forego their visit when a group of locals bolted into the barn, dripping wet but laughing. There were nearly a dozen men in the group, which surprised Holt.

"Come, sit," Major Colby urged.

The soldiers moved closer to each other and pulled out a few dusty hay bales for the men to sit on.

"Did you find any rabbits?" Gunnar asked.

Holt shook his head. "I'm afraid not. But there were a few fish pulled from the river."

Gunnar held out a large loaf of dark bread wrapped in a linen towel. "We don't have any butter, I am sorry to say. But we have some coarse bread to share."

"Thank you. That is very kind." Major Colby tore off a small piece and passed the loaf to the man sitting next to him.

"Will you tell us what you have done since you arrived in our country?" Gunnar asked, his eyes lit with hope. "How have you hurt the Germans?"

The loaf of bread moved down the line as Major Colby talked about blowing up the train tracks north of Steinkjer— twice. He described the explosions at the highway bridge, the Tangen Bridge, and the runway at the German airbase north of Trondheim.

The other soldiers chimed in with their own descriptions, and as the tales unfolded the men listening grew more excited.

"You are our heroes!" they said. "We thank God for you!"

Holt grinned and bit into his chunk of the bread. The consistency was indeed rough, and the flavor reminded him of how a forest smelled. He looked at those who had taken the bread before him and noticed that they were not eating with any sort of enthusiasm.

"What is this?" he whispered to Roald in English.

Roald took a tiny bite as if to confirm his answer. "Tree bark, I think. They grind it up and mix it with whatever grains they have."

Holt stared at Gunnar and his buddies, suddenly aware of how hard the last five years had been on the entire population of Norway. It was no wonder that they were so happy now, and so grateful that Hitler was dead and his army so solidly defeated.

This wasn't the first time Holt wished that America had acted sooner, but the fact that he was able to be here, now, meant the world to him.

He took a determined bite of the bread, and smiled at Gunnar.

Chapter Twenty-Two

June 4, 1945

Holt stood on the top of the mountain northwest of Oslo and nearly broke down in tears. The sight of the busy harbor in the Oslo fjord below, and the medieval fortress which overlooked it and the city, meant that their twenty-three-day ordeal was nearly over.

Not a moment too soon.

Holt had been pushed to the point that he was not certain he would ever see Oslo. The pain in his hip was so constant that he stopped thinking about it ever going away. He knew he'd lost weight—as much as a pound a day or more—and his uniform hung loose on his frame.

The men's once-white camouflage was now filthy and had taken on the dingy color of their surroundings. They had abandoned their skis about a third of the way to Oslo as the days grew longer and the snow disappeared on their nearly four-hundred-mile south-bound journey.

God, but he wanted a shower.

And a shave. His three-month beard was dirty and matted, as was his hair.

I bet they'll smell us coming.

Major Colby was looking through his binoculars toward the harbor below. "There's an American flag on that ship."

The other men pulled out their own binoculars and looked for themselves. Sure enough.

Thank God.

"How far out are we?" Holt asked.

Colby lowered his binoculars and consulted his map. "Not more than seven or eight miles."

Then he looked at his men and smiled. "And it's all down hill from here."

The decision was quickly made to head straight to the harbor and the ship with the American flag. Once the group identified themselves as the former Ninety-Ninth Battalion soldiers who transferred to the OSS and the NORSO group, they should be welcomed and taken care of by their countrymen.

The hike down seemed to take forever, probably because with every step the thought of imminent relief from his constant pain and gnawing hunger chipped away at the stoicism which had kept Holt vertical and moving forward ever since they jumped out of the plane and onto that frozen lake months ago.

Hold it together, man.

If Holt was honest with himself, his enlistment was as foolish as it was gratifying. Now that it was all coming to a very welcomed end the gratification would win out in the end, of course.

But there had been so many nights since jumping into Norway that Holt wondered if he had completely lost his mind.

Nights when the cold seeped so deeply into his core that he could not get warm.

Nights when he knew there was no way out of his situation, except to endure it or die.

Nights when dying sounded like a relief.

Since Nora died, Holt thought so many times that he wished he was the one killed in the accident instead of her. But as he trudged through the forests and headed down through the foothills around Oslo, he realized that those thoughts were foolishness.

He was meant to live.

He was meant to fight.

And he was meant to find love again.

The thought of Raleigh broke the barrier and tears began to run down his cheeks, unheeded. The war had been over for a month and she had no idea where he was, or if he was still alive.

If there was a way to call her, he would. But there wasn't. Trans-Atlantic phone calls were the purview of kings, presidents, and prime ministers. Mere mortals were relegated to pen and paper, with the flights of planes or slogging of ships to carry their news to their loved ones.

At least the censors would be less picky, now. Holt should be free to say he was in Norway and should be able to write more specifically as the men prepared to return home.

The first houses on the outskirts of Oslo popped up, their white wooden sides and glazed tile roofs much different than the sod-roofed log cottages of the rural areas.

Soon the soldiers were marching on paved streets. Those streets widened, the houses got bigger, and traffic that was common in a city rumbled past the soldiers. Occasionally, the driver would honk and wave.

Colby guided the group toward the harbor. As they got closer, they recognized the American Army uniforms on the soldiers milling around the docks.

"Hey!" Holt jabbed Roald. "Is that Sergeant Dagestad?"

Roald turned to face the stocky captain and nodded. "Looks like it's *Captain* Dagestad now."

Major Colby strode up to Dagestad. "Major Colby reporting in. Where's your HQ?"

Dagestad pointed to a building set back a little from the water, but he was staring at Holt. "Private Hansen?"

"Corporal Hansen now, sir." Holt grinned. "And you'll remember Rygg, Steen, and Lind, as well sir!"

The man appeared gobsmacked. "What are you all doing here?"

"Liberating Norway," a grinning Wilhelm piped up. "What are *you* doing here?"

"Is the rest of the Ninety-Ninth here?" Roald asked before Dagestad could answer.

"Yes—well—we're the Third Battalion of the Four-Hundred-Seventy-Fourth Infantry Regiment now." Dagestad still stared at the unexpected group of former Ninety-Ninth soldiers. "We've been assigned as the Honor Guard to welcome the Norwegian royal family back to Oslo next week. That's what we're here preparing for."

Major Colby interrupted the odd reunion. "Do you think my men could get food, showers, and a place to bunk, Captain?"

"Oh! Yes, sir!" Dagestad pulled his attention back to Colby. "HQ will set you up right."

Dagestad saluted Colby and the major returned the gesture. Then he turned to his ragged group.

"Come on, men. Let's go get treated like heroes."

*****

Holt stood in the shower—this one was hot—in the hotel which had been commandeered for the American Army soldiers after their post-German-surrender transport to Norway. As the water streamed over his body, Holt could not imagine ever stepping out of it.

He used the very plain soap to wash his hair and his beard first, and then scrubbed away the weeks of dirt and oil covering his body. He luxuriously clipped his toenails and fingernails, now softened by the water.

When his fingers were pink and wrinkled, Holt reluctantly turned off the shower and stepped out. As he dried himself, he evaluated his condition in the mirror.

Bones showed everywhere.

With a resigned sigh, he combed his overly-long hair straight back from his face. Then he picked up a small pair of scissors and trimmed off as much of his graying beard as he could before lathering his face and gripping the razor.

Stroke by stoke, he scraped away the reminder of the last months and revealed the clean pink skin that was hidden underneath.

When he finished, he stared as his reflection again.

He looked older. There were more wrinkles at the corners of his eyes. His cheeks were hollowed by the weeks of deprivation.

The cheeks would fill out as he ate regularly again, but the wrinkles were likely a permanent addition.

Holt left the tiny bathroom and walked to the single bed where a new set of fatigues waited for him. He dressed himself in the clean boxers, clean t-shirt, clean socks, clean pants, clean shirt, and new belt—knowing that he would never take such things for granted ever again.

He slipped on his old boots since new ones weren't available, glad that whatever he faced next would not be accompanied by the blisters of un-broken-in footwear. Then he headed down to the hotel dining room for supper.

What the NORSO guys learned since walking into Oslo was that the Americans sailed in, accepted the personal surrender and disarming of German officers, and then imprisoned them for extensive debriefing and possible charges. Non-officers were disarmed and corralled to be transported back to Germany.

"The king and his family are arriving in six days," Major Colby reported. "So your former comrades from the former Ninety-Ninth Battalion are pretty busy making the preparations."

"What will we do?" Holt asked between bites of an amazingly tasty fish soup. He tried to eat it slowly but without success. He looked around the dining room.

I wonder if I could get another bowl.

"I sent a message to OSS headquarters in Scotland, and I'm waiting for an answer," Colby said. "In the meantime, we'll rest and regain our strength."

"Can we write letters?" Holt pressed.

"You can write as many as you want…" The major shrugged. "But you can't mail any of them until we get back to Scotland."

June 10 1945

The NORSO guys received word that they would be transported back to Scotland on the ship that was returning King Haakon and his family to his throne in Norway. So for six days, all they had to do was wait. And eat. And bathe regularly.

And souvenir hunt.

That pastime became a passion for the Americans recruited for the original Viking Battalion and they were determined to return home with both German and Norwegian trophies. The fact that all the men spoke Norsk endeared them to the locals, who proved eager to trade for all sorts of items.

Holt and Roald spent the last six days in the grassy plaza between Stortingsgata and Karl Johans Gata in front of the royal palace, which stood empty for the first two years of the German occupation. Once the traitorous Vidkun Quisling stepped up and offered to run Norway on the Nazi's behalf, he set up his offices in the palace and remained there for the next three years.

Since the Germans' surrender last month, and Quisling's immediate arrest and imprisonment, local craftsmen had labored enthusiastically to remove any trace of the disgraced Norwegian leader and prepare the palace for their King's return.

And that meant they had access to Nazi paraphernalia.

Holt and Roald quickly realized that the locals coveted anything American, but especially if it was Army related. They each checked out several knit caps from the supply tent and traded them for anything with a swastika.

"I want something Norwegian for Raleigh," Holt commented as he stuffed another red-white-and-black armband into his pocket. "I know she's Scottish, not Norse, but I want to give her something pretty from here that's not related to the war."

"You might need to trade something more than a cap for that," Roald opined. "What do we have that these people want?"

That answer was obvious.

The next day Holt and Roald showed up with tins of rations.

"This one is beef. It's enough for a small stew." Holt handed a can to one of the men who passed them every day. "I'm looking for something pretty for my fiancée."

The man lifted a skeptical brow. "Jewelry?"

"Doesn't have to be..." Holt realized he shouldn't cut himself short. "But she would love that, I am sure."

The man held up the tin. "I'll need more of these."

"Sure. How many?"

The man hesitated, clearly weighing the wisdom of his answer. "Five."

Holt nodded. "I will bring you six tomorrow."

The next day the man reappeared with three brooches which Holt knew were worth far more than the seven tins of potted meat. But jewelry wasn't edible, and when your family was hungry that was the immediate problem.

Holt selected the smallest one, which he honestly felt was the one most suited to Raleigh's no-nonsense style. "Thank you. She will wear this at our wedding."

The man looked relieved. "I will tell my wife."

Then he walked off carrying the six tins of meat and whistling,

Today the NORSO guys stood at attention beside their former battalion-mates and waited for King Haakon to appear at the top of the gangplank. Crowds of cheering Norwegians and a huge band waited for their sovereign and for a moment Holt wished that American presidents were always greeted with such revelry.

When King Haakon stepped to the edge of the deck, the Americans saluted and the Norwegian band began playing the Norwegian national anthem. The salutes and the anthem continued long after the King stood on the dock and acknowledged both.

Holt considered the people in the crowd. Both men and women waved little flags and wiped tears. It had been a long and hard five years for them living under the German's tyranny, but now their world was being set back to rights.

He smiled softly and glanced at Roald. His young buddy was grinning from ear to ear.

It is a very good day to be Norwegian.

When the soldiers were dismissed, Holt hefted his rucksack over one shoulder and followed his group up the gangway and onto the ship.

June 20, 1945

Six full weeks after the war in Europe ended, Raleigh opened her salon's mailbox on a hot and humid Wednesday afternoon and slapped a mosquito before pulling out the black-and-white photo postcard from the little mail box beside her salon's front door. When she turned it over, she gasped.

I'm alive. I'm coming home.

Those simple words, hastily scrawled in black ink, were the most beautiful words Raleigh had ever read in her entire life.

Half laughing and half crying, she stumbled back into her shop before falling on her knees, weak with relief.

Thank you thank you thank you.

The shop door opened and Miss Whitley walked in gripping the arm of her niece Mary for support.

"Good Lord, child!" She looked down at Raleigh with a horrified expression. "Has something happened to Holt?"

Unable to speak just yet, Raleigh shook her head and handed the elderly woman the post card. Mary read the cryptic message aloud.

"Praise be!" The visibly relieved Miss Whitley fanned herself with the postcard. "Merciful heavens, you gave me a start."

"When will he be back?"

Shaken out of her jumbled reaction by the question, Raleigh looked at Mary and wondered once again if the girl was simple. "This is the first time I've heard from Holt since he went to Norway in mid-March. Every single thing I know is written on that postcard."

Raleigh regained her feet and retrieved the postcard from Miss Whitley. "This was postmarked in Inverness, Scotland on

June thirteenth. One week ago."

Still holding Mary's arm, Miss Whitley made her way toward her regular chair in front of the middle mirror.

"Post that on the door so everyone can see it," she urged. "Everyone in town will want to know our Holt has made it through."

Raleigh smiled and held the postcard to her lips.

Holt had this in his hand a week ago.

He's coming home to me.

Raleigh walked around the reception desk and opened the top drawer. She cut two pieces of clear cellophane tape and put one on each corner of the postcard. Then she walked back around to the shop's front door and taped the postcard to the glass so that the writing faced outward.

Hurry home soldier.

June 25, 1945

A proper letter arrived five days later. Raleigh tore open the thin envelope and unfolded the thin paper, noticing immediately that no thick black lines obscured any of the writing.

Dearest Raleigh ~

As you know from my postcard, we have returned from Norway and are back in Scotland. Once we are debriefed, we will be sent back to the States. Our commander thinks we could be on our way in a week or two, depending on how soon there is space available for us on a ship.

Sometime after we reach Camp Henry in Virginia, we will be discharged. That's all I can write at this time, but I can't wait to see you and tell you about our experiences.

Lord knows, I have missed you so much. You have no idea how just the thought of you and your love for me kept me going through some very hard and difficult times. Times when I questioned my own sanity, to be honest.

Why in the world was I so eager to join the 99th, and then the OSS, to go and fight in such an inhospitable climate? I can't adequately explain the miserable conditions which we endured for the months we were in Norway ~ but by God we survived. Every one of us.

I'm afraid I will look significantly changed when you see me again. I lost a lot of weight during our deployment, which I am currently striving to regain. But the man who looks back at me in the mirror has aged ten years in these last three. Please don't be shocked when you see me again, Ralls. I am your same steadfast Holt on the inside.

All my love,
H

Raleigh read the words over and over again through happy tears. She didn't have any confidence that an answering letter might reach Holt before he left Inverness, but in case it did she wrote back and mailed her missive the next day.

My dearest darling ~

I don't care if you hair has gone white or you're thin as a rail, I will love you no less. And as hard as your experience was, for you to have gone to do what you did is something you will never regret.

I am waiting for your return, happier than I can say to see you again.

Chapter Twenty-Three

July 7, 1945

Raleigh set down her scissors and comb and spoke to her client's image in the mirror. "Excuse me while I get that."

She hurried to the jangling phone on the salon's desk and grabbed the receiver. "Burns Beauty, how can I help you today?"

"Hi, Ralls. It's Holt."

"Holt!" Raleigh faced her shop full of ladies, all who stared back at her with wide eyes and open mouths. "Where are you?"

"I'm in Virginia. We docked last night."

"It's so good to hear your voice." *Don't cry.* "I'm so glad you're back safely."

She wished she could say more, but Holt did call her at the shop. He had to know their phone conversation would have an audience.

Holt heaved a deep sigh. "You have no idea how much I wish I was in Berlin with you right now."

Me, too.

"When do you think you will be?" she ventured. "Or is it too soon to know?"

"We are hoping to be discharged this week."

He sounds so tired.

"We aren't attached to any companies or battalions," he continued. "And the OSS discharged us from their service in

Scotland. So it's just Army paperwork that needs to be filed."

"Did you get my letter?"

"I did." She could hear the smile in his tone. "It came the day we sailed."

"I'm glad. I wasn't sure if it would arrive in time." Raleigh smiled, too. "Do you realize you're speaking with an accent?"

Holt coughed a rough laugh. "Am I?"

"A little. Yes."

"Well, I *have* been speaking mostly Norwegian for three years, so I'm not surprised." Holt chuckled again. "My mother will be pleased, I think."

"Will you let me know when you'll be on your way home as soon as you do?" *Really—do not cry!* "I'll meet you at the train station in Milwaukee."

"That'd be great, Ralls." Holt cleared his throat. "I better go. Guys are lined up to use the phone."

Audience be damned. "I love you, Holt."

"And I love you, more than you know."

July 18, 1945

The appearance of a Western Union uniform at Raleigh's door on a Sunday afternoon three days ago would have sent anyone with a soldier at war into an immediate panic. But the war was over. Holt was back in America.

No one is shooting at him or trying to blow him up.

Raleigh accepted the little envelope. "Thank you."

She closed her door and pulled out the yellow paper with its pasted-on message.

Boarding this AM stop. Arriving 18 July 130p stop.

Raleigh let out a whoop.

This morning she left Berlin for Milwaukee an hour earlier than she needed to because there was no way on God's green earth that she would be late to meet Holt's train. She'd spent the last three days working to tame her hair, polish her nails, and even applied extra cold cream at night to make sure her skin was as dewy as it could be.

Holt wasn't the only one who was afraid that the years of war had made changes in his appearance. Raleigh was already thirty when Holt enlisted, and now she was thirty-three.

And a half.

Did it show?

She didn't care a bit that Holt was halfway to his forty-second birthday. In the completely unfair world which they lived in, men who grew older were considered distinguished—while even at her obviously younger age, Raleigh was solidly in the old maid category.

None of that mattered anymore. The man she loved more than anyone on the planet was on his way home to her right this very minute. Whatever came after that, they would work out together and at their own pace.

Raleigh was prepared to wait for Holt if that was what he needed. After all, they really hadn't spent much time together since agreeing to marry when the war was over. Holt had more adjustments to make than she did—not only by taking a second wife, but in returning to civilian life.

War changed people. She had already seen that. Whatever Holt needed, Raleigh was determined to give him.

Raleigh parked her car in the train station lot and looked at her watch. Twelve-fifteen. She had more than an hour until the train was due.

She checked her appearance in the car's rearview mirror before getting out. Satisfied that she looked the best she could at this point, Raleigh got out of the car and headed into the terminal to get a bite to eat while she waited.

*****

Holt's knees bounced as the train slowed in its approach to the Milwaukee station. He had changed from fatigues into his returned corporal's uniform an hour ago, not wanting to look unkempt, or any more haggard than he already was.

He heaved a ragged sigh.

I'm going to sleep for a week.

On a bed that's long enough for me to straighten my legs.

He gaze reached across the narrowing space between his train car and the platform, searching for any sign of Raleigh. When he glimpsed her red hair, tied back with a scarf, his pulse surged.

Why am I nervous?

There is no reason to be.

Holt reached into his pocket and checked once again for the little Norwegian brooch, his special gift for the woman he loved with all of his heart. The train slowed to a stop. Men and women thronged the door.

Holt held back. He didn't want to greet Raleigh while being jostled by a crowd of strangers.

Not at a time like this.

*****

Raleigh waited near the end of the platform, scanning the face of each man who exited the train. As more people who weren't Holt climbed down the train's steps and walked past her toward the terminal, Raleigh had the sinking feeling that he wasn't on the train after all.

Please be here. Please please please.

A lone figure stepped from a car halfway back. He was tall. He wore an Army uniform.

And he was looking straight at her.

With a sob of joy, Raleigh abandoned all sense of propriety and ran toward Holt. He strode quickly toward her as well and held out his arms.

Raleigh launched herself into his embrace, sobbing uncontrollably. Holt held her so tightly she could hardly get her breath, but she didn't care. His face was pressed into her neck and he huffed with his own emotions. She never wanted to let go of him.

Of course, she finally had to.

Holt set her on the platform and slid his hands down her arms until he held hers in his strong, warm grip.

"You look amazing, Ralls."

Raleigh looked up into Holt's bright blue eyes, noticing the extra crinkles at their edges, and the gray which invaded his dark blond hair at the temples, and knew no man had ever been so handsome.

"And you are the most beautiful man in the world."

He winced a little. "I'm not too changed?"

"Changed for the better, Holt." Raleigh stood on her tiptoes and kissed him softly—they were in public, after all—and whispered, "I love you."

"And I love you." Holt smiled softly. "And I don't want one more day, one more minute, of our lives to go by without making this official."

Raleigh's heart seemed to skip a beat.

Still gripping her hands, Holt lowered himself to one knee.

As soon as he did, everyone on the platform around them stopped moving and stared openly at the soldier in uniform and the woman he was now kneeling on front of.

"What are you doing?" Raleigh yelped.

He grinned up at her. "I'm doing it right. I don't have roses, but I do have this."

He pulled a small brooch from his pocket. "Raleigh Burns, would you do me the great honor of becoming my wife?"

For a surreal moment Raleigh wondered if she was dreaming this entire scenario. She didn't answer, just stared down at the man she'd waited an entire lifetime for.

Holt flashed a crooked smile. "Should I take your silence as a yes?"

Startled back to her senses, Raleigh blurted, "Yes! Of course I'll marry you!"

Holt rose to his feet as the small crowd around them

applauded. He pinned the brooch—which Raleigh hadn't even looked at—to her blouse. Then he pulled her back into his arms and kissed her so long and so well that she didn't care if the entire population of Milwaukee was watching.

September 1, 1945

On the first Saturday in September, six weeks after Holt came home and three weeks after the war in Japan ended, Raleigh stood in the narthex of Trinity Lutheran Church in Oshkosh wearing a tea-length white dress and a short white jacket with the Norwegian brooch pinned to its lapel. She gripped her bouquet of pink roses and baby's breath with sweaty palms.

Holt's father offered his arm. "Are you ready?"

Raleigh nodded and flashed a nervous smile. "As ready as I'll ever be."

When Holt proposed, Raleigh assumed they'd be married in Berlin—but that plan immediately went out the door and down the road. First of all, because Raleigh had no living family, Holt's parents stated that they would pay for the wedding.

"He's our only child," his mother proclaimed. "And I had no say the first time. Now I can act as the mother of the bride *and* the groom."

Raleigh was happy to hand over the reins, even if that meant there were heavily Nordic influences in both the decorations and the food.

The second reason that the wedding was in Oshkosh was that so many people wanted to attend that the little church in Berlin simply didn't have enough room to hold them all.

"Holt's a hero, you understand," his father said to Raleigh the night he arrived home and announced to his parents that they were engaged. "His new-found happiness in the face of tragedy will give hope to everyone who's lost someone or something in the war. They'll want to be a part of that."

Raleigh had to admit that he made a good point. And as their plans expanded to include a buffet reception for the few hundred people expected, Raleigh decided to relax and let the Hansens enjoy the celebration of their son's happiness.

All that really mattered to her was that she and Holt were solidly married at the end of the day.

The organist inside the church finished the hymn, and after a brief pause, hit the opening chords of the Wedding March with gusto. The ushers inside the church opened the double doors, revealing the bride and her escort, and the crowd inside rose to their feet.

Raleigh pulled a steadying breath and tightened her grip on Holt's father's arm. Together, they took the first step.

As soon as they did, Raleigh looked into Holt's eyes and everything around her melted away. Standing in the front of the church with Jan Ramstad as his best man, Holt took her breath away.

He was the tallest, handsomest man in the room, proudly wearing his cleaned and pressed Army uniform, which was freshly adorned with a bronze star awarded for his service in Norway.

He smiled at her as she walked closer, but she didn't see the tears in his eyes until she reached him.

Raleigh thought it would be awkward for Holt's father to actually give her away to his own son, so the question of who gives this woman to be married was eliminated from the ceremony.

Instead, when they reached the altar, Raleigh simply kissed her soon to be father-in-law on the cheek and stepped to Holt's side on her own while he sat down next to his wife.

"My God, you are beautiful," he whispered.

She smiled, knowing she was blushing, and whispered back. "And you look like a Nordic god. Will you marry me?"

Holt's gaze flickered past her to the crowded church, and then returned to hers.

"I suppose so. I would hate to let all these people down," he teased.

Raleigh stood on her toes and whispered in Holt's ear. "I will give you a proper thanks tonight when we're finally alone."

Holt coughed, reddened, and turned to the pastor. "Let's get this thing going. People are getting hungry."

Then he winked at her.

Chapter Twenty-Four

November 6, 1946

"Mister Hansen?"

Holt looked up at the nurse. "Yes?"

She smiled at him. "Congratulations. It's a boy."

I have a son!

"Can I see my wife?"

"Of course! As soon as we move her to a room. Would you like to see the baby?"

Holt stood at the window and looked down at the red-faced, puffy-eyed, tight-fisted infant lying in the bassinette looking very confused about what had just happened to him.

He was absolutely perfect in every way.

"I think so, too." Raleigh smiled tiredly at Holt when he finally got to see her. "And almost nine pounds! He'll be a big man like his father."

"You have changed every single aspect of my life, Raleigh Burns." Holt leaned down and kissed his wife tenderly. "And I thank God every day for you."

"That's Raleigh Burns *Hansen*, soldier," she chastised. "Don't you forget it, especially now that we're a real family."

I won't. Ever.

NOTES:

The creation of units like the 99th battalion was first proposed by the War Department's most senior intelligence officer a month after Pearl Harbor. He proposed an "international combat force recruited of aliens in the United States." The 99th Battalion was the first of these "Foreign Legion" units.

The 99th Battalion was created in 1942 with nine hundred Norwegian-speaking volunteers: men of Norwegian descent, first generation Norwegians, and Norwegian immigrants. The original intent for the battalion was to liberate Norway and remove both Hitler's ability to cull her vast resources, and prevent him from attacking England from the north.

After training at Camp Hale, the 99th Battalion moved to northern England in 1943 to complete their training and prepare for Norway. In 1944, just before D-Day, General Patton was in England leading a "Phantom Army" in a massive deception plan called Operation Fortitude. Sadly, on D-Day six thousand American soldiers were lost on the beaches at Normandy.

After that tragic loss of so many military lives, the 99th was sent south to fight—and were forbidden from speaking Norsk because of its similarity to German. The 99th fought in France, Holland, and Belgium, saw heavy action in the bloody Battle of Aachen, Germany, and rushed to stop and hold the Germans during the Battle of the Bulge.

The recruitment of a hundred men by the OSS actually happened before the 99th left Camp Hale. Those men did train in England and Scotland, and the air drops into Norway happened as described in the story. In fact, half of all the men in the OSS Operational Groups came from the Norwegian-American 99th Battalion and its Greek-American sister "Foreign Legion" Battalion, the 122nd.

The rest of the 99th made it to Norway a month after the war in Europe ended, when they were tapped as the Honor Guard for the return of King Haakon and his family. Their last mission brought the 99th to Oslo in time to welcome the King's return and ensure the peaceful repatriation of over a quarter million German serviceman and 80,000 prisoners of war and slave laborers.

Politically, the presence of Task Force A in Norway inserted America squarely into Norway's political realities and the people's hearts. Hundreds of 99th soldiers were reunited with family they had never met and a hundred Norwegian war brides followed the soldiers home to America after the war.

Sixteen Silver Stars have been documented among the 99th soldiers—including the Italian, Pedar Olsen. Over eight-hundred soldiers received the Combat Infantry Badge, and the battalion was honored with the Belgian *Fourragere*.

In 2011, surviving members of the 99th Battalion received the Norwegian *Deltagermedaljen 9 April 1940—8 Mai 1945* for their service under two flags.

However…

After blowing up the Tangen Bridge, the OSS soldiers actually retreated into Sweden to find their misplaced comrades. On their way they discovered and buried the soldiers from the crashed drop—literally on the same day that Hitler killed himself. The war ended seven days later.

Actions in this story following the Tangen Bridge explosion are the creation of the author, who visited Trondheim while writing this book, and wished to expand upon and honor the Viking Battalion soldiers' mountain training, spy training, and indomitable spirit.

HANSEN FAMLY TREE

Sveyn Hansen* (b. 1035 ~ Arendal, Norway)

***

Rydar Hansen (b. 1324 ~ Arendal, Norway)
Grier MacInnes (b. 1328 ~ Durness, Scotland)

Eryndal Bell Hansen (b. 1327 ~ Bedford, England)
Andrew Drummond (b. 1325 ~ Falkirk, Scotland)

***

Jakob Petter Hansen (b. 1485 ~ Arendal, Norway)
Avery Galaviz de Mendoza (b. 1483 ~ Madrid, Spain)

***

Brander Hansen (b. 1689 ~ Arendal, Norway)
Regin Kildahl (b. 1693 ~ Hamar, Norway)

   Symon Karlsen (b. 1705 ~ Christiania, Norway)

   Skagi Karlsen (b. 1707 ~ Christiania, Norway)

***

Martin Hansen (b. 1721 ~ Arendal, Norway)
Dagne Sivertsen (b. 1725 ~ Ljan, Norway)

  Reidar Hansen (b. 1750 ~ Boston, Massachusetts)
  Kristen Sven (b. 1754 ~ Philadelphia, Pennsylvania)

   Nicolas Hansen (b. 1787 ~ Cheltenham, Missouri Territory)
   Siobhan Sydney Bell (b. 1789 ~ Shelbyville, Kentucky)

    Stefan Hansen (b. 1813 ~ Cheltenham, Missouri)
    Blake Sommersby (b. 1818 ~ Kansas City, Missouri)

    Kirsten Hansen (b. 1820 ~ Cheltenham, Missouri)
    Twain Kensington (b. 1822 ~ Cheltenham, Missouri)

    Leif Fredericksen Hansen (b. 1809 ~ Norway)

***

Holten Hansen (b. 1904 ~ Oshkosh, Wisconsin)
Raleigh Burns (b. 1912 ~ Berlin, Wisconsin)

Tor Hansen (b. 1913 ~ Arendal, Norway)
Kyle Solberg (b. 1919 ~ Viking, Minnesota)

Teigen Hansen (b. 1915 ~ Arendal, Norway)
Selby Hovland (b. 1914 ~ Trondheim, Norway)

Lucas Thor Hansen (b. 1918 ~ Sabetha Kansas)
Parker Williamson (b. 1917 ~ Denver, Colorado)

***

*Hollis McKenna Hansen (b. Sparta, Wisconsin)

Thank you for reading my book(s)! I hope you enjoyed the characters and their stories.

Please
consider leaving a review on Amazon.

Reviews are an author's only feedback regarding what our readers like and want more of.

Thank you for your support!

Kris Tualla is a dynamic, award-winning, and internationally published author of historical romance and suspense. She started in 2006 with nothing but a nugget of a character in mind, and has created a dynasty with The Hansen Series.

Find out more at: www.KrisTualla.com

Kris is an active PAN member of Romance Writers of America, the Historical Novel Society, and Sisters in Crime, and was invited to be a guest instructor at the Piper Writing Center at Arizona State University.

*"In the Historical Romance genre, there have been countless kilted warrior stories told. I say it's time for a new breed of heroes. Come along with me and find out why: **Norway IS the new Scotland!**"*